STALKING

A SEA STORY

MARK DAVID ALBERTSON

IRISH VIKING PUBLISHING

Other Books by Mark David Albertson

Steaming: A Sea Story
Spying: A Sea Story

Stalking: A Sea Story

ISBN: 9798352053935

Library of Congress Control Number: 2022919210

ACKNOWLEDGEMENTS

I think most people who are not writers have a vision of the author, finishing his or her book in a manual typewriter, pulling the final page out with a flourish and saying something like, "Voila! It is finished!" Little do most people know that the first draft is probably the easiest part of writing a book. Once the first draft is completed there are three, four or five more drafts (or more), a great deal of re-writing, and a huge amount of help from many people.

I would like to thank my wife and fellow writer, KE Meuir, for her many hours reading my writing, making kind suggestions, discussing *ad nauseum* details of plot and story, and, finally, being my first editor. Her selfless assistance made this book so much better, and although my name is on the front of the book, she is all over the rest of it. I treasure the hours we spent on the back porch sipping good Texas wine and discussing Matt and Randy and all of the paths the book could have taken.

I gratefully acknowledge the time and talents of my amazing editor, Ray Tuttle, who meticulously examined every word, phrase, and chapter, and, I'm guessing, who has the *Chicago Manual of Style* memorized. The great talents he applied to his editing magic improved the book immensely. His kindness in suggestions and critique is much appreciated.

Many thanks to the generous technical expertise Senior Master Sergeant (USAF Retired) Kevin FitzGerald lent to this novel. He reviewed all things that exploded in this book. Without his years of experience on the USAF Explosive Ordnance Disposal Teams, his active duty deployments in Iraq, which led to being awarded the Bronze Star for meritorious service in a combat zone, and his post-retirement work with the federal government, this book would be relegated to fantasy, rather than being plausible and accurate.

I also want to acknowledge and give appreciation to all of the western movies, actors and writers from whom my villain stole ruthlessly. They are too many to acknowledge, but if the reader has an interest, start watching old westerns and reading western books, and you'll see many of those words. I also want to give credit to Anne Dingus, who wrote an article that was published in Texas Monthly Magazine in 1994 entitled, *More Colorful Texas Sayings Than You Can Shake a Stick At.* Most of the Clay Young-isms were memorialized in that article, although I can tell you that many of my friends here in Texas use them on a regular basis, and I love hearing them.

For my Astóre

Prologue

Thursday, April 6, 2000, 0030 hours

Tiny, almost unrecognizable bubbles floated to the surface of Sweetwater Channel, which flowed into San Diego Bay, just south of Naval Base, San Diego. It was just after midnight. In the darkness, the bubbles curiously traveled slowly, in a line. At first, the bubbles traveled west, toward the western edges of the bay, then turned right, to the north, toward the piers that contained some of the United States Navy's most formidable warships. The bubbles continued moving north in virtual silence.

The insignificant burps of air concealed a malevolent presence beneath the surface of the water. If one could see through the murky water, they would have seen a human in a dark wetsuit and SCUBA gear, the bubbles emanating from the regulator in the person's mouth. The dark figure was holding a short, torpedo-like device with a headlight and handlebars. A propeller in the rear pulled the diver as it glided silently underwater. At a depth of twenty feet, the light on the Diver Propulsion Vehicle (DPV) would not be detected in the dark water, yet the shadowy figure could easily see the same distance ahead.

Having spent days studying the maps of the naval base to the end point and etching them in his memory, the diver noted where he was as he passed pier 13: the outer edge of Naval Base San Diego. Two salvage ships were moored to this pier. He again took note as he moved beyond Pier 12, Pier 11, getting nearer to his goal of Pier 7. When the diver reached Pier 7, he turned right and guided the

DPV a few feet deeper. As he expected, the diver saw through the murky water the screws of a long-hulled guided-missile frigate. This was his target.

The diver's destination was the USS *Stilton*, FFG 62, an *Oliver Hazard Perry* class frigate. The ship was a formidable weapon in the Navy's fleet. She was 453 feet long, with a 22-foot draft. She carried a Mark 13 Missile Launcher with a 40 missile magazine containing SM-1MR anti-aircraft guided missiles, Harpoon anti-ship missiles, Mk 38 Naval Gun Systems, and anti-submarine warfare torpedo tubes, and that was just the start. The ship had cost the US taxpayers $122 million to build.

The *Stilton* was moored to the pier in traditional style, with six heavy mooring lines, which kept the ship that displaced 4,100 long tons from moving away from the pier, even in heavy winds. The diver stopped his DPV at the approximate point of the forward breast line and attached it to the hull with a short line and suction cups. He quickly removed his buoyancy compensator, a vest holding his two air tanks and regulator, his fins, and mask. He unhooked a waterproof backpack from the DPV and put it on, took one last deep breath from his regulator, then allowed himself to surface quietly. As expected, it was dark, and no one was nearby. All the lights on the pier were aimed at the ship, not the water.

The diver, skilled in penetrating a ship, used a tool with large suction cups and handles to climb the side of the floating fortress. With a button under his index finger, he could depress a trigger to create suction and release the trigger to release the suction. With these tools, he gradually climbed the side of the ship, releasing one side and moving it higher, then pulling himself up and doing the same with the other side. When he reached the mooring deck, he silently climbed over the railing. He rapidly headed to the headline. He took the backpack off and withdrew six strips of flexible sheet explosive. In the days before this attack, he had cut the flexible sheet into strips and wrapped them in duct tape. The man had cut one strip for each of the five lines mooring the ship. He wrapped the explosive strip around the headline, brought out a shock tube detonator assembly with a mechanical timer, and an assembly to pull the firing pin. He duct taped the detonator to the line, inserted the small detonator under the sheet explosive and pushed a button to arm the assembly, removing the safety pin manually. The head line completed, he moved to the forward line and did the same, repeating the process for the head spring, the back spring, the aft breast line, and finally, the stern line. Once he completed all the lines, he returned to his suction climber and made his way back down to the surface of the water. He donned his SCUBA gear, unmoored the DPV, and without a sound, glided back the way he came, small bubbles leaving the only trace of his presence.

Ten minutes later, five detonation charges fired practically simultaneously. All five mooring lines splashed into the water by the pier, the sounds of the splash drowned out by the whirring of the generators powering the ship. The detonators were loud enough to be heard from the quarterdeck of the ship, and the Officer of the Deck (OOD) turned to the quarterdeck watch. "What the hell was that?" said the OOD. Almost immediately, the USS *Stilton* began drifting away from the pier, first a few inches at a time, and then gradually gaining momentum.

As the ship slowly drifted away, the gangway between the vessel and the pier began groaning. The quarterdeck watch stood stunned as he saw the gangway gradually pull off the ship's quarterdeck, then fall into the harbor. The OOD and the Sentry watched for a moment, dumbfounded. They looked at one another, and the OOD ran to the 1MC, the ship-wide announcement system, and called general quarters. "General Quarters, General Quarters! All hands man your battle stations. This is not a drill. General Quarters, General Quarters! All hands man your battle stations. This is not a drill." USS *Stilton's* bow turned out slowly and grazed another moored ship, tugging its ship to shore power lines from the pier. Emergency power generators came online after the Stilton went dark, which provided a modicum of light.

As the ship continued to drift, the crew watched in horror. The OOD called on the quarterdeck's sound-powered phone to the radio shack to be certain there was emergency power to the ship-to-shore radio. The radioman in the shack confirmed it was working and patched the radio to the bridge. Without hesitation, OOD ran to the bridge, calling the harbormaster for help.

Within a few minutes, Harbor Control dispatched two tugs to stop the movement of the frigate. Coming alongside, the tugs tied to the *Stilton*, brought it to a stop and held her in the harbor until instructed to bring her back to the pier. Two hours later, the Stilton was towed to the dock and re-tied. The damage from grazing the other ship appeared to be relatively minor, although large gouges and bends were apparent on both ships.

It was then the Officer of the Deck found the note. In plain sight, attached to the quarterdeck door, was a white piece of copy paper with computer printing on it. The words read:

This is just the start. Prepare yourself for greater pain.

Wilson

The OOD shouted to the captain, who was watching the completion of his ship's re-mooring. The Commanding Officer (CO) read the note attached to the wall and turned to his Executive Officer (XO) with a grimace. "XO, Call the Naval Criminal Investigative Service (NCIS)," said the captain. "This was sabotage."

THE LAND OF ENCHANTMENT

Monday, March 27, 2000, 0800 hours

S upervisory Special Agent (SSA) Matthew Bertram always enjoyed attending training conferences at The Federal Law Enforcement Training Center (FLETC), Artesia. FLETC Artesia, named for the town where it was located, was in the heart of southeast New Mexico's oil and dairy belt. The training center was on a sprawling 3,620-acre site that included a full range of facilities for conducting basic and advanced law enforcement training and served the Federal Bureau of Investigation (FBI), Central Intelligence Agency (CIA), US Marshals, United States Secret Service (USSS), the US Forest Service (USFS) and the Naval Criminal Intelligence Service (NCIS), among other federal law enforcement agencies. It contained numerous buildings with training rooms, shooting ranges, tactical courses, and more.

Matt had grown up in Northern New Mexico in the town of Los Alamos. Known to most Americans as "The Atomic City," was formerly a top-secret laboratory where the atomic bomb had been designed and built during World War II. Matt had grown up camping, hiking, and fishing in the Jemez Mountains, a place that still lived in his heart. With his current duties as SSA of the Criminal Division of the NCIS in San Diego, Matt only occasionally visited his home state. A training conference in New Mexico gave him the excuse to return to the home that had never left his heart. Any time he attended a meeting there, he would try to couple it with at least a few days in Northern New Mexico to visit friends, camp in the Jemez or the Sangre de Cristo Mountains, fish, and saturate himself with the unique and ecstatic delights of Northern New Mexico cuisine.

As a bonus at this conference, his long-time companion (and lover), Randy Glasscock, would be attending. They had been a monogamous, if distant, couple since they had met twenty-four years before.

A short, paunchy, gray-haired man walked to the front of the classroom. Although he was 68 years old, he had the countenance of a man much younger, and on his face was an irresistibly winsome smile. Wearing a light blue sport coat and khaki trousers supporting a sizable belly and sporting a mustache that covered his entire upper lip and most of his lower lip, he exuded an air of calm control and authority.

"Alright, everybody, please take your seats, and let's get going. We've got an action-packed agenda during our conference, and we aren't here, *mostly*, to socialize. For those of you who don't know me, and I think it's probably nobody here, I'm Aldrich Sowles, Special Agent in Charge (SAC) at NCIS San Diego. We've got three days to cover quite a bit of ground. Tomorrow, we'll have an update on changes going on with our authority as NCIS agents, and yes, I mean finally, after only 118 years in existence, we are being given the authority to execute warrants and arrest perpetrators." A series of whoops and rebel yells came from the attendees. "We'll talk about these changes and what we will be required to do to keep from getting our asses handed to us on a fu-, er, a friggin' silver platter. Day three will be firearms training, field search and arrest practices, along with an afternoon of fun and games with SSA Bertram in the gym, where he'll teach you some effective hapkido moves. I figure I had to throw that in to keep you from sleeping through the entire third day."

"Today, however, I've got a special presentation for you. As most of you know, I was assigned to the 'Paris of the Orient,' better known as Saigon, during Vietnam. What you may not know if you've never had a beer with me is that the Office of Naval Intelligence (ONI), our mother organization, provided a mountain of logistical support to the forces in Vietnam from the outset of our boots on the ground there. What you also may not know is that ONI had no friggin' idea of the shit storm of counter insurgency in South Vietnam that put us in harm's way. We had bombings of ships in the harbor, attacks on our offices, and much more, and we had zero weapons, zero combat training, and zero experience in jungle warfare. If it had not been for the CIA's covert efforts, we'd have all come home in body bags."

"In 1970, I met Jake Packer, the man who will train you today. At the time we met, Jake was a CIA agent and special operator. Jake was an amazing guy to meet. He was not only a covert operations specialist, but he also spoke Vietnamese, Mandarin Chinese, and Russian fluently. He could not only speak those languages, but he was also proficient in reading and writing in those languages. Jake knew everything we did not, and rather than letting us get ourselves killed, he took us under his wing. Jake procured weapons and ammo for us, and he taught us how to do the job our superiors had expected us to do, but somehow forgot the fact that we didn't know how to do it. This man knows more about special operations than any man I know, and I've asked him to spend the day teaching you how to think like a special operator when the need arises. So, without further ado, let's welcome former CIA Officer, current lecturer, and author of the bestselling book, *Never Fear Anyone Again*, Jake Packer."

Matt turned to SSA Randy Glasscock, who was sitting next to him. He whispered in her ear, "I hate *fucking* CIA Officers. They are all a bunch of Ivy League pricks with heads as big as basketballs." Randy gave Matt a scowl and said, "Give him a chance, Matt. I think this will be interesting." Matt simply shook his head and rolled his eyes.

The tall man standing at the podium looked like someone straight out of the movies. He made James Bond look like Jackie Gleason. His full head of grey hair was perfectly coiffed. His posture was that of an Olympic diver, and his voice was deep and resonant. Matt thought to himself that if he were casting a spy movie, this guy would be the perfect hero. Packer was probably the same age as his friend Aldrich Sowles, but Packer was obviously slim and fit in his $1000 Brooks Brothers suit. Matt immediately hated this man.

"Now I know, guys and gals, you all are highly trained professionals, and I respect your skill set in the NCIS. I'm not here to tell you how to do your jobs. I am going to tell you how to survive worst-case scenarios and how to use simple skills to avoid them. I'm also going to give you a crash course in some interrogation techniques and a few covert operations 'secrets' you might not know. Now, I know Special Agent, um Bertram, is it? Is going to be working with you on some tactical martial arts moves, but I'm going to throw in a bonus. I call it the *Trinity*. It is a simple technique, but if you master it, you can take down anyone, any time."

Matt again glanced at Randy, who was listening intently, and rolled his eyes. His lips formed the word *bullshit*, but he said nothing out loud.

In Matt's opinion, the rest of the morning was a combination of self-promotion, book promotion, ego, bragging, telling sea stories, and pure fantasy. Matt spent time doodling, yawning, and thinking about the fact that he and Randy would be spending a week in Santa Fe, Bandelier National Monument, and Jemez Springs following the conference. His mind drifted back to his childhood and the many days and hours spent backpacking, fishing, and camping in the mountains he loved. He pictured the tall Jack pine trees, the Piñon pines, and the cool, clear Jemez River. It startled him out of his daydreaming when Randy raised her hand to ask a question of Packer. "Mr. Packer?" Randy said.

"Please call me Jake, Special Agent...?" Packer replied.

"Glasscock, Jake. My first name is Randy. And I'm a Supervisory Special Agent, or SSA, with the Protective Service Detail for the Chief of Naval Operations (CNO) and Secretary of the Navy (SECNAV)."

"Go ahead, Randy; I've noticed you are taking quite a few notes today."

"Your information is fascinating, Jake," Randy stated. "I have a question about what you said a minute ago. You mentioned that foreign spies live among us in numbers larger than we suspect. As you know, our agency stopped the largest Komitet Gosudarstvennoy Bezopasnost (KGB) spy ring in history twenty-four years ago. The younger agents in the room may not know it, but Komitet Gosudarstvennoy Bezopasnost in English translates to Committee for State Security, and was composed of security and intelligence personnel and their own secret police force. NCIS has been diligent in safeguarding our national secrets, as far as the navy goes. Do you have an opinion on whether they currently embed spies in the military, or have our safeguards worked?"

"Everyone knows about the Morris Lester case, which I believe you and SSA Bertram played some part in, so I don't want to sound like I'm dismissing the NCIS's efforts in this regard. But it's my opinion that you would be shocked at the efforts the Russians are still making to gather intelligence from US sources.

Even though the Union of Soviet Socialist Republics (USSR) fell in 1991, in the last nine years, a very powerful *Sluzhba vneshney razvedki Rossiyskoy Federatsii*, or as we call it now, the SVR, has become just as active, if not more active than the KGB ever was. The SVR mission is to conduct intelligence and espionage operations outside Russia and as such they've just learned to fly much further under the radar. Not to mention the fact that we've got the Chinese, the Arabs, the Islamic fundamentalists, and even the Israelis working overtime to spy on us."

Matt turned to Randy and whispered, "*Played some part*? The two of us brought the spy ring down! What an asshole!"

"Shhh," said Randy, giving Matt one of her famous scowls.

Randy stood up when the group broke for lunch and said, "I'm going to invite Jake to sit with us for lunch. I really want to pick his brain. Are you with me?"

"Pass," said Matt, forcing what he hoped would resemble a smile. "I have some business with Director Sowles."

"He's still working on you to take the promotion when it comes, isn't he?" said Randy with a smile.

"Enjoy lunch with Captain America," said Matt as the two went in separate directions.

Matt not only reported directly to SAC Sowles, but they had become good friends over the years. Matt's respect for Aldrich Sowles was higher than any other man he knew, and Sowles had taken Matt under his wing when he was a novice Special Agent (SA). "How do you like Packer's presentation?" asked Sowles as they set their lunch trays on the table.

Knowing that the two went back over thirty years to Vietnam, Matt, never a great diplomat, but having no desire to seem unappreciative, mumbled, "Well, he certainly has some interesting ideas and stories."

"Great," said Sowles. "I'm glad to hear that. NCIS has decided to contract with Packer for some continuing consulting. Headquarters feels he can add a measure of skill to our field staff. And you'll be glad to hear that I've asked him to shadow you in San Diego for a few weeks so that he can get a feel for the way we operate. He'll check in with you when you get back from your leave."

Matt could feel his face getting hotter, which meant that it was possibly eight shades of red. With every bit of diplomatic energy he could muster, Matt mumbled, "Wow, Aldrich, that's quite an honor. I'm sure we'll have plenty of opportunities to show him how we work in the field." Matt took a long, deep breath in an attempt to lighten his assuredly flushed face.

"The other thing I want to let you know is that I've set a date for retirement. I've given notice that I'm going to be on a fishing boat in Cabo six months from now, giving not one thought to NCIS."

"My god, Aldrich, you've talked about retirement, but I kind of believed you'd always be here," said Matt. "We're going to miss you terribly—*I* am going to miss you terribly. It won't be the same organization without you here."

"It won't be such a big hole, Matt. I've written letters to Deputy Director of Operations Montague and Deputy Director of Operational Support Klugman recommending you for the job. I know we've talked before about this, and even if you don't think so, you are the right man to sit behind that desk."

Matt once again took a moment to find diplomatic words to express his disdain for management work. "Aldrich, you know that I am honored that you want me to take the position, but Dugan is Assistant Special Agent in Charge (ASAC), and he should have it."

"ASAC Dugan is retiring, too. He is just waiting for me to make the announcement. That will give you a chance to participate in the process of choosing your second."

Matt paused, trying to sound as honored as possible. "It's a big job, Aldrich, and you were the one who said I'm the right man to *sit behind the desk*. You know I don't want to sit behind a desk at all. I should have been sitting behind a desk as SSA, but I'm still in the field taking cases, I know, much to your dismay. Aldrich, I am not a *desk* kind of guy.

"I understand, Matt, but the truth is, you're no spring chicken yourself. You are 44 years old, and even though you're in great shape, a black belt in Hapkido and all that, it would be a wise decision to make the change. Your agents and investigators are as loyal as any I've ever seen. I've already gotten the word. The job will be yours if you want it."

"Thanks, Aldrich. I will give it the consideration it deserves, and I'll let you know when I get back from vaycay, alright?"

Aldrich smiled. "I hope you will give it serious consideration, Matt. I'm counting on you."

When they reconvened after lunch, Packer wasted no time resuming his stories of daring and intrigue. He was obviously well-practiced in speaking to audiences of civilians who wanted to pretend they were patriotic militia members dedicated to stockpiling semi-automatic weapons, survival food, and camouflage. His audience today was a bit different, and from Matt's perspective, Jake was only delivering one big commercial for Packer, Inc.

As Packer had promised, he ended what Matt considered to be eight hours of his life he would never get back, with the demonstration of his "ultimate defense move," the *Trinity*. "Now, this is a simple three-step move that even your granny could do," Packer said confidently. "Can I get a volunteer?"

Randy was the first (and only) person in the class with her hand up and rushed to the front like a thirteen-year-old teen at a Raven-Symoné concert.

"OK, Randy, here's how it goes. I'll explain it, then demonstrate it in slow-motion for everyone. Then each of you can pick a partner and do a slow-motion practice with it. If SSA Bertram allows, I'll be at the gym when you do the hapkido thing the day after tomorrow, and we'll do it on the practice dummy or, if we're lucky, a live victim!"

Packer began by explaining the process of his defensive technique. "The key to this move is to make surprise the most important aspect. Your target must not see it coming. Step one of the Trinity is to strike the assailant's head, specifically the eyes. *Not* with a fist, but with your hands in a clawing posture, like this." Packer demonstrated the posture, holding his hand in the shape of an eagle's talon, and slowly reached for Randy's eyes.

"Step two is almost simultaneous with step one but delayed just a split second. As soon as you claw the eyes, quickly punch your assailant's throat with the other hand balled into a fist. I know that sounds drastic, but keep in mind that you are responding to someone who is trying to dispatch you with prejudice." Matt smiled and shook his head. *This guy has been watching too many thrillers,* he thought to himself. Packer demonstrated slowly on Randy.

"Punching the throat is amazingly effective," Packer went on. "The automatic response is to back off and withdraw whenever your air intake is threatened. You *have* to do it, and you can't stop yourself."

"The third movement uses an appendage you are not otherwise using: your knee. Almost simultaneously with the other two moves, give a swift knee to the groin. This alone sends most people to the ground, but in conjunction with moves one and two, it will ensure that your attacker will not get back up."

"The key to this working for you is to move as fast as possible, going from the eyes to the throat, then to the groin. That will give you time to make your escape or subdue your attacker and get restraints on him. He or she, will be a helpless little baby. Now, everybody grab a partner and give it a try. SLOWLY! With your instructor's permission, I'll show you the move at true speed when you're in the gym.

After the day's presentation, Matt and Randy walked back to the housing building. "I know you thought Jake was a little smarmy, Matt," said Randy, "but you have to admit, he knows his stuff. Tell me you got something out of the day?"

"Sure. I got a good nap after lunch, and a good chuckle as Packer was teaching you his 'secret' move. I'm sorry, Randy, but we could have spent our time today doing much better things. I know SAC Sowles is giving his old friend a break, and probably some much-needed consulting income, so I'm willing to grant you that he does seem to be experienced. I think maybe he's a better marketer than he was a CIA officer, however. The man reeks of bullshit."

"My little skeptic," Randy said with a smile. They sat down on a bench in front of Randy's housing, and Randy took Matt's hand. "I've missed you, Bertram," Randy said with a smile. "Sowles offered you the SAC job, didn't he?"

"How did you know that? Did he talk to you?"

"No, it doesn't take a CIA agent to figure out what you two were talking about at lunch."

Matt smiled and gave Randy a loving look. He took his finger and brushed her hair back over her ear. "I can't wait for us to spend a week in Northern New Mexico together. I've really missed you, too."

Randy, known far and wide for her blushes, did so. "I'm very much looking forward to catching up. I know we talk on the phone all the time, you in San Diego and me in D.C., but it just isn't the same. Can we talk more about the position when we're on our own in your *motherland*?"

Matt smiled. "Of course, but I'm hoping we spend most of our time *not* talking, if you get my drift!" He gave Randy a long, tender kiss. Finding it difficult to end the day, they walked to Randy's dormitory. Matt opened her door for her, gave her one more kiss, and walked back to his dormitory building. Randy's desire to maintain professional decorum didn't allow for much more in public. He looked forward to climbing the wall of her dormitory and walking the narrow ledge to her window. Although some would consider walking the ledge very dangerous, the risk only added another level of enjoyment to the evening for him, since he had loved rock climbing and mountaineering from his early teens. Randy also was thrilled by the idea that her man was willing to crawl ledges and scale fire escapes when necessary to spend some time with her. So, when she arrived in her room, she opened her window in preparation for her nocturnal visit from Matt.

Day two of the conference was much more interesting than the first for Matt. Sowles gave the official announcement. NCIS Special Agents had finally been granted authority to execute warrants and make arrests. For all of Matt's 24 years at NCIS, they could do investigations, but they had to bring in other law enforcement to make the actual arrest or to execute a warrant. It had always felt a little like being junior rangers shadowing the *real* professionals. Matt couldn't count the times he had said to Sowles, "They arm us, and then they don't let us do our job. Why don't they just issue us water pistols?" This amendment in policy would change the entire tenor of his staff and would be a big boost in morale. NCIS Special Agents would now have the same status as other law enforcement agents.

They spent an hour going through protocols for warrants and arrests, and Sowles laughed when he said that each special agent would be going through further training on properly restraining suspects. He laughed because, even though they weren't allowed to make arrests before now, they had all had dozens of hours of training on how to arrest someone properly.

Sowles also discussed the other significant change that was coming. The Department of the Navy had decided to integrate the Marine Corps Criminal Investigation Division, (MCID), into NCIS. The navy and the marine corps had signed a memorandum of agreement the year before, but there were so many details being negotiated that Matt thought it would never happen. Matt was happy that he would have a pool of ex-USMC CID agents to integrate into his staff. The Marine CID agents were well-trained and highly professional. It was a long process to recruit Special Agents, train them and put them in the field. It would be great to have his new agents walk in the door with proven skills and experience.

The afternoon of day three was Matt's, and he was excited to have this time with thirty other special agents. Matt had been practicing Korean Hapkido since joining NCIS and advocated for Hapkido training for new recruits. Unfortunately, the NCIS had closed its own training facility and used the Federal Law Enforcement Training Center, so his advocacy went unanswered. US Marshals, FBI agents, and other similar federal law enforcement agents now received the same basic training. The FBI had mastered training agents, so, unfortunately for Matt's belief in the effectiveness of Hapkido, everyone received training in the way the FBI saw fit.

As the attendees gathered in the gym, Matt supervised the set-up of mats, punching bags, and practice dummies. When they were ready, Matt shouted to everyone to gather around. "I know that several of you, with my encouragement, have been learning Hapkido. I personally believe it's the best possible martial art for law enforcement professionals to know."

"For those of you who don't know much about it, let me just give you a quick summary. The Korean character □(hap) loosely means *harmony*; □ (ki) literally means air, gas, or breath. I was taught that it is something more like *spirit* or internal energy; □(do) means *way* or *art*. It sounds awkward in English, but people often interpret these Korean words *as the way of coordinated power*."

Matt continued briefly. "Hapkido is a hybrid of many forms of martial arts. My opinion is that it took the most kick-ass, bad-ass, ass-whooping techniques of the most bad-ass martial arts forms and combined them. It uses joint locks, grappling, pressure points, throwing, kicks, punches, and plenty of striking attacks. When you see the few things I'll teach you today, those of you who have training in other areas will recognize Aikido, Judo, Jiu-jitsu, and Krav Maga, among others. Now let's get started!"

Just as they were beginning their lesson, Jake Packer arrived (fashionably late), wearing, in Matt's opinion, possibly the most hideous lime-green suede running suit ever, and was sporting a white tennis headband. Packer looked to Matt, like he had just beamed in from a 1980's 'B' movie. Despite the utterly out-of-date jogging suit, Jake participated in all the exercises, giving Matt the opportunity to teach the class what he knew. With reluctant respect, Matt thought to himself that, all things considered, Packer had reasonably good skills in martial arts, and even though he had to be in his sixties, he moved like a much younger man.

As they were wrapping up for the day, Jake approached Matt. "Hey Matt, would it be alright if I showed your students the *Trident* at full speed?"

Matt looked at the attendees, shrugging his shoulders at them, and questioning their interest. It slightly disappointed Matt when the attendees indicated they wanted to see it.

Packer put the practice dummy front and center and demonstrated his three-part move, allowing others to try it as well. Matt watched Randy at Jake's side, and she took a stance when it was her turn. Jake reached around Randy's torso from behind, correcting the stance a bit. A rare injection of jealousy surged in Matt, and he completely lost his composure and felt tingles in his limbs. His face felt like it was going to melt right off. Matt would look back on the moment, realizing that the feeling was, in fact, common sense leaving his brain.

Jake was finishing the demonstration as Matt was seething quietly. "Now, as far as I'm concerned, your *little* hapkido is cool and all, but the *Trinity* is an atom bomb," Packer said, chuckling.

"Well, if it's so good, Packer, why don't we do this for real and put your trinity up against hapkido?" Matt said. A voice inside Matt's head said, *did I just say that out loud*?

"If you're up to it, special agent, I guess I can't refuse!" Jake said with such a degree of confidence that Clint Eastwood might have backed down. They donned protective headgear, padded gloves, and groin protectors and stepped to the center of the mat.

Before Matt could react, they were squaring off in front of twenty seasoned NCIS Special Agents. Standing face to face with Packer, Matt felt his adrenaline flood his body. *I'm going to show this joker the floor*, Matt thought. Before Matt approached, he said quietly to Packer, "It's *Supervisory* Special Agent Bertram. That means something here." Matt approached first, having already planned a swift elbow to the side of Packer's head. He made his move and, in a stunning flash, found fingers in his eyes, a fist to his throat, and a knee to his groin. Even with the protective gear, Matt lost his wind for a moment. Stunned, he realized he was looking up at Packer from the ground.

Packer looked down at Matt, smiled, and said quietly, "Well, *Supervisory* Special Agent Bertram, you need help getting off the floor?" Packer helped Matt up and in a demonstrably kind voice, said to the group, "Don't get me wrong; hapkido is excellent, and I highly recommend it. But sometimes, an old guy can teach you young bucks something of value."

Matt put on the best face possible, reluctantly gave a glove bump to Packer, and dismissed the class.

Jemez Bound

Wednesday, March 29, 2000, 1600 hours

As soon as the conference was over, Matt and Randy put their luggage in the back of their rented Ford Edge and headed out of Artesia. They decided to take a more scenic route, so they drove west on Interstate 82, through the Lincoln National Forest and Cloudcroft, then skirted White Sands, northbound for Santa Fe. They planned to spend a couple of nights at their favorite bed-and-breakfast, the Four Kachinas Inn, take a day hiking the Nambe Lake Trail in the Sangre de Cristo Mountains north of Santa Fe, and a day taking in the Georgia O'Keefe Museum, then head to Los Alamos and connect with Matt's childhood friend, Tadg Goldman. Tadg would provide them with some of his camping equipment, and they would head into the Jemez Mountains for a night in Bandelier, then a night camping by the San Antonio River, before driving to Albuquerque for their respective flights back to work.

It had been four months since they had seen one another, which meant they had other business to attend to first. *Personal* business. As soon as their room door at the Four Kachinas had closed, Randy pushed Matt onto the bed. Forgotten luggage on the floor was soon draped with clothes randomly tossed willy-nilly, the separation ignored as they touched skin on skin like two teenagers in the back seat of their father's car. Finally, Matt made the "time out" sign with his hands, too out of breath to talk, and they cuddled together, talking and laughing.

"Marry me," Matt said, looking into Randy's eyes.

"Not on your life, sailor," Randy replied, trying to look as resolute as possible.

"No, I really mean it," Matt sighed.

"Matt, you've asked me to marry you at least a hundred times over the last 24 years. Each and every time, I say no. Although I have to give you credit for hanging in there."

Matt sat his pillow up and took Randy's hand, interlocking his fingers with hers. "Why is it that we haven't married?" he asked, partially rhetorically.

"You know exactly why, Matthew Bertram. We are married to our jobs and our careers. You are heading the largest criminal division in NCIS, and I am Supervisory Special Agent to the NCIS Protective Service Detail for the Chief of Naval Operations and the Secretary of the Navy. Those are both huge jobs, and if we were married, one of us would have to give their job up. You're in San Diego, and I'm in D.C. You want to move there, give up your position, and what? Become a Capitol Cop?"

"Sure, or a professional dog-walker for all I care. I'd give it up in a second," Matt defiantly replied.

"Look, Sweetie," Randy said, touching Matt's cheek, "I like what we have right now. We've been together for 24 years, and it's worked well. I'm as committed to you as I would be with a ring on my finger, and I believe you feel the same way. Why screw it up with legal papers? I see people change when they get married. Suddenly their spouse feels they can control them just because of the ring. And I'm never, and you know this, going to allow myself to be controlled by another person." Randy stopped and gave Matt a tender kiss. "Even if that person is as cute and sweet as you. And I could never live with the guilt of causing you to decide to give up your career for me. That just wouldn't work for me."

"But you're still in agreement that when we hit retirement age, we'll move to the Jemez and buy some property, right?" Matt inquired.

"Of course; I know how much you love the Jemez, and with you as a tour guide, I've come to love it too. There is a Starbucks and a Macy's there, right?" Randy said with a smile.

"My camp coffee beats any Starbucks in the world, and nothing beats Clement and Benner Department Store in Los Alamos," Matt replied.

"I'd love to see you make a triple shot caramel macchiato in your camp pot."

"I don't even know what you just said," said Matt.

Quickly trying to change the subject, Randy said, "Speaking of important jobs, Sowles told you the SAC job is yours, didn't he?"

"Yeah, he did," Matt said with the sound of dread in his voice.

"So, what do you think?" Randy whispered enthusiastically.

"I'm–I'm just not sure, Randy. It would mean that I would have to start sitting behind a desk, going to lots of meetings, and spending my time doing mountains of paperwork. It just doesn't sound like me," Matt said.

"You're supposed to be behind a desk right now, Matthew," Randy remanded. "They only let you continue to participate in field investigations because you're a legend at NCIS. 'The man who brought the big spy down,' they say, in hushed tones, as you walk commandingly through the halls."

"Stop," Matt said, smiling. "I've never walked a 'commanding' step in my life. They tolerate my involvement in the field because I'm damn good at solving crimes. I'm giving the promotion due consideration, but I need you to know that I've been giving some thought to leaving the service completely."

"What the *fuck*?" Randy said, mouth gaping open. "Are you serious about becoming a professional dog-walker? I'm kidding. What in the hell would you do, and why?"

"Here's the thing, Randy. I've never made my own choices in life. They've always been made by my circumstances, and not simply by my decision. I'm 44 years old, and I'd like to make a few of my own choices in life."

"What do you mean you haven't made your own decisions? Nobody ever forced you to do a single thing," Randy said defensively.

"OK, even though I've made the actual decisions, I've just gone the direction the tide was flowing in life. I joined the US Navy three weeks after graduating from High School, filled with the anticipation of adventure and travel, but primarily because my father had informed me that money for college was non-existent, and living at home was not an option."

"And, as it turned out, the kind of travel and adventure I experienced had been far from what the navy recruiters marketed. While I was serving as a radioman and on deployment, I was written up for calling the quarterdeck and telling them there was a race-riot happening on the mess decks so that I could dive into

Subic Bay to retrieve my chief's dentures the chief had chucked, and which I had promised the chief's wife I would protect with my life. I could have earned myself a dishonorable discharge, but the CO needed a 'volunteer' for something called a Landing Force Deployment Team. In order to avoid punishment, I took the "opportunity" to join the team. which transported me to Cambodia just after the Vietnam conflict was "officially" over. Although the conflict in Vietnam was over for all intents and purposes, I had found myself in combat, coming to the aid of a platoon of stranded marines. The operation had resulted in combat and casualties, neither of which the US Government intended to disclose to the American public.

"Because of the training I had received during that time, I was then recruited by the Naval Criminal Investigation Service, which in 1976 was called the Naval Investigative Service (NIS). They placed me in an undercover operation aboard a cruiser in Japan and tasked to find the source of significant leaks of Top-Secret materials from the ship's radio shack. Completely over my head, I, along with a certain Special Agent named Randy Glasscock, managed to expose the spies so we could bring them to justice."

Randy chimed in, saying, "As I recall, SSA Bertram, things went pretty well for you from there. Following the Morris Lester case, they offered you a helluva job. You were discharged from the navy directly into a position as a Special Agent with what was then the NIS, which became the Naval Criminal Investigative Service in 1991. You did your job pretty damn well and managed to be given more responsibility over the years. With twenty-four years of service in the NCIS, Matt, you are heading the criminal division of the NCIS Regional Office in San Diego, with 75 special agents and investigators who report to you."

"You know, I've heard this before, more than once. You always do the right thing, and I'll go out on a limb and bet on your good judgment to do the right thing now. Whatever you decide, you know I'll support your decision, but you're doing great. Don't take the promotion, do take the promotion. It doesn't really matter to me. I'm just afraid that what keeps us together right now is the NCIS, and if you leave, we'll drift apart. I don't want that. I want you, just in case you're interested. Even though our relationship is a little unconventional, it's worked for us for a couple of decades."

The two kissed and showered, then headed to Matt's favorite Santa Fe Restaurant, Tomasita's. The restaurant is one of the Santa Fe icons, and while there are fancier and more famous restaurants, Matt loved the building next to the railroad tracks and the old Santa Fe Railroad Station. He particularly liked the casual atmosphere and the excellent service. Sitting for an hour in the bar drinking margaritas, then gorging themselves on stuffed sopapillas drenched in green sauce was a true delight. The night was lovely, and they walked around the plaza before heading back to their bed and breakfast, stuffed with the food in their bellies and a few too many margaritas.

Duty Calls

Friday, March 31, 2000, 1000 hours

After spending two wonderful nights in Santa Fe, eating fantastic food and doing a little hiking in the Sangre de Cristo Mountains above the city, the two traveled north on I-25. They took the turnoff for Los Alamos, their car climbing the narrow road up the side of a tall mesa. As they reached the top of the mesa, they passed what used to be the main gate into the secret city of Los Alamos. The machine gun tower still stood at the site of the gate. By the visitor's building, there was another building that Matt fondly remembered as the site of Philomena's Mexican Restaurant, which his family regularly visited when he was a child. They passed the small municipal airport and headed up Central Avenue, pulled into the parking lot of the Los Alamos Police Department, got out of the car, and walked into the lobby.

"I demand to see Chief Goldman immediately, or there will be hell to pay!" growled Matt as he stepped up to the front desk.

"Shut your yap, Bertram!" replied the sergeant at the desk. "You've always been too big for your britches!"

"Well, Bobby Swenson, as I live and breathe!" Matt said back. "When did they let you out of prison?"

"Ah, shut up and give your old friend a hug," he said, stepping around the desk. "And who is this lovely person who has judgment bad enough to be seen in public with you? And it's *Sergeant* Robert Swenson to you, Bertram!" The officer held out a hand.

"I'm Randy Glasscock, Sergeant," Randy replied, displaying her ability to blush. "I work at NCIS with Matt."

"*You* can call me Bobby, Randy. Well, any friend of Bertram's is a suspect in my book," Bobby replied, adding, "But I'll give you the benefit of the doubt this time."

A side door of the lobby opened, and out walked the Chief. "Hey Bertram, you got that $5 you owe me?" the man said, holding out his arms and grabbing Matt. At seven feet even and easily 250 pounds, Tadg Goldman made 6'5" Matt Bertram look like a hobbit. He turned to Randy, gave her a big bear hug, and said, "Randy, it is always a pleasure to see you. I don't understand why you're still hanging out with this delinquent! You still doing protection detail for the CNO?"

"Hey Tadg, good to see you too, and if you can believe it, they put me in charge of the detail last year and included the protection detail for the SECNAV."

"Woh, ain't nobody touching a hair on the old man's head with you around, Randy! Really, it's great to see you guys. Unfortunately, I've got a hectic day fighting crime in the metropolis of Los Alamos. With 12,000 people in this city, mostly geeks with PhDs, crime is rampant here! I've got to head to the library to see about an overdue book ring. I think I've got everything you need in the back of my truck, so you guys can get camping."

As they were walking to the truck, Tadg turned to Matt. "How's the job going, my friend? It must be fun in the big leagues. I know I sure miss it."

"And I'm pretty sure the FBI misses you, too. Things are going really well. I'm up for a promotion, which, don't get me wrong, is great, but actually, Tadg, I'm thinking of moving on. I've given thought to buying a place up in the Jemez somewhere, have a couple of horses and dogs, and get back to my mountains."

"That will be the day, Bertram. I've heard this one before, but, I'm calling bullshit. Frankly, my friend, you like adrenaline a little too much to sit and stare at the sky all day. But I'll tell you this, the second you want a job fighting urban crime in a big city like Los Alamos, I've got a detective badge just waiting for you."

"That's good to know," Matt replied. "I just might take you up on it. We'll be at Bandelier tonight and San Antonio campground tomorrow. We'll bring your stuff back before we head to Albuquerque."

Bandelier National Monument was about six miles from where Matt grew up, as a crow flies. As a teenager, he spent hours, days, and weeks there hiking, camping, and exploring the ruins and cave dwellings of the ancestral Puebloans. Hunter-gatherers had lived in the area for over 10,000 years in a pristine spot with water, which is a rare thing in New Mexico. Somewhere after 1000 AD the Ancestral Puebloans began farming the canyon floor. They carved impressive cliff dwellings into the volcanic tuff, including an entire apartment complex on the canyon floor and a huge kiva in a cave for their ceremonies.

Around 1500 AD probably due to lack of water, they moved out of the canyon and into pueblos along the Rio Grande, such as Cochiti, San Felipe, San Ildefonso, Santa Clara, and Santo Domingo, which they still inhabited. The ruins they left behind made for hours of climbing and hiking adventures.

The Frijoles River wound through the bottom of Bandelier Canyon and was lined with giant cottonwoods. Matt never missed an opportunity to camp there, at least one night, when he was in town. He preferred backcountry camping, but at least he was close to the home he had never stopped loving.

Matt and Randy set up camp, then drove down into the canyon to take a walk beside the Frijoles River. Randy grabbed Matt's hand, interlacing her fingers with his. She looked at him, thinking he was getting more handsome the older he got. She smiled and said, "I can understand how much you love this part of New Mexico, Matt. It's absolutely enchanting. It would be nice to have a place in the Jemez Mountains someday. Gosh, you're just eleven years from retiring; not many jobs you can retire at 55."

"We'll see if I make it that long," Matt replied.

"Of course you will. You'd be crazy to give up that pension before then."

"Well, you know," Matt said with a smile, "Jimi Hendrix said, 'You have to go on and be crazy. Craziness is like heaven.'"

"And we all know where Jimi Hendrix is now, Bertram," Randy shot back without hesitation.

Just as Matt and Randy arrived back at their campsite, an unexpected visitor drove up the road. Matt immediately spotted the Los Alamos Police cruiser, which was out of place in a federal park. The car parked in front of their campsite and out climbed Chief Goldman, looking like an unfolding chaise lounge far too big for the little car. "Matt," Tadg said, "I just got a call from your office. They told me there has been some sort of major crime in San Diego, and they need you to get there pronto. It looks like your holiday is going to be cut short."

Matt looked at Randy with a long face of disappointment. Randy smiled and shrugged. The three broke camp, putting the equipment in Tadg's trunk. Matt searched his bag for his cell phone, a piece of equipment he had reluctantly accepted and rarely used. "There won't be any mobile service here, my friend," Tadg said. "You won't get any until you are on I-25."

Matt and Randy said their goodbyes, and Matt forlornly said *adiós* to his homeland. Randy took the wheel, and as soon as they had cell service, Matt called his office. He was immediately put through to Aldrich Sowles. "I'm sorry to have to ask you to cut your leave short, Matt, but we need to have you here as soon as you can get here. There was an act of sabotage on the USS *Stilton*," Sowles said. "Someone cut her loose from her moorings and drifted into the harbor."

"Aldrich, that's something my staff can handle without me," Matt said. "What *aren't* you telling me?"

"Looks like the work of a professional. A *serious* professional, and he left a note indicating there is more to come, which we are taking very seriously. When you see the evidence we reviewed, you'll no doubt agree. We need you here ASAP. Albuquerque International is also home to Kirtland Air Force Base. They will have a jet waiting for you. Time is of the essence."

As they finished the call, Matt turned to Randy. "I'm sorry for cutting our romantic camping trip short," he said.

"I'd have done the same thing if they called me," Randy said. "I told you that you are married to this job, and I was right!"

"Well, the job and I are going through a rough patch, if you ask me."

"Sweetie, I love you. Go and do what you do best. The CNO is going to be visiting San Diego in a few weeks, and we'll have a bit of time to get together."

"You know," Matt said with a quizzical look on his face. "It's a little ironic. They named the USS *Stilton* after Admiral James Stilton, a hero of a huge battle during World War II."

"What's so ironic about that?" Randy inquired.

"James Stilton was the father of my commanding officer when I was stationed on the USS *Robert E. Peckham*. Kind of a weird coincidence, don't you think?"

THE BEGINNING OF THE NIGHTMARE

Saturday, April 7, 2000 (0800 hours)

I t almost seems that there are unwritten procedures for military transportation, especially during times of emergency. One of those is that acquiring proper transportation is an excruciatingly slow process. When Matt arrived at Kirtland Air Force Base only to find that they were having difficulty arranging for a jet to fly him back to San Diego, he wasn't all that surprised. After waiting most of the night for a plane to appear, his ride finally touched down at 8 a.m. He had never been good at sleeping on planes. The pilot announced over the P.A. that they would be landing in approximately fifteen minutes, Matt having had no sleep for twenty-four hours.

The Regional Office of NCIS San Diego was located on the sprawling Naval Base, San Diego. Also known as 32nd Street Naval Station, the base was the second-largest ship-based facility in the US Navy. It was the operational headquarters of the US Navy's entire Pacific Fleet. Although NCIS had been a military organization for most of its existence, it had been gradually staffed exclusively by civilians over the years. In 1997, the last military director of the service retired, and the first civilian director of the NCIS took command. NCIS had become an almost entirely civilian organization while remaining under the authority of the US Secretary of the Navy.

Matt watched the city of San Diego appear out the window as his plane made its final approach to North Island Naval Air Station, a short five-minute drive from 32nd Street Naval Station. As the jet taxied to the terminal and he walked off the jetway, he was met by two of his NCIS special agents, who took him on the short drive to the NCIS regional office.

As they walked into the office, the receptionist let him know that SAC Sowles was in Matt's office waiting for him. Matt walked in the door, greeted Sowles, then looked to his left to see Jake Packer seated next to the special agent in charge. Matt gave him a scowl and turned to his friend Sowles. "What is *he* doing here?" Matt said, unable to control the sound of incredulousness in his voice.

"We discussed this at the conference, Matt," Aldrich said, attempting to sound conciliatory. "Jake is here to shadow you for the next two weeks as a part of his contract to consult with us. I think he'll provide a lot of help to your division in the next few weeks, and he will learn how a well-run criminal division is led."

Matt turned to Packer, attempting to give him an intimidating stare. "Well, that's just peachy," he said sarcastically. "I hope you take the word *shadow* seriously."

"Don't worry, *Supervisory* Special Agent Bertram," Packer said, with more smarminess than Joe Pesci could ever pull off. "I'll be a veritable fly on the wall."

"I don't doubt the fly part," Matt blurted out and immediately regretted it.

"OK, children, stop right now," Sowles said. "We have some trouble here that could signify something even more severe being thrown at us. I need you to muster as much professionalism as possible, Matt, and the same goes for you, Jake. Like it or not, the two of you are going to be spending substantial time together in the next few weeks. Now let's head to the conference room. We've got forensics and our bomb experts there, and I'll give you the whole story."

When they reached the main conference room, Alban Harrett, a team leader from the Office of Forensic Support (OFS) met them. Also in the room were a dozen or so of Matt's top criminal special agents. Alban was a stereotypical geek wearing a suit two sizes too small, his pink socks showing between his pants cuff and shoes. Matt liked Alban, and his "geekiness" helped, in Matt's eyes, to enhance his credibility. The geekier, the better when it came to forensics people. It gave Matt a sense of comfort when talking to them. Matt and Alban had worked on hundreds of cases together, and he was a man that Matt trusted immensely.

Next to Alban was a man that Matt had not met before. Sowles shook his hand and turned to Matt. "SSA Bertram, please meet Jakob Gerver. He's with the FBI's explosives division, and the FBI has kindly loaned him to us to help with this case. I'll start by briefing you on the situation and let Alban and Jakob fill you in on their findings."

Sowles began the presentation. "On Tuesday, April 6th, the USS *Stilton*, a guided-missile frigate, homeported in San Diego, drifted away from the pier where she was moored, and grazed a ship with its bow as it floated into the harbor. There was damage to both ships, but, fortunately, it was superficial, probably to the tune of a couple of million dollars each. Once they moored the ship, the Officer of the Deck found a note taped to the bulkhead next to the quarterdeck."

Flashing a slide on a screen at the front of the room, a photograph of the note appeared. "It's a little cryptic, but it definitely indicates the perpetrator has plans for more shenanigans, and by shenanigans, I mean damage. I'll let Alban and Jakob take over from here."

Alban Harrett stood, cleared his throat and pulled copies of his notes from a folder, which he passed to the others. "I'm going to leave the bomb stuff to Jakob. I'll brief you on what we know so far from a forensics standpoint. The perpetrator apparently approached the ship about amidships from the water. The *Stilton* was berthed at Pier 7, which is approximately the center of the naval station piers in San Diego. There are some counter measures in place to alert the harbormaster in the event of a large incursion. Still, someone with the proper SCUBA gear and a sea scooter could, most likely, bypass these fairly easily. I'm not sure the navy anticipated a one-person attack on its ships. In this case, unless the perpetrator had access to the base, he would have had to approach by water. The subject left behind a fairly sophisticated set of suction cup devices with handholds, which were what he probably used attach to the hull of the ship, lock, climb, unlock, move higher, and climb until he reached the railing."

Jake Packer chimed in, "Wow, that would have taken someone with some upper body strength to make it, what, twenty feet up the side of the ship?"

"I thought you said you were going to be a *shadow*," Matt responded with irritation."

Ignoring Matt's comment, Alban continued. "Good point, Mr. Packer," he said. "It would have taken some strength and also access to some technical tools in order to reach the top, especially considering that he was carrying explosives, which Jakob will explain in a moment. The suction devices were hand-tooled, so the perpetrator also had access to some rather sophisticated machining devices."

"So, we took some time to analyze the note. It was printed on a computer printer, so there's no handwriting to identify. The note was attached to the bulkhead with scotch tape, which the perpetrator probably retrieved from the supply drawer inside the quarterdeck. This also indicates a high skill level in penetrating the quarterdeck without being seen. There were no fingerprints on the paper. The paper is office paper you can get at a million places, and the note was printed on a laser printer, not a typewriter. Because they found the climbing gear at water level, we can only assume that the perpetrator left the same way he came. I'll answer questions in a second, but first, Jakob, would you talk about the explosives?"

Jakob walked over and stood next to Alban. Matt couldn't help but think that they were the crime-fighting equivalent of Dean Martin and Jerry Lewis. Jakob was tall, dark-skinned, and muscular, with a face that looked like it had been chiseled in stone. His confidence preceded him, and his voice was deep. He chose his words carefully.

"The person who did this knew bombs like nobody I have ever seen. He carried onboard five strips of something called 'flexible sheet explosive.' Here is a sample." Jakob held up a thin, sheet-like material that was soft and pliable much like clay.

"The explosive was originally developed primarily for breaching and demolition needs. The explosive is equally powerful as a C-4 explosive but, because of its consistent performance and properties, exact cutting of the sheet can target the amount of blast damage. It's flexible and waterproof and is easily cut to the size needed for the job. In this case, they cut it into strips one inch wide—just wide enough to slice a mooring line in half. Ironically, it is the US Navy that invented the explosive, and holds the patent on this material.

"The detonator is also very interesting. It's what we call a "robust shock tube assembly," and has an integrated M81 firing device and a military strength detonator. The shock tube is precision coiled and encapsulated in a thermoplastic 'skin,' eliminating the spool, reducing the overall weight of the unit and simplifying deployment." Jakob held up a sample of the detonator.

"The detonator is deployed by pulling the tab from the bottom of the device, releasing the detonator. A shock tube pays out of the bottom of the detonator as the user retreats to a secure location. The unit is fired by removing the safety pin from the M81 integrated firing device and pulling the pull ring. When deployed, the 'spool-less' design of the detonator results in only the initiator left in the user's hands. In this case, our bad guy went one step further. He machined a mechanical lever attached to a timer that pulled the ring back and released it, causing the device to detonate after he was safely out of the area. It was absolutely brilliantly engineered."

With a quizzical look on his face, Matt said, "Jakob, how available is this flexible sheet explosive these days?"

"Because of its ability to cause destruction, it's pretty difficult to get it privately. There are demolition and construction companies that use the explosive, but it is a highly controlled weapon. I would assume that the perpetrator would have needed to steal it, either from a seller, the military or a demolition company."

"Thanks, Jakob. Alban, one quick question. Is anybody trying to analyze the authorship of the note, and, in particular, the name 'Wilson?'

"Yes, SSA Bertram," said Alban. "Several of your special agents are already working on that. It's not my place to say, but besides the forensic clues we have, I'd bet dollars to donuts that the name 'Wilson' must also be some sort of clue."

"So, let me be sure that I understand what you're telling me," said Matt. "Here's what we do know. We have a person who is in excellent physical shape, who knows how to SCUBA dive, who can build a sophisticated bomb perfect for the type of sabotage he's attempting, who has machine skills to build a climbing device, who intends to do something again, and who wants to give us a clue as to who he is. I guess nobody knows the answer, but we need to go on the assumption that it's *not* just one person. I'm not sure that one person could pull all that off, and I doubt that any single person has all those skills."

Matt turned to his agents. "OK, we've got some work to do. I want a report on your research on the name 'Wilson' as soon as possible. If possible, I want you to find where he put into the harbor and how he got there, and I want interviews with anyone and everyone who might have had contact with him or who saw anything suspicious that evening. It will be hell waiting to see if he's serious about further crimes, but I don't want us twiddling our fingers waiting for the next attack."

Jake Packer stood up. "It seems like it would be a good idea to find companies that sell or store the sheet explosive , too."

Matt paused, staring at Packer. "Yeah, that was the next thing on my list. Let's get on that. I'll put together a list of assignments for everybody that you'll have in half an hour. Captain America here will be with me *and will stay out of the way*." Matt gave a sideways glance at Packer, who raised both hands in a gesture of surrender. Matt had a feeling he wouldn't be able to keep Packer quiet. It was going to be a very long two weeks.

Saturday, April 7, 2000 (2100 Hours, Pacific Time)

The attendant pushed the wheelchair down the hallway of Shady Palms Assisted Living Center in Chula Vista, California. Sitting in the wheelchair was an older man, perhaps in his 80s, who appeared to be napping. A plaid blanket was on his lap, and he was wearing a sweatshirt and sweatpants. The attendant reached a door. On the door was a small sign bearing the name *Jack Wilson*. She opened the door and pushed the man in. "May I help you get into your easy chair, Mr. Wilson?" the attendant asked, slowly and loudly.

"Huh? What?" the man said.

"Your easy chair. Do you want me to help you into it?" She stated again, this time with a tinge of irritation in her voice.

"Uh, yes, I guess so," the man said slowly. He had the trace of a foreign accent, but it was difficult to place its origin.

The attendant, with great difficulty, helped the old man into the chair as he groaned, winced, and moved slowly. Once he was in the recliner, the attendant parked the wheelchair next to the man's chair. "Is there anything else that I can help you with, Mr. Wilson?" The man grunted something that sounded like a 'no'. Wilson's attendant said, "Then, please have a good night, Mr. Wilson." The attendant turned and left the room.

As soon as the door shut, the man took a deep breath. He then stood up out of the chair, his movements lithe and easy. Standing straight with perfect posture, he pushed his shoulder blades back and reached his arms in the air, stretching them as far as he was able. Although he was in his eighties, he moved quickly and confidently, much as someone sixty years younger would have. The man who called himself "Jack Wilson" had grey hair, neatly combed, and not a hint of a belly underneath his sweatshirt. Wilson walked to the bed in the bedroom, got down on his hands and knees and from under the bed brought out a bar. He stood without using his arms and walked to the doorway of his bedroom. He took the bar and placed it on brackets in the doorway just below the top door frame. The man grabbed the bar with both hands, lowered his body to stretch his arms and quickly completed fifty pull-ups without stopping. Once he completed this exercise, he went back to the bed and pulled out a jump rope and skipped rope for five minutes. He followed this with fifty pushups. When he completed the pushups, he was barely winded. The man showered, dressed, opened his bedroom window, and left his room through the open window.

Wilson walked off the property of Shady Palms, being careful not to be seen. This time of night few people came and went. The staff was in the middle of their shifts, and family and visitors had gone home for the evening, so the odds of being seen were minimal. Shady Palms was on the edge of a suburb of San Diego, and within a couple of blocks there was an industrial park where Wilson was headed. When he reached the park, he used a key to enter an unguarded outside gate, and walked to one of the five buildings in the park. He came to a section that contained a large garage door, large enough for a truck to enter. Next to the large door was a pedestrian door without a window. The door had a padlock in addition to the lock in the doorknob. He opened the padlock, inserted another key into the door lock and entered the building.

As he entered, he flipped a switch that turned on two large mercury vapor lights. The room was large and laid out in sections. There was what appeared to be a living area, a kitchen area, a bathroom, and a workshop. The workshop had two metal lathes, a wood lathe, welding equipment, a drill press, a band saw, and various hand tools. Notably, there was a metal fabrication area with metal forging equipment. There was an industrial sewing machine and a variety of handheld tools. With the equipment in the workshop, virtually any part for any sort of equipment could be fabricated.

There was another section of the workshop, separated by a steel wall. On the far side of the wall were boxes with various chemical names, some of which were marked "Danger: Explosives."

Wilson sat down at a large work bench containing electronic fabrication devices, including small motors, radio-controlled receivers and transmitters, and several soldering irons, some of which were mounted on stands. He took a breath, opened a schematic, turned on the soldering irons, and began his work for the night.

A Perplexing Challenge

Monday, April 10, 2000, (0900 hours)

Matt and Jake walked the few blocks from the office on base to the piers where the USS *Stilton* had been moored. Approaching the pier, Matt stopped and looked at the ship from a distance. They slowly walked along the pier from the fantail of the ship to the bow, noting how the mooring lines had been placed. They stopped at the bow, examined the crumpled steel, then walked back to the quarterdeck where they requested permission to come aboard following naval tradition. After receiving permission to come aboard from the Officer Of The Deck, they identified themselves and were promptly escorted to the ship's XO by the messenger of the watch. The XO was awaiting them in the wardroom, Matt always enjoyed being onboard navy ships. His work with the NCIS allowed him to do so every so quite often. Each time he went aboard a ship, volumes of memories of his time as an enlisted radioman came rushing back. Ships were a bit more comfortable in 2000 than they had been in 1975, with the crew having just a modicum more privacy than he had during his time on the *Robert E. Peckham*. The navy had changed in the twenty-four years that had passed. Most notably, women now served on warships. Perhaps, thought Matt, women onboard might have been the reason berthing compartments were a bit more comfortable now.

The two men spent the remainder of the morning and most of the afternoon interviewing the enlisted sentries and the OOD who was on watch the night of the sabotage. To their frustration, they received very little new information.

Each person they interviewed had not seen anyone or anything out of order until the ship began drifting from the pier. It was evident that the saboteur had been completely stealthy, managing to infiltrate a US Navy warship docked in the middle of a secure naval base without being seen by any of the fifteen officers and 190 enlisted sailors billeted aboard, a seemingly impossible feat.

As Matt and Jake were leaving the ship, Matt's cell phone rang. It always took Matt a moment to remember that he was carrying a mobile phone, and the ring indicated he should locate it and answer it. Matt had been a late (and reluctant) adopter of cell phones, but the device had become a necessary tool in his line of work. Once Matt learned how to use it, he realized that stopping at pay phones each time he needed to connect with a colleague, his office, or a contact had been a hindrance in his job, and he grudgingly appreciated the newfound convenience. Just two weeks earlier, he had received his second cell phone, a Nokia 9210 communicator. The phone was state-of-the-art for the year 2000, and the government had managed to procure them before Nokia's scheduled release to the public in November. This one, Matt was told, had the technology to send and receive SMS messages, whatever the hell those were. Matt had yet to learn how to use this feature. He was barely getting used to learning how to make and receive calls and did not feel in any rush to enhance his technical skills.

On the line was a special agent from the office, who said they had discovered some important information. Matt informed him they were on the way back. The NCIS office was just a few blocks away from the pier. As they reached the NCIS building, Special Agent Simon Danforth accosted them before they were in the door. "We've discovered that there is an explosives dealer outside of Pine Valley, just off I-8. Yesterday they reported to the police that they discovered a roll of sheet explosive and a dozen detonators were missing. We've sent a team there to investigate."

Matt looked at Jake, who was standing with a shit-eating grin on his face. "I guess the *shadow* knows, huh, Sherlock!" Jake said, gloating.

Matt simply gave Jake a scowl and turned back to Danforth. "Update me as soon as the team reports in."

"There's more," Danforth said, with a look of dread on his face. "They informed us while you were at the *Stilton* that there has been another break-in.

Freedom Distributors, a military contractor, also had a break-in. They aren't sure when, but in doing inventory, they discovered that they are missing nitroamine, dioctyl sebacate, polyisobutylene, and process oil."

"I don't know what those things are, but it doesn't sound good," Matt said, rubbing his forehead.

"C-4," said Jake. "Those are the ingredients to make C-4; you know, plastic explosives."

"I know what C-4 is, Captain America," Matt said with more than a little bit of irritation, although a grudging admiration was building in him for the wily old man. "It sounds like we have an idea of what's coming next," Jake said.

"You know, for a shadow, you sure talk a lot."

"Just trying to help, Matt," said Jake. "I know stuff."

As the two headed back to his office, Matt, mostly talking to himself, said, "If this was Wilson, I don't understand why he would steal the ingredients when he could have just stolen the C-4. He seems to have the skills to do that."

"I know you don't want my input, Matt, but there are possibly two reasons. First, perhaps the C-4 might have been under more strict protection than the individual ingredients. Secondly, and worse from my standpoint, from the expertise this guy showed with the sheet explosives, he might have his own, more powerful recipe he wants to use."

Matt grabbed the phone and called Aldrich Sowles, informing him of the progress in the investigation and the information they had just received. After a pause, Aldrich said, "Thanks, Matt. I'm going to let the base commanders know that the threat of another attack has become imminent. I'm sure they will increase security to the maximum extent possible." Upon receiving the information from Sowles, the base commander immediately ordered the highest level of security possible at the base. They transported three hundred marines to 32nd Street, and each ship increased its armed watches.

"What's next, Sherlock?" Jake said to Matt.

"Why the hell do you keep calling me *Sherlock*?" Matt said, his face reddening.

"Just thought I'd put a little levity on the situation. Seems only fair if you are going to call me Captain America, I can call you Sherlock."

"Don't you have an infomercial to film or another book to write, Packer?"

"This is *way* too much fun for me to leave now," Packer responded.

Monday, April 10, 2000 (2300 hours, Pacific Time)

The old man approached a large door in his shop on a back street in an industrial park just a mile from Shady Palms Assisted Living Center. At 11 pm, anyone else who might have been working in the complex had gone home, which allowed him to unchain the heavy door, unlock the three Chrome-plated steel body key locks and pull the door open. He shut the door behind him and then turned on the lights. The noisy and bright mercury vapor lights illuminated his workshop's spaces. He went to the kitchen, which contained an industrial stove and oven, two full-size refrigerators, and two chairs. Next to the kitchenette was a space that held a single chair. In this space, an old wooden wheelchair sat with a high back. The old man had modified the wheelchair to include wrist and foot restraints, with a large hole in the seat under which he had placed a bucket. A very large tank filled with water was farther away, three feet deep and 25 feet in diameter.

In another corner of the room was printing and laminating equipment and a computer attached to a printer, a camera and sufficient equipment to create ID cards. On the table next to the computer were photographs of the IDs for active military, retired military, civilian contractors, and naval civil service employees.

The man had covered the walls of the entire shop in cork, over which he had attached four-inch thick foam rubber. He had then affixed thick moving blankets to the foam rubber. He had covered the floor with thick carpet. Below the carpet was a thick pad. The entire room was virtually sound-proofed.

The old man went to the workbench, turned off the mercury vapor lights, and clicked on two adjustable shop lights, one containing a large magnifying glass in the center. On the workbench was his current project. When he completed his soldering, he walked to a large materials shelf with different types of metal, and picked out some titanium pipe. He then moved to a metal lathe and then to a drill press. He meticulously turned slender tubes of varying sizes on the lathe. These he carefully inserted into one another until he had created a smoothly telescoping rod. He cut pieces of wood on a band saw and used a soldering iron to install electronics into his creations. With great concentration and intensity, he worked meticulously on his projects, fashioning several items. He worked well into the night on his projects, as he had almost every night for the past two months.

Standing and stretching, he took the creation and walked to the water tank. Setting it in the tank, he watched it carefully to ensure it did not take on water or sink. He smiled, thinking of the creative way he intended to use his new weapon. *They won't know what hit them*, he thought. *There's more than one way to break a dog from sucking eggs.* Just before dawn, he shut off the lights, locked the shop, and walked the mile back to his home. He would be back a good hour before the nurse came in to awaken him, shower him, put him in the wheelchair, and take him to breakfast.

A Spy is Gone

Tuesday, April 11, 2000 (0900 hours Central Time)

Fort Leavenworth, Kansas, Army Installation is the second oldest active military base west of the Mississippi River. Built in 1827, it served as the last outpost for cavalry, explorers, and surveyors traveling west in the 1800s. By the year 2000, the base was known best for two things. First, the base served as the intellectual center of the military, housing the US Army Training and Doctrine Command (TRADOC) and the US Army Combined Arms Center (CAC). More widely known to the public, however, the base served as the home of the United States Disciplinary Barracks (USDB), known to most simply as, *Leavenworth*. It was the military's penitentiary.

Leavenworth resembled a medieval building in many respects. Prominent stone placements and a castle-like entrance were daunting to new prisoners entering the prison. The largest building in the facility was commonly known as *The Castle*. The bulk of the work initially building the penitentiary had been through the forced labor of the prisoners themselves. Completely outdated, the US Government had allocated plans for building a new facility, but completion was over two years away. In the meantime, Leavenworth was home to 1,500 prisoners, including twenty-two women. The inmates included forty-two officers with ranks as high as lieutenant colonel. Leavenworth had become a consolidated prison for all the service branches, and the prison was operated by the Federal Bureau of

Prisons (BOP). The prisoners included marines, coast guard, air force, army, and navy service members.

The most notable prisoner at Leavenworth was a former Senior Chief Petty Officer named Morris Lester. Lester, a radioman with a top-secret clearance, had created a spy ring aboard the USS *Oklahoma,* in which they passed the most sensitive intelligence the Navy possessed to the KGB, compromising countless naval operations. His spy ring lasted almost ten years. Lester and his minions had been brought down by a young third-class radioman, Matthew Bertram, who had been reluctantly recruited by what was then the Naval Investigative Service as an undercover agent to investigate and root out the source of the massive leak.

Leavenworth had been Lester's home for the past 24 years, and, in typical Lester fashion, he had made the most of his time there. Lester had always been a passionate poker player, and while incarcerated, wrote a book entitled "Poker Spy," which was number five on the New York Times Bestseller List for fifteen weeks. They made the book into a movie, netting him $5 million, part of which went to the Federal government and part to his ex-wife, which upset Lester to no end. Lester had written nine books on poker strategy up to this point in his life and, for a time in the late 1970s, was a celebrity of sorts, having been interviewed by Morley Safer on 60 Minutes, among other network television shows.

While Lester was serving out his sentence of life without parole, he spent much of his time playing poker for cigarettes, chocolate, and assorted "favors." Besides his unusually intense and energetic flatulence, which caused others to avoid him as much as possible, he got along well with other inmates and the guards. Before prison, Lester had been a workout junkie and was one of the very few Chief Petty Officers (CPO)s in the navy whose six-pack was in his abs, not his refrigerator. At 62 years old, however, prison had taken its toll, as he had not kept himself in shape physically. In addition to a large belly, Lester had a number of health issues, the most pressing being significant coronary artery disease. Just a few weeks earlier, the physicians at Leavenworth had determined that he needed bypass surgery and stents. The closest facility able to handle such an operation was the Cardiothoracic Surgery Center at the Dwight D. Eisenhower Veteran's Medical Center. The hospital was just six miles away from the prison.

Lester was sitting at a table, playing cards with three other inmates, chain-smoking, and spending most of his time, as usual, bragging about his poker skills. "And," Lester continued, "I'm the most famous spy the navy ever experienced. I guess you might say, I'm an all-around badass."

The inmate sitting across from him laughed. "You got caught, Dude. I wouldn't really put that in the badass category. And you're about to go to the hospital for heart surgery. If I didn't think you'd drop dead from breathing too heavily, I'd put your badass skills to the test!"

"Well," Lester continued as though the inmate had said nothing, "I'm going to have four days of R&R from this place, and I'll be eating hospital food, which has got to be better than the shit they serve in this place."

Lester left the table and headed to the telephone bank to make an essential call to his ex-wife, Maddie. Maddie had divorced Lester after his conviction and the divorce judge had awarded her 75% of his book royalties and movie rights. She was living in the Cayman Islands with a string of young boyfriends, abandoning each as they "aged out" in her eyes. Maddie never answered Lester's calls, and a week prior, her cell phone had been stolen when she was visiting friends in San Diego, all information Lester did not have as she had not spoken to him, except through her lawyers, for the entire time he had been in prison. Undaunted, Lester continued calling her and leaving voice mails that were alternately pleading for her to come back to him and threatening her if she didn't call him. "Maddie, sweetie," Lester said, this time in pleading mode, "I'm going to have surgery tomorrow, heart surgery. It's not looking good. I need you to be with me, baby. All is forgiven."

The person listening to the voicemail he left wasn't Maddie, however. It was an 84-year-old man with a plan.

Late in the afternoon, four correctional officers arrived in the cell block to transport Lester to the hospital and maintain guard while he was recovering from surgery. Shackled hands and feet, wearing the traditional brown uniform bereft of any insignia, Lester was led out of his barracks and into the back of a waiting van. There were two guards in the front seats, an armed driver and another armed guard, along with the four correctional officers, each carrying a 9 mm Parabellum

CZ 75 automatic pistol with 20-round magazines and fitted with a horizontal rail in front of the trigger guard with a spare 20-round magazine.

The van approached the main gate and slowed to a stop. The guards at the gate opened the back of the van, ensured there were no stowaways, and everything was as it should be. They checked and double-checked IDs and transport papers. Although escapes from Leavenworth were rare, security was tight, as diligence had paid off on several occasions and contributed to keeping the successful escape rate lower than any other penitentiary. Once the guards satisfied themselves that everything was in order, a sentry opened a first gate, and another sentry waived the van through to a holding area. Only after the first gate had been shut and locked did they signal the guards operating the second gate to open it. Another sentry manning the second gate opened the gate, and the van proceeded through and left the Leavenworth containment area. Upon leaving the containment area, the driver turned the van toward the VA hospital. The heavy gates shut behind the van as it turned onto North 13th Street, rather than entering Interstate 73. The prison authorities preferred to transport prisoners on back streets and avoided the major arterials and highways, the theory being that there was less chance of mayhem. Unfortunately, the driver didn't see mayhem approaching in the form of a nondescript brown Chevy, which turned behind him from one of the side streets. The Chevy passed the van a mile or so down the road.

"Any of you guys play poker?" inquired the shackled Lester.

"I read your book," said one guard.

"Which one? I've written nine."

"The one on Texas Hold 'em," replied the guard. "It's made me some good money at the table," he said, smiling.

"Well, good. My ex-wife got all the proceeds from that book, the bitch."

"Maybe you should have stuck to poker instead of spying," said another of the guards.

"Hindsight," mumbled Lester.

About three miles into the six-mile journey, they heard a loud bang, and the van began wobbling on the road. Being naturally suspicious, the four guards looked at one another. The driver, remaining calm, said casually, "Damn BOP vans. They won't spend the money to maintain these vehicles properly. This happens a lot."

The driver pulled the van over to the side of North 4th Street. "Just stay put. I'll get it fixed in a jiff," he said. "I've got to come around and open the back."

The driver exited the van and walked to the back of the van, where the spare tire was located. The guard riding shotgun exited also, following the driver with his rifle at the ready, keeping his eye on the surroundings. It was necessary to open the back of the van to get the jack and lug wrench. He smacked the rear door twice with the palm of his hand, unlocked the door, and opened it. A moment after the driver opened the door, a dull pop sounded, and the driver fell to the ground. The The other guard raised his weapon and put it to his shoulder, looking through the scope for the assailant. His head exploded before he could orient himself. Each of the guards in the back raised their weapons, but before any of them saw the threat, in succession there were four more pops, and each guard fell dead, the recipients of bullets directly to their heads.

Six men died from bullets to the head in less than ten seconds. Lester sat in a bench seat on the side of the van, trying to comprehend what had just happened. As the door opened, an older man carrying a suppressed fully automatic Colt AR-15 aimed directly at Lester smiled, and with a distinctive Russian accent, said, "Easiest shooting range I ever been to. There's no law west of Dodge and no God west of the Pecos. Right, Mr. Lester?"

Lester's jaw dropped. His lips started quivering, and he was having difficulty making a sound. Finally, with a look of confusion and fear, he said, "Who the hell are you? What do you want with me?"

The old man smiled. "Well, Moe, this is going to be a very harsh and unpleasant business and will take an equally harsh and unpleasant person to see to it. Now step out of the van." The man escorted Lester, still in shackles, to a car twenty feet behind the van. He pushed Lester into the back seat. Lester felt a prick on the side of his neck, and the world became dark.

Tuesday, April 11, 2000 (1300 Hours, Pacific Time)

Consciousness gradually returned to Morris Lester before he could open his eyes. He realized as he slowly regained consciousness that he could hear a buzzing sound. He recognized the sound as the distinctive buzzing of mercury vapor lights after a few seconds. In the background of the noisy lights, he could hear what sounded like a small electric tool. His eyes felt as though they had been locked tightly closed, and because of the foreign sounds, he was afraid to open them. A memory flashed briefly in his mind of muffled rifle sounds and the sight of heads exploding around him, but the rest was too fuzzy for him to recall clearly.

As he gradually regained consciousness, Lester relaxed his eyes and forced himself to open them. The surroundings were blurry at the beginning. As he started to focus, he saw he was in a large room. On the other side of the room was equipment; a drill press, lathe, forging equipment, and other machines he could not identify. There was a man with his back turned to Lester sitting at a workbench, meticulously using a hand-held motorized tool with a small grinding head attached to it.

From behind, the man looked to be in good shape, with gray hair tied in a ponytail reaching to the middle of his back. The man was wearing a tight black

t-shirt. Lester could see the ripped muscles bulging through the shirt, his back forming a distinct "V" shape from his waist to his shoulders as the man's latissimus dorsi muscles strained against the shirt. As Lester's awareness returned, he realized he was seated in a wooden chair with a high back and wheels. As he looked down, he could see that he was still wearing his prison uniform, which was covered with blood and the remnants of brain matter from the guards. He looked more closely at the chair and recognized it as one of those old-fashioned high-backed wooden wheelchairs he had seen in the movies. His hands had been shackled to the arms of the chair and his feet to the legs. His pants were pulled down to the ankles. There was a large hole in the chair's seat where his bottom was. A sudden wave of terror washed over Lester. It didn't take a genius to understand that this was not a good place to be. He immediately panicked, screaming, "Help me! Help me! Somebody help me!"

The man at the bench slowly turned his swiveling chair toward Lester. "I soundproofed the room, Moe. Nobody can hear you but me, and I'm trying to concentrate," said the man with a recognizable Russian accent. Lester could see the man as he turned into the light. His face was much more aged than his body disclosed. Judging from the wrinkles, the guy had to be at least 80.

"Who the fuck are you, and what the fuck have you done?" Lester shouted, panic in his voice.

"Well, lookee what the cat dragged in: former Radioman Senior Chief Morris 'Moe' Lester. You have kept your sailor's potty mouth, I see," said the man. "Convicted spy, lifer in Leavenworth, and now a federal escapee on the FBI's ten most wanted list. Quite a resume, eh, Moe?"

"I said, who the *fuck* are you?" Lester repeated.

"What, you don't recognize your old friend? Damn, hombre, if brains were leather, you couldn't saddle a flea."

Lester suddenly recognized the cowboy parlance. A signature of only one man he had ever known. "Shit. *Makarov*? Is that you?"

"There you go, sidewinder. It's your old compadre. A little bit rode hard, but it's me!"

Lester stared at Pyotr Ivanovich Makarov, *Major* Makarov, in the KGB, and formerly Lester's "handler," in the most extensive compromise of intelligence in the history of the US Navy. Over more than a dozen years, Lester had provided thousands of top-secret documents, crypto codes, and more to Makarov. As a senior chief petty officer in the USS *Oklahoma City* radio shack, he was privy to thousands of bits of top-secret information that the Soviets used liberally in their quest to be the world's greatest superpower. The *Okie*, as she was lovingly nicknamed, was the flagship for the commander of the seventh fleet, which meant that she not only handled communications for the ship, but she also handled communications for the Fleet Admiral. That meant that the quantity of information was exponentially higher than most other navy ships. Lester and Makarov had a twelve-year relationship that Lester believed had been a strong working partnership and even a friendship.

As Lester came to full recognition that his former handler was now his captor, he attempted to push his panic down to a manageable level. After taking a few breaths, he decided his best strategy was to pull out the Lester charm on his old friend. "Well, Pyotr! It—it's just damn good to see you after all these years. You are looking fit as a fiddle, my friend! And thank you so much for breaking me out of Leavenworth. That was something to watch. But I have to ask, what are you doing here, and why did you break me out? Do you need a partner in whatever spying you're doing now? Boy, I was pretty sure you were sore at me back so long ago. We parted in—in a rather awkward way. You left me on that runway while you jetted off to safety—not that I'm upset about that in any way. I completely understand. You had a mission to carry out, and I had helped you quite a bit over our long relationship."

"Safety?" Makarov lowered his head, shook it back and forth, then looked directly into Lester's eyes and smiled. "You have no idea what your stupidity cost me. Safety was not so plentiful when I returned home, in shame. Safety was that they demoted me. Safety was that they sent me to Dikson Island, a desolate, horrible place, and the KGB left me to freeze my ass off, doing nothing of importance. Then came 1991, when the greatest tragedy to my nation happened, and the USSR was no more. No, we were *Russia* again. The 'new' Russian government decided that I should just become invisible. Safety for me meant no pension, no way to earn a living, and no family. Nothing. Broke. Broken. There are worse things than dying, my friend. Safety was starving and freezing until I finally found a job sweeping floors in the shipyard. I worked my way up to working in the machine shop. And, after years of being treated like a nobody, I was running the machine shop. To those in the shipyards, I was nobody, and my past was meaningless to them."

"My 'meaningless' past was a past of distinction: distinction, Lester. I served in the KGB since they discharged me from the Army, after serving heroically in World War II. I have a master's degree in International Relations from the University of Moscow State Institute of International Relations, and I speak *six* languages fluently. I became one of the top leaders in the First Directorate. I ran the most successful spy recruiting organization in the history of the world and my peers and superiors respected me, not to mention my adversaries."

"You and I worked together for a dozen years, and it went fine as frog fur. And then you, the *great* Morris Lester, a man who couldn't knock a hole in the wind with a sack full of hammers, let your disproportionately huge ego cause it all to come tumbling down. If you had not screwed the pooch, amigo, life would have been happy street for me. You and that mangy pole-cat Bertram, who had a ten-dollar Stetson on a five-cent head, that Glasscock mare who was always itching for something she couldn't scratch for, and your lackey, Clay Young, who helped them to escape when I had them all wrapped up with a bow. You all ruined me. You took my life away."

Makarov walked over to Lester, pushing his nose against Lester's and narrowing his eyes until they were barely slits. "I've had 24 years to plan to set it all right. And you, my friend, are going to help. You see, in this world, there are two kinds of people, compadre: those with loaded guns and those who *dig*. I've got a loaded gun, and it's time for you to dig. You are going to dig and dig and dig for your life. Now, just maybe, if you help me to give that revolving son of a bitch his comeuppance, you might just walk away with your scalp. We'll see."

Makarov could see the terror in Lester's eyes. *Good. Not the end, but it makes my heart sing to see that egg-sucking dog suffer.*

REMEMBER THE ALAMO

Thursday, April 20, 2000 (0800 hours Pacific Time)

Three horn blows sounded from the top of the mast as the USS *Alamo*, CG-74, dropped its mooring lines from the pier at Naval Station San Diego. With the help of two large tugs, the *Ticonderoga* class guided missile cruiser was underway. The *Alamo* was the second ship to bear the name of the famous Texas battle and was the last ship in its class to be built. The 557-foot-long warship was formidable. She was designed to be used for multiple purposes. Four gas turbine engines powered the sleek, fear-provoking ship with two variable pitch propellers and she was capable of speeds over 38 knots. She carried Tomahawk missiles that could be used against both land and sea targets, a Light Airborne Multi-Purpose System (LAMPS) helicopter for anti-submarine missions, and a state-of-the-art, AN/SPY-1 phased radar system. She had proficiency in both mobile anti-ballistic missile and anti-satellite weaponry platforms. With a crew of 300 enlisted personnel and 30 officers, the ship was one of the most sophisticated warships in the world.

The *Alamo* was headed on a West Pacific Deployment, known to the sailors as a "Westpac." She would be on deployment for five months and was scheduled to visit Subic Bay, Hong Kong, Pusan, Korea, Bangkok, Thailand, and several other ports during the deployment.

Most ships homeported in San Diego carried a minimum of armament when not on deployment. It was customary to be armed entirely before heading west to the Pacific Ocean. For that duty, the Seal Beach Naval Weapons Station (NWS) was a mandatory stop. Inside a harbor in Anaheim Bay and about seventy-eight nautical miles north of San Diego, abutting the pristine Seal Beach National Wildlife Refuge, Seal Beach NWS, one of the most significant weapons armories in the world, provisioned warships with the weapons any navy ship might need to conduct the business of war.

The navy had not upgraded seal Beach since 1956. The base greatly needed modernization, including a new wharf for ships to dock at while bringing armament and munitions aboard. Its piers needed rebuilding and new cranes to load armament. Plans were being made to do so, but the bureaucracy of the US Navy and the US Congress made such changes happen at a snail's pace.

The trip to Seal Beach would take about four hours cruising at 25 knots. Following the coastline, *Alamo* would pass Laguna Beach and Huntington Beach and would make a starboard turn into the bay south of Long Beach.

Just before noon, the USS *Alamo* lumbered slowly northward toward the weapons station, past large yachts with the millionaires of Beverly Hills and Los Angeles aboard, in addition to smaller boats of all sizes. The navy restricted civilian craft entry into the inner harbor because of the sensitive activities near NWS. Despite the restrictions, the area outside of the inner harbor was a great place for boaters to hang out, watching the massive warships come and go. Occasionally, a sailboat would wander too close to the restricted area. When that happened, a coast guard patrol boat would quickly intercede.

As the warship made its final turn to starboard heading into the harbor, it passed a small sailboat with sails furled and an older man fishing from the bow. He waved to the ship as it passed 200 yards from him, and the harbor pilot and lookouts waved back, envying the leisurely day the man was having in the warm Southern California sun. Once the ship passed the sailboat, the man stood up, stretched, and casually walked to the stern of the boat. He untied what appeared to be a tiny raft, perhaps two feet long, with long pontoons on each side. In the center of the raft was a box just smaller than the sides of the raft and about three feet high. The man turned on two switches, then stepped into the sailboat's cockpit. He picked up a radio-control transmitter, turned it on, and extended a long antenna. Using his thumbs, he began moving a control stick. The raft powered on and began moving toward the *Alamo*. The man had designed the raft to be small enough that it would go unnoticed by any of the lookouts or watches and would not be detected by any electronic equipment onboard the ship. Even if it could have been seen, the *Alamo's* enormous radar array was not running, and the crew had shut down the sonar, as the ship would be quite close to massive amounts of explosive material.

The small raft was amazingly swift in the water. It had been built with precision and contained two electric motors, each with a propeller. The pontoons on its side had been crafted much like the bow of a boat so that it would cut through the water with grace. Within two minutes after its launch, the raft had reached the *Alamo's* fantail without notice.

The man guiding the boat had a specific location on the *Alamo* he had targeted for the raft to come alongside. The raft passed the fantail of the ship, heading forward. It passed the helicopter deck located about one-third of the ship's length from the fantail. As it reached the end of the helicopter hangar, he continued to move the raft another few feet, then steered the raft to abut the side of the ship. Powerful magnets attached to the robot boat were positioned so that as soon as the pontoons touched the ship's metal, they attached directly to the ship to hold the raft in place firmly. Once the raft was solidly attached, the man used a second transmitter with two control sticks. His thumb pushed one forward. As he did, the top of the box in the center of the raft opened, and a telescoping rod with a ball on top about the size of a volleyball began extending upward. The rod had several collapsed joints so that it lengthened past the main deck to the O1 level of the ship. Once the rod reached its full height, the man pushed the second control stick, which leaned the rod over the railing until the ball on top touched the bulkhead of the ship. The ball had a powerful magnet attached to it. Once the ball had firmly attached itself to the bulkhead, the man retracted the rod, which separated the ball from the rod. The rod returned to the raft. Once the rod was retracted entirely, the man brought out yet another device. He extended the antenna and pushed a button on the device. He threw each transmitter overboard, unfurled his sails, and began sailing south, away from Seal Beach.

Ten minutes later, the Alamo had passed the inner harbor. As the captain and the pilot of the *Alamo* were bringing the ship closer to the pier to moor, the massive guided-missile cruiser lurched, and the entire ship tilted to starboard as though a massive wave had hit her. The ship's tilt was followed quickly by an almost deafening sound of an explosion. The captain looked at the pilot completely dismayed and received a shocked look back from the pilot. "All stop!" shouted the captain.

"All stop, aye!" shouted the helmsman, the order relayed to engineering to stop the screws from turning.

"What in the hell just happened?" The captain shouted at the pilot, who simply stared back. The lookout on the flying bridge screamed into his microphone for the captain to look outside. The CO ran out the bridge door to the wing, scanning the ship's port side. It took no time to see the cause. The O1 deck forward of the helicopter hangar was burning. Some sort of explosion had blown off at least thirty feet of bulkhead, creating an inferno cascading from the ship's side. The flying bulkhead metal had torn off the railing, part of the deck, and the entire mid-ship gig. The force of the blast had blown its rigging a hundred feet into the harbor. The inward force of the explosion created a fireball with the heat to melt the equipment inside the space, igniting any fuel source, including paper, rubber decking, insulation, and humans. The explosion was loud enough that it could be heard five miles away. What could not be heard from that distance were the screams of wounded and dying sailors inside the space. Instantaneously, the compartment became a raging oven, cooking the flesh of the sailors inside.

The captain shouted to his XO to call for general quarters. The XO grabbed the microphone of the 1MC, the ship's announcement system. Trying to keep his voice from breaking, the XO announced the emergency: "Now General Quarters, General Quarters. This is *not* a drill. I repeat, this is *not* a drill. All hands, man your battle stations. General Quarters!"

Sailors trained for general quarters regularly, and even when it was a drill, it infused each crew member with a rush of adrenaline. The explosion had been significant enough that even before GQ was sounded, every sailor aboard knew there was a big problem.

The ship was only about 200 feet from the pier, and stopping the massive cruiser was critical. The last thing they needed to have happen would be more explosions so close to the stockpile of munitions sitting on the pier. Onboard firefighting and damage control teams were dispatched. Ambulances were called to the pier. The damage control team sprayed molten metal with water, and it was almost thirty minutes before they deemed the space safe enough to enter.

Once the damage control team considered the space safe, the operations officer was the first to enter the compartment. What remained of the bodies of the sailors working inside the space was strewn across the room. The young officer vomited, realizing that he could never *unsee* the devastation the scene revealed. It was apparent there was no one left alive in the compartment.

Meanwhile, Back in D.C.

Thursday, April 20, 2000 (0600 Hours Eastern Time)

Randy had just passed the five-mile mark on her morning run. Running had become her ritual and her sanctuary. With the responsibility for supervising the protection of the SECNAV and the CNO, it felt as though she worked twenty-four-hour days. When she really thought about it, she was always on call, and her staff, in addition to both SECNAV and the CNO, did not feel the slightest compunction to call her at any time during the day or night. In many ways, she was a victim of her own ambition. Both her staff and her charges understood she had no family to care for at home. She did have a pet turtle named Myrtle, but, frankly, Myrtle needed very little time and attention. Although she and Myrtle had long philosophical conversations. Randy did most, if not all, of the talking. However, she made it clear to her staff that if anyone called during her morning run, it had better be an emergency.

Randy made a habit of regularly working ten or twelve-hour days, with frequent shift hour changes when either of the two men was on the road. She usually insisted on being part of the travel security team, because she felt it was not only her responsibility, but an honor to accompany the team. Unfortunately, both men often traveled at the same time, and they rarely traveled together. When that happened, she preferred to travel with the CNO, Admiral Myricks, mostly because he was an authentic and proven leader and had found himself in the highest position in the Navy through grit, guts, courage, and determination. By contrast, Secretary Poe was a presidential appointee and couldn't tell a forecastle from a fantail. No matter whom she was protecting, she took her job seriously and with absolute loyalty.

Randy's job was made a bit easier because both men had offices in the Pentagon, which meant they were in a secure facility during working hours on most days. NCIS assigned each man two special agents to be present at all times they were out of the Pentagon, and they rotated in ten-hour shifts, which meant that it took eight to ten special agents per protectee in order to give all of them time with their families. The pool of Special Agents on her team was far less than those on the President's team, which made scheduling shifts easier and protection much more difficult. Fortunately, at least currently, neither man was a high-profile target, and her teams were competent and well-trained. Each not only had significant experience in the field, but everyone on the protection detail had received advanced training. There was a standard training program on entry into service with NCIS. Each agent also went through the same training that the Secret Service provides, including the Criminal Investigator Training Program (CITP) at FLETC, and an 18-week Special Agent Training Course at the Secret Service's training academy outside of Washington, D.C. The training was crucial for the special agents, as a protection detail required specific training in protective intelligence investigations, physical protection techniques, protective advances, and emergency medicine. Their training augmented the core curriculum with extensive courses in marksmanship, control tactics, water survival skills, and physical fitness. It was a rigorous program that had a high drop-out rate.

Randy had helped to design the training program for the protective details, and as SSA, implemented regular continuing education for all of her SAs. Matt had lobbied Randy unceasingly for her agents to become proficient in Hapkido without success. Ironically, the Secret Service was very fond of the Russian martial art called Systema. Because her special agents trained so closely with the USSS, most of Randy's agents chose to become proficient in that system.

Randy usually ran at the Army Navy Country Club, situated just next to the Arlington Village Condominiums, where she lived. She had gotten lucky and bought the condo from a retiring special agent for a reasonable price. Not having a family allowed her to build a more significant nest egg than her SAs with children.

Her space needs were low, so a two-bedroom condo was a good fit for her. The condo was close to work, and she could ride the Metro to work, as there was a Pentagon metro station. Arlington was a wonderful, quiet place to live, even though she often traveled.

Randy finished her run at the door of her condo. Arlington Village was a beautiful area. The condos, originally built as apartments in the 1930's, were two-stories each, with red brick exteriors and black shutters. The area was peaceful and most of her neighbors either worked for or had retired from the government. She entered the condominium and placed her keys in a ceramic tray on a table by the door. Randy had furnished the condo modestly, but with taste. It contained just enough furnishings to feel "homey," but it was far from cluttered. On the walls were paintings she had purchased at her past duty stations including Yokosuka, Japan, Pearl Harbor and Subic Bay. On her fireplace mantle were mementos of her time spent on the Chicago police force prior to joining NCIS, along with photographs of her father and brothers, who had all served in the "family profession," the Chicago PD. On her nightstand were two pictures of her and Matt enjoying time together camping. The apartment had taken on a fusion of Asian and mid-western with an overlay of cop, but it worked well for her. Although not minimalistic by any stretch, visitors considered it tidy and ordered, which Randy enjoyed.

Although Randy had grown up around and loved dogs, her lifestyle simply wasn't conducive to traditional pets. She compromised in a weak moment window shopping at a pet store and came home with a pet who would complement her busy profession.

She went to the cabinet and got some turtle food out of the cabinet. "How's your day going so far, Myrtle?" she said as she sprinkled some food in the turtle habitat. She pushed her face down to about an inch away from the turtle, waiting for a response. Myrtle seemed to say things were OK as she was gobbling up the food. While Myrtle was having breakfast, Randy fixed some Greek yogurt, poured Grape Nuts on top, and she and Myrtle finished their breakfasts together. Randy showered and dressed for work. The thought crossed her mind to give Matt a call which was dashed when she calculated it was four a.m. in San Diego. The whole east coast/west coast time difference made phone calls more complicated.

Randy finished her breakfast, said goodbye to Myrtle and walked the half-block to the Metro station. She watched out the window to see the imposing edifice of the Pentagon approaching. Randy exited the Metro at the Pentagon station. After passing through security, Randy headed directly to the beverage area in B ring, poured herself a very large coffee with a dash of cream. She took a quick slurp of the overheated beverage, then headed straight to her office in B ring.

To say the Pentagon is an immense building is an understatement. It is, in fact, the world's *largest* office building, with over 6.5 million square feet of floor space, of which 3.7 million square feet are offices. In the center of the Pentagon is a five-acre park. Every day, somewhere in the neighborhood of 23,000 military and civilian employees and another 3,000 non-defense support personnel work there. The building has five sides, five floors above ground, two basement levels, and five concentric ring corridors per level, labeled A through E. The only offices with windows are on the E ring, which, like almost every office building in the world, are coveted, and usually occupied by the most senior personnel.

Randy's assistant, Special Agent "Duck" Kuryaken, followed her into her office with the day's schedule. Duck had received his moniker from an investigation when he was a field agent, in which he had shot a suspect who was aiming for his partner. Duck screamed to his partner, "Duck!" which his partner obliged, which allowed Duck to fire on the suspect, saving his partner's life. From that moment, everyone on the team called him Duck.

"How was your night last night, boss?" Duck said.

"Considering I was here until nine, it was pretty short. I heated a leftover enchilada, enjoyed a glass of wine, and read for about five minutes until the book hit me on the face. How about you, Duck?"

"Charlie started T-Ball this year," Duck replied. "I don't know if you've ever watched a T-Ball game, but watching five-year-olds play baseball is more entertaining than a Patton Oswalt concert! If you're ever depressed, I highly recommend going to one. You'll bust a gut!"

"Yeah," said Randy. "I have a nephew who played, and you're right. Watching little kids with zero ability to focus, zero skills, and zero competitive drive is pure comedy!"

Morning pleasantries out of the way, Duck knew his boss would be eager to get to work. "We've got a pretty quiet day, from the looks of things. SECNAV has a cabinet meeting at the White House, and we detailed Hanes and Shotsy to escort, but the CNO will be at Ground Zero all day." Ground Zero was the unofficial nickname for the Pentagon and had been since the Cold War began not long after World War II ended. People started calling the building Ground Zero as it was a widely held assumption it would be the first target in a Soviet nuclear attack.

"Good. That will give us some time this morning to go through our intel and get our threat list in better order," replied Randy.

The two spent the morning reviewing the reports and enjoying an unusually calm day. Randy spent the early afternoon returning calls and pouring over the mountain of paperwork to which she needed to attend.

At 2:30 p.m., the calm evaporated. Randy's phone rang. "Randy, it's Don. We have a *situation*. I need you in Admiral Myrick's office ASAP." Captain Donald Hemminger was the CNO's adjutant, and the sound of his voice indicated that something big had happened.

"Do I need to bring back up?" Randy inquired.

"No, just you. But hurry," Hemminger replied.

Randy grabbed her notebook, rushed out of the office, down the B ring hallway, and turned right at Corridor 4 toward E Ring. Once she reached E Ring, she turned right again and walked halfway down the hall to the CNO's office, where she was ushered in, and took a seat at the Admiral's conference table. Several high-ranking naval officers sat at the table.

"Welcome, SSA Glasscock," said the CNO. "I believe you know everyone here. Dan, I think we can get started."

"Thanks, Admiral," said the Adjutant. "About half an hour ago, one of our Navy ships was severely damaged from an explosion at Seal Beach NWS. We don't have much information at this point, and we don't have a complete damage assessment, but we do know that sailors died in some sort of blast. Early theories are that it was an external attack. We do not yet know who was behind the attack." Captain Hemminger explained the details they knew, where it took place, and what was happening at that moment. "We don't know a lot, but NCIS forensics teams and investigators are being dispatched as we speak. We do know the damage is extensive. This will most likely be something the CNO will need to visit, so I'd like you to make travel arrangements ASAP. Secretary Poe is in a cabinet meeting at the White House, so we don't know if he will also travel at this point. We have contacted the President's office, and he is being informed as we speak. We will provide you with details as we learn them. Any questions?"

Randy asked, "Do you have any idea when you'll be leaving, Admiral?"

Admiral Myricks looked at his adjutant, then at Randy. "I think we should plan to get there tomorrow."

Captain Hemminger chimed in, "Provided it's been secured. You all know your jobs, so you are dismissed to get started."

As Randy made her way back to her office, she speculated whether this might be another act of the perpetrator of the *Stilton* sabotage. Too early to tell, she thought to herself. When she arrived at her office, she picked up the phone to call Matt, assuming he would have more information. The phone went to voicemail, which was a good sign that he was knee deep in the incident. "Hey Matt, it's Randy," she said when his voicemail beeped. "We've heard about the *situation*, and it looks like the CNO wants to visit. I know you're probably up to your ass in this right now, but when you have a second, please call me. Be careful, and I love you."

"What's the emergency, boss?" Duck inquired as she entered her office.

"USS *Alamo* has had an explosion of some sort. Early indications are that it was *not* accidental. Admiral Myricks wants us to put plans in motion for travel to Seal Beach NWS. Let's get things rolling on our side."

WHERE DO WE GO FROM HERE?

Thursday, April 20, 2000 (1130 hours Pacific Time)

Two weeks after the sabotage of the USS *Stilton*, Matt, two of his criminal division senior special agents, and Jake Packer sat in a conference room at the NCIS San Diego Regional Office. Scattered in front of them were paper records, summaries of the interviews conducted, and a report on the break-ins at the phosphorous dealer and Freedom Distributors. Matt looked at the scant evidence with dismay.

"So," Matt said, a wave of frustration in his voice, "We have no witnesses anywhere, no video camera footage, no alarms tripped, no fingerprints, no physical evidence whatsoever, other than the climbing devices found on the side of the *Stilton* and the note taped to the quarterdeck. We've discovered that the climbing devices were privately manufactured, and the note was printed on an inkjet printer that could be purchased practically anywhere. We've brought in experts, who suggest that it took a high skill level to make the climbing devices, and extreme proficiency in explosives. So, our bad guy not only has skills as a commando but also as an engineer and machinist. Or, he has help. OK, I'm open to suggestions about where to go from here."

"I'd suggest that–" Jake started.

"From anyone *except* Captain America," Matt interrupted. The room was silent. An anxious pause was ended when Matt looked up at Jake, shook his head, and reluctantly said, "OK, Jake, I guess you have the floor."

"Since this is my last day with you as a shadow, *Supervising* Special Agent Bertram," Jake said with more than a modicum of sarcasm, "I'll give you one last suggestion. You need to build a good profile of our suspect. Take a look at all of his skills, behaviors, and actions, and begin to create a picture of him. You might know that most profilers work on serial murder cases, but I think a profile will be useful. You have to develop a profile because this guy is unique. He has given us clues; by how he has behaved and the completely incredible and varied skill set he has displayed. I believe that the language in his note and the way he signed it should reveal more information about him to aid us in identifying who he is. He hasn't left physical evidence sufficient to reveal his identity, so we need to examine all of his actions to learn more about him. The more we can build a picture of him, the more avenues we will have to pursue. That's it. That's all I have."

To the surprise of everyone in the room, especially Jake, Matt said, "Well, it's a sound suggestion. Let's begin with that." Matt turned to his special agents, both of whom had astonished looks on their faces that belied their surprise that their boss had said anything complimentary to Packer. "Let's see if we can get someone from the FBI's Behavioral Science Unit in ASAP."

As the two SAs left the room, Matt smiled at Jake. "You know, Packer, I think you are a completely arrogant asshole. You puff yourself up like a male peacock trying to impress the hens, and I think about half of what you say is complete and utter bullshit. But I have to admit it, and only in private, I think I'm going to miss having you around."

It was Jake's turn to have a look of astonishment. He sat back down at the table, lowered his head for a moment, and looked into Matt's eyes. "You're not exactly the easiest guy to get along with either, Sherlock. Much as you don't want to admit it, you've gotten used to being the alpha dog around here, and you are supremely jealous, or maybe fearful, that Randy has a thing for me, which is entirely irrational because it's obvious she adores you. If you knew anything about me, you would know that I'm not a threat to your position or your relationship with Randy. I *am* here to help you."

Pausing for a moment and taking a deep breath, Jake continued. "But you are right. I know I come across as an arrogant asshole. It's, I guess, a way to protect myself from myself. The truth is, Matt, much of my demeanor is bravado, and I know it."

"In the interest of full disclosure, I'll let you in on a little secret. I wasn't precisely liked at the *Company*. Although I believe I did my job very well, I never quite fit in with the Yale *Skull and Bones* crowd that has the CIA by its balls. I felt, sometimes, that they were placing me in positions where I would fuck up just enough that they would have justification to have me dismissed. I saw it time and time again. We had very little support and guidance in Vietnam and were often given jobs that history just might have recorded as cruel and far outside the Geneva Convention. But then, those were the days when the CIA had little or no accountability to anyone. Hell, Congress wasn't even allowed to see our budgets!"

"Well, it was confirmed in 1990. That year was a terrible year for me. They accused me of something absolutely unacceptable to the US Government in general, and my agency in particular. I was on assignment in Northern Iraq at the same time Saddam Hussein attacked the Kurds. It was a freaking mess. The Kurdish forces were revolting against Hussein, and I was there as an 'advisor' to them, obviously covertly. My bosses wanted me simply to observe and report, as the US was concerned that Hussein was going rogue and would do something drastic to eliminate the Kurdish insurrection. Sometimes you can see things when you are present in the area that you can't see from intel reports. Once I embedded with the Kurds, I grew to like them and built some very solid relationships. I could also see that without help, they would not have a snowball's chance in hell of getting what they needed and wanted, and most probably would get themselves killed. So instead of simply observing and reporting, I did a bit more than that. The Kurds and I fought in several skirmishes. I taught them how to use their arms wisely and effectively and took part in several missions against Iraqi forces. I didn't realize that this information was getting back to my superiors. The fighting was ugly. Worse than anything I saw in Vietnam. The Republican Guard ruthlessly slaughtered thousands of Kurds.

"Although that landed me in hot water, something worse happened. Somehow, a reporter got ahold of classified information about the specifics of the attacks and the CIA's involvement with the Kurds. If you know anything about any government, the people in power do *not* want to be exposed to public embarrassment, and this definitely embarrassed the government, most especially the President. It left my former CIA Director, who was by then the President of the United States, no choice but to pressure Iraq to withdraw from the northern border area. The US leadership found themselves in an embarrassing position. Against popular will, they had to expend the resources to set up a security zone for the Kurds in northern Iraq. Hussein responded in kind, both against the Kurds and by setting the oilfields in Kuwait ablaze. As we all know, on August 2nd of that year, the President launched the Gulf War when Iraq attacked Kuwait.

"My superiors suspected I was the one who provided the classified information to the reporter, although they had no direct evidence of that. They knew that I was very sympathetic to the cause of the Kurds. My superiors gave me an ultimatum. I could 'choose' to resign quietly or be fired. I chose to leave.

"I want you to know that it I did not provide that information to the reporter, but I completely agree with the outcome. I had been an active CIA officer since Vietnam. I watched my career evaporate over baseless suspicions and a CIA that makes its own rules, even when they don't have a former *Skull and Bones* Yaley sitting in the oval office."

Jake looked up at Matt with an imploring look. "Now that my career was gone, I went through a hell of a time trying to figure out what a person with my skill set could ever possibly do to make a living. On the surface, it could go two ways. I could sell life insurance, or I could hire myself out as a professional assassin. OK, I'm kidding, but you get the point. What I did know was that, somehow, I had to reinvent myself. And that's when I found *my* people. I was asked to write an article for some obscure prepper newsletter on personal protection. I received thousands of letters and notes asking for more. I discovered that *my* people are all those paranoid people in the world. Those folks who listen to the crazies spout their bullshit about conspiracies and the overthrow of the "American Way" of life. They loved me! I started writing books, speaking at conferences, and being a guest on radio shows dedicated to scaring the shit out of people and then selling them stuff. I found my niche helping paranoid people feel more protected in the world and supplying them with education and gizmos that would accomplish that. As it turned out, I was pretty good at it. It's not that hard to write books, and I'm a natural at public speaking. It also turns out there are a *lot* of paranoid, conspiracy theory weirdos who will buy just about anything I recommend, even if it's a rehash of public information. I help people feel safer, and while I've been accused of being an awful person, I think I've done a lot to help people feel more secure and prepared in their lives. I like to think of myself as the Tony Robbins of the paranoid prepper crowd."

Packer continued, "But I'll tell you this, Matt: I miss my old job every day. Every single day I wish I could make it right. Every single day I feel like a complete and utter failure. And it doesn't matter how much money I make, how many conferences I keynote, or how many interviews I get on Rush Limbaugh. My 'bravado,' as you say, is 90% bullshit. I'd never sell another book if my loyal fans knew how insecure I am. There. And now you know my dirty little secret."

"Wow, Jake, I, I had no idea," Matt said, putting his hand on Jake's back. "For what it's worth, most of my animosity toward you was because I saw you as one of those guys whom God gave an extraordinary tap of the *talent* stick, not to mention the great body and good looks sticks, which completely missed me. Yeah, I did get a little jealous of the way Randy became your adoring fan, and I did throw my weight around more than I usually do. Believe me, though, when I tell you, I don't like being alpha. I'm here just because I learned to do a certain job competently and nothing more. I apologize for being such a jerk."

At that moment, SAC Sowles opened the door. He stood for a moment, mouth gaping open in shock. "What the hell am I seeing here? Brotherly love between you two? Will wonders never *fucking* cease!"

Sowles sat down at the table and took a moment to gather himself, took a deep breath and slowly exhaled. "Well, that will have to wait. Matt, we've had another attack. It looks very much like it's Wilson again. This time it's *much* worse. There's been an explosion on the USS *Alamo*. At least thirteen sailors are dead. It's docked at Seal Beach Naval Weapons Station. There's a helicopter waiting for us. A forensic team is already on its way, and we need to get our eyes up there as quickly as possible."

"Damn it!" Matt shouted. "What the hell happened?"

"I'll brief you on the way, but we've got to get up there pronto," Sowles replied. He turned to Jake and held out his hand. "Jake, my old friend, it's been great to have you around this place. I know that today marks the end of your two weeks of shadowing Matt. When I get back, we'll sit down and discuss some projects I think you can help us with here in San Diego."

Matt looked at Jake and smiled. He stood and took Sowles by the arm, looking him directly in his eyes. "Aldrich, Jake has been a real asset for the last couple of weeks. I know it's weird for you to hear me say this, but he's been very helpful in our investigation so far, and I'd hate to lose him at this point. He's up to speed, and I consider him to be a great resource. You suppose I could have him for a couple more weeks?"

Sowles looked at Matt, then at Jake, then back at Matt. "Romulus and Remus are buddies now? This world gets crazier by the minute. Yeah, we can use all the help we can get. You good with that, Jake?"

"I suppose I can push a few projects off for the time being," Jake said with a smile.

"Then let's catch that helicopter and see what kind of cluster fuck we're dealing with."

QOI

Thursday, April 20, 2000 (1300 hours, Pacific Time)

The Bell UH-1Y Venom, also called Super Huey, piloted by a US Marine Corps First Lieutenant, touched down on the widest point of the wharf a few hundred feet from where the USS *Alamo* was moored. Jake, Aldrich, and Matt all exited the helicopter and ran, bent over out of habit to avoid the blades of the chopper, which were in fact thirteen feet off the ground. As the chopper powered down, they were met by two NCIS Special Agents.

"The forensics team is onboard and looking at the damage," said one agent. "Of course, we first thought it was an equipment failure that caused an explosion, but we ruled that out quickly. From my vantage, it looked like it could have been a missile attack, but the forensics team has indicated they believe it was a bomb detonated from the ship's exterior. This theory was bolstered about half an hour ago when we discovered some interesting evidence at the ship's side that you'll want to see. SAS Bertram, twelve enlisted, including the CPO, are confirmed casualties. The bomb also killed the communications officer, bringing the total to thirteen. It directly hit the radio shack. All the enlisted dead were radiomen."

Matt paused for a moment, thinking about the magnitude of the tragedy, simply shaking his head. He had spent several years in a radio shack much like this one. His shock was increased by the fact that those killed held his rating. Memories of the hours spent patching radios, monitoring the fleet broadcast, repairing teletype machines, and trading sea stories with the radiomen on watch flooded his head. He imagined for a moment what the radiomen were doing during the blast. The ship was headed on deployment to the West Pacific. In his mind he could see the radiomen discussing the exotic ports they would visit, the alcohol they would consume, and the adventures they would find along the way. His heart hurt for the women and men whose families would never see their loved ones again. "Matt, are you OK?" asked Jake.

Coming out of his momentary vision, he cleared his throat and told the special agent, "Let's see what evidence you found at the side of the ship."

They walked over to a small motor whaleboat tied to the pier. A boatswain's mate untied the boat, then backed it away from the pier. He shifted into forward gear and piloted around the fantail of the *Alamo* and up her port side. The special agent pointed to an object in the water alongside the *Alamo* just below where the blast had occurred. The object was attached to the ship by what appeared to be large magnetic legs. To Matt, the object looked like a small raft with pontoons. The other Special Agent said, "We didn't want to take it out of the water until forensics has given us the go-ahead, but it looks to us like it's radio-controlled. It appears to have a telescopic rod on it with a radio-controlled motor. It is solidly attached to the side of the ship. Whatever was on top of the rod is now missing. Obviously, we'll need experts, but it looks like this was most likely the delivery device for a bomb. But brace yourselves. There's a note attached to it."

Matt bent over and looked at the note, apparently laminated and taped to the raft:

This was a small display compared to what is coming.
I want $5 billion to stop

QOI
Wilson

Aldrich read it out loud. "He wants to extort the US Government? That's what it's about? Money? This guy is either the stupidest human on earth or the craziest. There's no way he could successfully extort the US Navy. It's ridiculous!"

Jake was leaning over the others, looking at the note. "But what the hell does QOI mean?"

Matt immediately recognized the three letters, suppressed a surge of panic, and swallowed. "It's a communications abbreviation. Back in the days of morse code, sailors created "Q" and "Z" codes to shorten common communications phrases to make sending messages faster. The codes were carried over into the teletype age. There are a bunch of them. We used them all the time onboard ship when we communicated ship to ship or ship to shore on the teletype. 'QOI', as I recall, means, 'Your work is finished.' It seems to me to be pretty clear he wasn't targeting just any old place on the ship. He was specifically after the radio shack."

"Who's got something against radiomen?" Sowles questioned, looking from Matt to Jake. "OK, let the bomb guys and forensics finish here, and we can mull over the radioman thing. They can get this little bomb machine to the lab and go over it with a fine-toothed comb," said Sowles. "I'm not sure who we bring in for the extortion piece, but I'll send it up the line."

At that moment, Sowles' cell phone began ringing. He answered, said *yes* several times, and finished with a *yes, sir*. "The CNO wants a conference call this afternoon for us to bring him up to date. It's three hours later in D.C., so we need to get moving. This is going to break big in the media, and we've got to prepare for the public's reaction. I don't think there's much we can do here right now except to let the experts comb over it. We'll fly back to San Diego and re-group before the phone call. Maybe forensics will have more for us. And call the FBI again, Matt. We need their profilers ASAP."

When the helicopter landed at Naval Base San Diego, the three men headed directly for the regional office. As Matt and Jake walked into his office, they were met by Matt's assistant, who was hanging up Matt's phone. "Matt, I know this is awful timing, but something else has happened."

"Well, go ahead and pile it on top of this growing pile of shit. Nobody will probably notice," Matt said, sounding both weary and sarcastic simultaneously.

"We got news that Morris Lester has escaped from Leavenworth."

"What the f-?" Matt shouted. "When? How?"

"He was being transported to surgery at the VA hospital two days ago when the van was attacked. Six corrections officers were shot in their heads, and Lester vanished. It's pretty apparent that he had help—high-quality help, and it was from someone or a group with remarkable shooting skills."

"And I'm just now learning about it?" Matt said with incredulity.

"It was a Bureau of Prisons (BOP) issue. They were investigating and waited to make it public."

"And it took them two days to figure out the insignificant detail that if Lester is on the loose, it just might be wise to inform the person who put him there?" It was a rhetorical question that nobody in the room attempted to answer.

"I've got to be in a conference call in less than an hour with the Secretary of the Navy, the Chief of Naval Operations, and so much brass we could have our own marching band. While I'm in there, I want you to call the BOP and get all the information you can on this and where they are at with the search for Lester. I don't think it's any kind of coincidence that he escaped in the middle of this current business. I can't help but imagine Lester's jailbreak has a direct connection to our current situation, and if I were a betting man, I'd say Lester has been behind much of this. The extortion piece sounds especially capitalistic, and we know Lester loves money." Matt kept to himself the incredulity he felt that Lester could have plotted and conducted these acts of espionage while incarcerated in one of the top prisons in America. "Check on all Lester's visitors and get phone records of anyone that he may have called. If he is the brains behind these acts of sabotage; he had to have help!"

The conference call was brief. SECNAV and the CNO would be on a plane in the morning to make their presence and concern known to the public and the media. The press was already on the story, and Public Affairs Officers (PAO) would arrive with the leadership to put the Navy's best face forward on the chaos. Matt, although preoccupied with thoughts about Lester and the repercussions of his escape, was happy that the brass would be in San Diego. It meant he would have the opportunity to see Randy, and at that moment, he could not recall ever needing her presence more on both a personal and professional level.

He checked his voicemail and saw that Randy had called. He hit his speed dial, and Randy answered. "Anything interesting happening in your day?" Randy said, attempting some humor.

"I hear I'm going to see you tomorrow," said Matt.

"I wish it were under different circumstances," Randy said, attempting to be consoling.

"Me too. Definitely."

"Matt, you've been out to the site, and I haven't been briefed on the entire situation. I just know it was a bomb."

"Yeah, it was a bomb, all right," Matt said with a sigh. "Some kind of crazy robotic delivery device ingeniously planted it on the ship on a radio-controlled raft. It blew up the radio shack."

"Oh, Matt, I'm sure you didn't know anyone in the shack, but it must bereave you that it was radiomen that were killed."

"Yeah. It gets worse. There was a note on the device, and it was signed 'Wilson.'"

"Oh shit, Matt. Then the first warning was true. This Wilson is orchestrating sabotage and now murder."

"The note says that he wants 5 billion dollars. He's making it look like extortion is the motive."

"What?" said Randy. "That's ridiculous. The government isn't going to allow itself to be extorted."

"Exactly. And this guy is smart enough to know that. It feels like a red herring to me. But we aren't at a point where we can even venture a guess about his true motives." Matt paused for a moment, struggling for words. "Randy, this kind of stuff just doesn't happen to the US Navy."

"I know. And I can hear the gears cranking in your brain, Bertram. You'll get him, I know."

"Randy, there's more. It's not about the bombing—or it might be. Morris Lester escaped from Leavenworth two days ago. I just learned about it."

"Oh my God, Matt. How—how could that happen? And just before the *Alamo* explodes? Holy crap, this makes things even weirder, doesn't it?"

"That's one word for it," Matt replied.

"Baby, I'm sorry, but I've got to go. We have two weeks of planning to do in about twelve hours. I'll see you tomorrow, and we can discuss all of this further."

"Sounds good," Matt said. "Knowing you're going to be here makes a big difference."

A Visit From the Brass

Friday, April 20, 2000 (0800 hours, Pacific Time)

"We'll be arriving at North Island Naval Air Station (NAS) in just under an hour," Randy said over the Airphone on the Gulfstream G200.

"We've got three choppers waiting at the field to fly everyone up to Seal Beach, and the PAOs have set up a press conference there. I'm sure they have statements ready for the brass," Matt responded. "I'm glad you're going to be here. I need some of those wonderful, beautiful brains to help me with this one," he said.

"Matt, I don't know if we'll have much time to talk. We've got both the CNO and the SECNAV onboard. They each have an adjutant, which left seats for only four of us on the security detail on the plane. There's a second plane with six more of my special agents that will arrive in a couple of hours, but both men will observe the damage, make some remarks, and will probably head back to D.C. in the morning. We have escalated the threat index for these men, and that requires additional protection for the time being. With the menace of Wilson we are dealing with, I'm going to have my hands full just keeping everyone safe."

"I understand, Randy. I'm not looking for a hot night in bed. Well, actually, I am, but at least you've got to eat dinner at some point. Maybe we can talk a bit then."

"Let's play it by ear. This is big," Randy said, a tinge of disappointment in her voice.

The planes landed and taxied to the awaiting helicopters at the Air Station. The Secretary of the Navy, Jefferson Poe, exited wearing his self-made "field uniform" of navy-style khaki pants, a navy utility jacket from the USS *Hornet*, and a blue ball cap with double rows of scrambled eggs on the brim with the word "SECNAV" prominent.

Poe, as a political appointee of a President who had never served in the armed forces, had himself never served. He was a Harvard College graduate with an MBA from the Wharton School of Business. When he was drafted, he was rated "4F", which meant he medically could not serve. The examining doctors found a "bone spur" in his foot that the doctors surprisingly discovered under pressure from Poe's father, former Congressman and billionaire oilman George Poe. It had been a common rumor that this was an orchestrated maneuver to keep Poe out of Vietnam. Nevertheless, Poe loved the uniform he had created for himself after being appointed by President Bill Clinton in 1999.

Next to the SECNAV was Admiral Dylan Myricks, who presented a spectacular contrast to the SECNAV. Myricks was a highly decorated career officer and Navy SEAL who had distinguished himself in Vietnam, being awarded the silver star, the bronze star, the purple heart, and the meritorious service medal, among several dozen others. He had entered the US Navy as an E-1, or enlisted seaman recruit, and had worked his way up to the highest job in the navy. It took no more than a few minutes watching the two men interact that it became apparent to everyone except Poe, how much Admiral Myricks despised his boss.

The commander of Naval Base San Diego greeted the two men and escorted them to the helicopters along with Randy, three other security agents, and two PAOs who would brief the two men on the trip up the coast.

By the time the two men arrived at Seal Beach, the press had become a swarm of cameras, people speaking into microphones, and large trucks with satellite antennae on top. Randy had opposed allowing the press on base at Seal Beach, but Poe had specifically encouraged it. It was his opportunity to be the lead face on the evening news, something a man with considerable political aspirations could not pass up.

With cameras rolling, several local and national television personalities followed the men as they inspected the damage to the ship. A podium was set up on the pier. The SECNAV gave his speech verbatim from the notebook the PAOs handed to him, mispronouncing the names of three dead sailors. When it was Admiral Myrick's turn, not once did he look down at the speech that had been prepared. He looked into the cameras with the face of a man who had seen suffering, death, and agony.

"I'm speaking today directly to the American public and the families of these heroes who gave their lives for their country," Myricks said. With tears in his eyes, he cleared his throat and, stared into the cameras, emphatically stated, "I vow to you we will find those who perpetrated this act of paramount evil, and we will eliminate the possibility of them ever causing harm to our servicemen or our country again."

With that, the entourage loaded into the helicopters and headed back to San Diego where they would give several "exclusive" interviews to all the major network broadcasters, then meet with the NCIS Director, the Criminal Operations Directorate executive assistant director, Aldrich Sowles and Matt for a briefing on the progress of the investigation. Unfortunately, there would not be much progress for Matt and Aldrich to report.

When Poe and Myrick were tucked safely into the VIP guesthouse on base, Randy called Matt. "I've got an hour," she said.

"I can't offer you stuffed sopapillas and a view of the Sangre de Cristo's," said Matt, "but I know a nice little officers club close by where we can talk."

They greeted one another in front of the officers club. Having never been a commissioned officer while in the navy, even 24 years after leaving the service, Matt felt like a little kid sneaking into the movies whenever he went into an officers club. At the doorstep, Randy glanced around her to be sure none of her people were present and then gave Matt a passionate kiss that washed away practically all of Matt's angst of the last few weeks. "I don't know why you're shy to kiss me in public," Matt said, smiling. "Everybody has known about us for years."

"Decorum, my love. Decorum."

They walked in and ordered some small bites. Matt also ordered a double Jack Daniels Single Barrel Reserve, while Randy asked for lemonade.

Matt had enjoyed Jack Daniels since he was a navy enlisted man. He tried the fancy single malt scotches, the Irish whiskeys, and the small distillery bourbons. Still, a visit to Lynchburg ten years earlier had made him a fanatic about Jack Daniels Tennessee Whiskey. Watching how they carefully filtered the alcohol to give it a smooth taste, then discovering they made top-shelf reserve whiskeys, made him a true convert and evangelist for Jack Daniels. Anytime some pompous scotch or bourbon drinker gave him the snob routine, they were in for a lecture on the difference between Tennessee whiskey and the swill for which they were paying too much.

When the server brought the drinks, Matt took a good pull on his whiskey, took a breath, and waited for that familiar warm feeling in his chest. Someone once had called it a "Tennessee Hug," and what a hug it was for him.

"I know we don't have much time, Randy. But you've been briefed on everything we've got, which isn't much. We will hopefully know more once we get the forensics back. This was a sophisticated device, and I know we'll learn a lot from the evidence.

"And then there's Lester. The man escaped from Leavenworth two days before the *Alamo* explosion. The timing just screams that he is involved in all of this. Randy, I really need your thoughts on this."

Randy took a sip of her lemonade. "Next time I'm having a whiskey with you, Bertram. You're kind of an asshole to drink that in front of me when you know I can't."

"Yeah, I know. But it's only for medicinal purposes," he replied, smiling.

Randy took a breath before speaking. "Yes, it seems like it's too weird of a coincidence for Lester to escape right now. But it raises far more questions than answers. We are two weeks out from the first sabotage. Lester was clearly in prison then, so that couldn't have been him. And we know that he's barely able to walk with his heart condition. If he is behind this, he has some major help. In addition, the attack on the *Alamo* wasn't something he could have put together in two days. And besides, it's *Lester,* for God's sake. He doesn't have the skills or intelligence to pull something like this off. Have you reviewed his communications from prison over the last few months?"

"Yeah, it was the first thing we did," said Matt, shaking his head. "He's had no visitors in over a year, and in the last few weeks, he made three calls to his ex-wife, Maddie, none of which she answered. Two of the calls, he left voicemails blaming her for his being in prison. The third was to tell her he was going to the hospital for heart surgery. According to the staff at Leavenworth, the accusatory calls are a regular thing for Lester. Two days before he escaped, he also made two calls to NBC's Today Show asking to speak with Matt Lauer, which is also a regular thing. Funny, but neither of the calls were returned. Once again, according to BOP, he's been a model prisoner while he's been in Leavenworth, and because of the nature of his crime and his media exposure, he's something of a celebrity there."

"It occurred to me, though," Randy said pensively, "The bomb took out the radio shack on the *Alamo*. He was a career radioman, and it would be just like him to target the people who ended up being his demise."

"Why didn't he just try to kill me, then?" Matt inquired. "I'm the one who put him behind bars, *and* I was a radioman!"

"I've got nothing for you, Baby, other than to tell you to watch your back. You could very easily be a target. I'll keep my ears to the ground from my position, and I'm happy to keep you informed if any new information turns up on this. But in the meantime, it looks like 'Wilson' plans to strike again, and most certainly will when the government fails to cough up five billion dollars. All of that means I have to double up on my diligence in protecting Poe and Myrick. I know our wonderful camping trip to New Mexico was completely messed up, and I'm despondent about that. I was so looking forward to sitting around campfires, hiking, and fishing, and soaking in the hot springs, besides having some quality time for you and me. We really needed it. Make me a promise, Bertram, will you?"

"What's that, SSA Glasscock?"

"When this is all over, let's resume that trip to the Jemez and really take some time. Like, ten days or so. What do you say?"

Matt smiled and said, "I hope it's over soon."

WHEN A BOAT IS A BOMB

The conference room at the NCIS Regional Office was standing room only. The screen in the front of the room had been lowered, and a PowerPoint slide with the NCIS logo was on the screen. Aldrich Sowles stood to speak, and the conversation in the room stopped.

"I want to thank each of you for being here today and participating in what may be one of the most critical investigations we have had at NCIS in the last twenty years. I am incredibly grateful to the FBI personnel in the room and your willingness to deploy your expertise in this matter.

"Each of you in this room has been appointed to the task force to stop and capture Wilson. At the moment we don't know if Wilson is a group, a man, a woman, or all of the above. Each of you will be working on this case full-time, without distraction. I am appointing SSA Matthew Bertram, Task Force Leader, so each of you will report to him. He, in turn, will report to me, and so on. You will give him your unfettered support in this investigation, as Wilson must be stopped, and quickly before he has the chance to do anything else. I'll turn it over to SSA Bertram to start the briefing."

Sowles sat down, and Matt stood up. "We've put together this team because you are our best. This is a national emergency with the heinous murders of more than a dozen of our sailors. We consider this crime to be one of terrorism, probably domestic, and so we have brought you together from a variety of operational directorates to work together. I appreciate the sacrifice that those of you are making who have traveled here from other locations, and we'll get you back to your homes and families as soon as humanly possible. We have fifteen Senior and Special Agents, ten agents, and ten operational representatives on the team, in addition to members of the FBI's Office of Forensic Support (OFS). In an act of interdepartmental cooperation, the FBI has loaned us two of its best profilers: Dr. Dexter Barber, a clinical forensic psychologist with the FBI, and Agent Piero Ferri, who leads the Behavioral Sciences Division."

"Let's start with forensics. I think you all know him, but this is Special Agent Aiden Morris from OFS. Aiden, please take it away."

Aiden Morris was not only a career NCIS Special Agent, but he also held a doctorate in criminal science and a doctorate in forensic science. The man oozed nerd from every pore of his body and, at the same time, was the most respected of the Criminal Directorate's forensic scientists. The challenge for SA Morris in briefings like these was that he had difficulty reducing vastly complex subjects into understandable information for people who didn't have two doctorates, which was everyone else in the room.

Morris pushed a button on the remote in his hand and teed up the first slide. "Let me give you a summary of the forensic evidence that we have found to date and what we've learned from it. The evidence discovered after the sabotage of the USS *Stilton* provided very little information. The perpetrator covered his tracks very well. The only physical evidence we have is two homemade climbing devices with suction cups, the remnants of the sheet explosive devices that caused the ship's tie lines to fail, and the note which was found on the quarterdeck. We have no witnesses and no way to trace the note. The sheet explosive was very novel in that the perpetrator wrapped strips of the explosive encased in duct tape around the lines. The explosives were connected to a shock tube detonator and a timer, so he could be long gone when they detonated. My assessment is that this person has a superior level of knowledge in bomb-making.

"We have traced the sheet explosive and detonator to a company north of San Diego that reported the theft of this material. Although there were video cameras, locks, and armed guards, the person who broke into the facility was not recorded, seen or heard. Because the hand climbers were homemade, we have attempted to trace the source of the material used to build them without success, at least so far. Our inspection reinforces our suspicions that whoever built the climbing devices was a highly skilled machinist."

"With the *Alamo* blast, we have a bit more to go on. The delivery device was a very creatively built raft with magnets on the pontoons and two radio controlled motors. The radio control device had a maximum range of about a half mile—maybe a bit more."

Matt said, "Hate to interrupt, Aiden, but I will say that this shows that the perpetrator was very close to Seal Beach at the time of the explosion. We have reached out to the coast guard and are interviewing the sailors on visual watch at the time to see if they noticed anyone onshore or in a vessel that might have been suspicious. Sorry, Aiden, please proceed."

Morris continued, "Once the raft touched the *Alamo*, the magnets on the raft held it tight enough to keep it immobile. The raft contained another radio-controlled telescoping device that extended high enough to reach the 01-level aft of SSES, the Ship's Signal Exploitation Space, then CIC, or Combat Information Central. Radio Central was forward of the helo hanger, and that's precisely where the pilot of the raft attached it to the ship."

"We've tested the device and found that it could lift five pounds of C-4 explosives to the O1 level of the superstructure. We found shreds of what we believe to be a volleyball. Our examination of the delivery device forces us to conclude that this was the container for the explosives. We did the math on C-4, which yielded interesting results. One pound is 454 grams in human-friendly units, and the effect can be easily calculated from the formula $p = k*c*d*w^3$, where p = mass of the explosive needed, k = kilograms' explosive quality coefficient (1 for C4), c = hardness of the target (1 for softwood, 10 for reinforced concrete), d = coverage (1 for sunken charge, 4 for surface charge), w = radius of effect." Morris looked around the room and realized he had lost everybody with that description, so he tried a different approach.

"Let me put it this way: One pound is close enough to half a kilo, which can easily blow a car into smithereens. It can also destroy a single-family house, snap a railway track, or blow up a light traffic bridge."

"The bulkhead of the superstructure of the *Alamo* was made of 1-inch-thick aluminum with steel strips as reinforcement. The Navy some time ago determined that aluminum cracks too easily, and as such, future superstructures will, once again be built with steel in the future as was common in World War II combat vessels. The warships of World War II had high steel superstructures to allow the commander a clear view of the action. After the war, new advanced electronic systems required more space, and the Navy found it could provide that space by building lighter but larger aluminum superstructures atop steel hulls. The *Alamo* was equipped with Kevlar splinter protection in critical areas, but there was none at the point where the bomb was placed. The placement of the bomb with magnets indicates the perpetrator knew exactly where the steel strips were located, as the magnets would not have adhered to aluminum."

Morris advanced the slides to show the formula. "Here is the application of our equation for the damage. Rather than do the math for you, I'll just give you the bottom line: Five pounds of C-4 placed directly against the aluminum bulkhead would have done precisely the damage caused in this case."

"Once again, the ingredients to manufacture the C-4 were indeed stolen from a US armament supplier in the San Diego area. The results of that investigation are the same as with the sheet explosive."

"Our perp has demonstrated, quite completely, that he has an extraordinary skill set. Questions?"

Matt stood up after all of the questions were answered. "We'll have one more presentation from the FBI as soon as they arrive, then we'll break and start assignments. We will meet back tomorrow at 9 am sharp."

Matt's assistant gestured to let him know that the FBI had arrived. Although there were a hundred things that Matt needed to attend to, the resources of the FBI's Behavioral Science unit were tough to come by.

Matt signaled for two FBI agents sitting in the room's rear to come forward. Matt had met both on several occasions. The NCIS did not have its own profiling unit, although Matt had been advocating for full-time profilers for some time. "Let me introduce Dr. Barker and Agent Ferri from the FBI Behavioral Science Division."

Matt introduced Dr. Dexter Barber, a clinical forensic psychologist with the FBI, and Agent Piero Ferri, who had been with the FBI's behavioral science unit since the 1970s. He had been a part of a group of FBI agents who had intensely interviewed 39 serial murderers in an effort to develop theories about their personality traits to categorize offenders.

Both men stood up and changed the PowerPoint to their presentation. Doctor Barber said to the group, "I think we'll just jump into where we are at with developing a profile."

"Before we get started, Dr. Barber," Matt said, "my colleagues are not as well-versed in your unit and what you do. Just to be sure we're all on the same page, can you give us an introduction to your job?"

"Happy to, SSA Bertram," Dr. Barber said with perhaps too much formality. "Criminal profiling is a common and valuable tool to law enforcement today. Our unit at the FBI has been fully staffed since 1974. But criminal profiling is, in fact, nothing new. The first recorded instance of criminal profiling dates back to the 1880's when two British physicians analyzed crime-scene evidence in an effort to make predictions about Jack the Ripper's personality."

"Caught somewhere between psychology and law enforcement, we forensic psychologists are most useful in serial homicides and serial sex crimes. The entire premise of criminal profiling is that behavior reflects personality. At the FBI, we have gradually developed the idea of the 'organized/disorganized dichotomy.' In lay terms, this means that organized crimes are premeditated and carefully planned, so rarely is any valuable evidence found at the scene. According to our classification scheme, organized criminals are antisocial, but they also know right from wrong. They aren't insane, and yet they show no remorse. Disorganized crimes, in contrast, are not planned, and criminals usually leave such evidence as fingerprints and blood. Disorganized criminals may be young, under the influence of alcohol or drugs, or mentally ill. It may simply be spontaneous and not premeditated."

"Your perpetrator, in this instance, is quite easily categorized as 'organized.' We would expect little to no direct usable evidence to be left at the crime scene, unless he does so intentionally, which is mostly the case here. Our job now is to develop a profile of this person based on his or her behavior and use whatever is left behind at the crime scenes to deepen our understanding of the offender's mind. In your case, we ask many of the same questions we ask when looking at a serial murderer, as we can safely assume that this person is at least a serial criminal. First, we look at the antecedent: What fantasy or plan, or both, did the perpetrator have in place before he did what he did? What was it that triggered the crimes? We look at their methods and manner: Who were the victims of the crimes, and are there commonalities? And we look at post-offense behavior: Is the perpetrator trying to inject himself or herself into the investigation by reacting to media reports or contacting investigators? If so, what clues do those acts give us?"

"Based upon all that, relying on the research of hundreds of criminals, we develop a theory of who this person is, so you can better do your job of investigating the crimes, and even, perhaps, narrowing the field of suspects down significantly. We aren't here to solve the crime. We are here to help draw a map that will help to lead you to the person who committed the crime."

"Thanks, Dr. Barber," Matt said. "Special Agent Simons will be working with you on your work and will provide you with every bit of information that we now have and all new information that we come across. I must let you know that it seems pretty clear that this guy or these people aren't finished, which means that a successful conclusion to this investigation is absolutely exigent. I don't know that the term 'serial terrorist' is a thing, but that seems to be what we are looking at."

Dexter Barber continued. "Based upon our correlation with our profile database, and looking at all of the available data, including what little evidence we have, we have an incomplete picture of the offender's behavior, which has at least allowed us to begin to build a profile.

"Contrary to what other events have happened, we believe that we are dealing with one person. A man. He may have some help, but it is essentially one man who is running the show. The man is in excellent physical condition, lives alone, and has few, if any, relationships. He is not young. We believe him to be at least 50 years old based on the mechanics of his delivery. He is former special forces or black ops, and we believe that he is most likely foreign-born, as all of the evidence indicates measurements were made in metrics, not imperial. Even though he claims to extort money, he is most likely motivated by a desire for revenge. He has no remorse and no need to advertise the righteousness of his cause beyond his intended targets. He has no hesitation in killing and is trained and experienced in ending human lives. The man has killed before, probably dozens of times. He is methodical, and we believe he has chosen his targets for a particular reason. We have turned that over to you to investigate any points of similarity in the two crimes. From a behavioral standpoint, we are still working on his pseudonym, 'Wilson.' I know your agents are working on the name from another direction. The bottom line is that this is a dangerous man on a self-perceived mission with tenacity beyond measure. The two crimes he has committed thus far required planning and execution beyond the capacity of most people, so we believe that he may very well have come out of the intelligence or the special forces community."

Dr. Barber answered questions, then sat down. Matt stood up and addressed the special agents in the room. "I'm passing to you an initial assignment sheet. I'll be meeting with the individual small teams this afternoon one-on-one at the assigned times. Now, let's go get this guy."

Matt and Jake walked out of the conference room and into Matt's office. "What do you think about the profile?" Matt asked.

Jake smiled and said, "I thought to myself, that sounds a lot like me."

"Now that you mention it, I think maybe I'll put a tail on you!" Matt said with a smile. "But to that point, I think that can work to our advantage. I really need you, Jake, to look at what we uncover and view it as though you were the offender. I want you to try to see things through *his* eyes. You are also really good with analysis, so I want you to work on what, or who, if anything, or anybody, connects the USS *Stilton* sabotage to the USS *Alamo* bombing. I've got a special agent just working on the name Wilson. That has *got* to be an intentional clue. He's working with some internet thing called Google to try to get information."

"Don't know what a Google is, but hope it helps," said Jake. "And I'm thrilled to get to participate somehow other than just watching."

You Want to Extort the US Navy?

Tuesday, May 16, 2000 (1000 Hours, Pacific Time)

Matt sat behind his government issued metal desk. Several of his senior special agents were sitting on the other side of the desk, each giving reports on their assigned areas. Distracted, Matt looked at his desk, realizing that he had been using desks precisely like this one since he was assigned to his first ship in the navy. He thought about all the military and government offices that contained the same desk made by the same manufacturer. *Some company has made a killing selling the government these desks.* Matt forced his attention back to matters at hand. The door opened, and one of his investigators came in. "A knock would have been nice, Woodhouse," Matt said with obvious irritation.

Visibly shaken by something, the investigator said nothing. Instead, he handed Matt an opened envelope and a piece of paper. After reading a few words, Matt set the letter down, opened a drawer, and took out blue gloves, which he put on. He began rereading the letter. "Get forensics up here ASAP!" he said. "Where did this come from? Why was it opened?"

"It was just in the routine correspondence and was opened like any other letter. A secretary and I, and now you, are the only ones who touched it."

Matt started looking at his desk, muttering, "Now, where did I put that camera? Ah! There it is." He opened one of the drawers in his metal desk, pulled out a polaroid camera, and took two pictures of the letter, just as forensics arrived. They put the letter and envelope in plastic bags. "Let me know if you find something," Matt said.

Meanwhile, Jake and the two special agents sat with looks of intense curiosity on their faces. He turned the pictures toward those sitting at his desk. "It's a note from Wilson. You can see he seems to be serious about the extortion part. The note read:

If you had any doubt about my capabilities, the Alamo should have convinced you. That was just a small example of what I can and will do, unless you follow my directions. Electronically transfer 5 billion dollars into the Cook Islands Trust Account "Wilson Trust 29384792749237, no later than midnight on Thursday. The Alamo bomb will look like a sparkler if it doesn't arrive.
Wilson

Within the hour, agents from forensics, the FBI, and the Internal Revenue Service were sitting at the conference room table. "Because Wilson is maintaining the *look* of a good old-fashioned extortion gig, and because it *looks* like he wants to funnel the money through an offshore account, you all are here to help. We don't get much of this in the NCIS criminal division, so we're looking to you on this one," Matt said to each in the room. "All I can tell you is that the government is *absolutely not* going to pay this in any way, shape, or form."

"SSA Bertram, I'm Agent Cunningham, FBI extortion unit. I asked Agent Barrow from the IRS to come because of their work with offshore financial havens. I'll tell you right now, this guy, on the surface, doesn't look terrifically sophisticated in finding a way to collect the money. Through international law, we can freeze assets, even in these offshore havens, when it is clearly the proceeds of criminal activity. Up until a year or so ago, our hands were tied, but we are making progress through the use of computers and the internet."

Agent Barrow stood up. "We've been doing the same thing, tracing money that Americans are trying to hide from taxation. I'll tell you we are just beginning to be able to trace such funds, so it's not foolproof, but we do have a few methods at our disposal. Each day the offshore banking industry is making more and more use of computer technology. Their customers want it so they can manage their accounts from a distance. It wasn't too many years ago that you had to physically travel to the bank to manage your money offshore. This technology has its upsides and its downsides for users. The downside is that we are becoming increasingly more sophisticated in tracing these funds electronically, too. And we may just be able to find your perpetrator's prints on this if we do it right."

"What do you suggest?" Matt inquired.

"What we do, is we go ahead and deposit a small amount of money in the account. We can trace where that money goes from there and ensure that the account is real. If it moves out of the account to somewhere else, which is likely, we can keep following the money path, hopefully to the doorstep of this guy."

"How long will this take?" asked Matt.

"A matter of hours," said Barrow.

"That's good because it's Tuesday afternoon, and if we don't catch him by Thursday, we may witness something horrific."

With the help of Aldrich Sowles, the ordinarily sluggish bureaucracy of the government moved at record-breaking speed. Within the hour, they had permission to transfer $5,000 to the account. The IRS prepared for the movement, as did the FBI. By 5:00 pm, the money had been moved. Within fifteen minutes, Barrow was on the phone with Matt.

"What did we learn?" Matt inquired, hoping for good news.

"The money did indeed go into a valid account in the Cook Islands. From there, it was immediately transferred to an account in the Cayman Islands. Twenty seconds later, the money moved to Panama, and thirty seconds later, it moved to another account, but we couldn't find it. My colleagues think it's either Israel or Russia, but the money flat disappeared. We don't have a clue where it went."

"Shit," said Matt.

"We'll keep on it and let you know if we find anything."

"I appreciate the effort. I guess we still have a way to go in this area." Matt hung up the phone and turned to Jake. "We have only one course, and that's to find this guy. And quickly."

The situation was briefed up the entire NCIS chain of command, then onto the Department of the Navy, then to the White House. To the person, the response was clear. The government does not pay ransoms. Period. As Matt surmised, there was only one thing to do, and that was to find and stop Wilson.

An Unparalleled Act of Terrorism

Monday, May 22, 2000 (0500 hours, Pacific Time)

The gray van with US Government license plates pulled up to the guard gate at North Island Naval Air Station. An older man in a ball cap with a bushy gray beard smiled as he rolled down the van's window, handing the marine on duty his credentials. "How's your watch going, corporal?" the affable man said.

"It's been kind of a shitty couple of days, Mr. –" the marine looked at the man's credentials. "Mr. Eastwood. Everybody's got their tail feathers in a knot with increased security. I'm afraid I'll have to take a look in your van, sir."

The older man got out of the van and walked to the rear where he opened the doors. "Just cleaning solvent; Nothing very intriguing," he said.

The marine took the shortest of looks and replied, "Yep, looks that way to me. Sorry to make you get out."

"No problem, son," the man said, getting back into the van. "Y'all have a blessed day," he said as he put the van back in gear and drove through the gate.

Once the van cleared the gate, he drove down the road, turning toward a supply warehouse. When he found what he was looking for, he pulled up to an open bay, looked in and found exactly what he was searching for; a forklift operator placing pallets of supplies on large shelves in the warehouse. Parking the van and getting out, he walked casually into the warehouse, giving the driver a wave. It was surprising to see anyone this time of day, so the driver shut down his forklift and walked over to the man. "Sorry to bug you, hombre, but I was told to deliver some supplies, and I think this is the place. Do you have a supervisor I can show my paperwork to?"

"I'm the only person in the place right now, mister," said the forklift driver. This was just what the older man was hoping to hear. He started to hand some papers to the driver, and as he reached out to take them, the man jabbed his fingers into the driver just above his sternum, which caused the man to collapse.

"Well, I'm your Huckleberry," said the older man as he smashed the windpipe of the driver. Once he was confident the man was dead, he dragged him to a closet, changed his clothes into the dead man's coveralls, and started up the forklift. Using the forklift, he slid the forks into the pallet in the van, bringing three 50-gallon barrels out. As he drove down the street with the barrels, he said to himself, "*It's a hell of a thing, killing a man. You take away all he's got and all he's ever gonna have.*"

Monday, May 22, 2000 (0700 hours, Pacific Time)

Naval Computer and Telecommunications Station (NCTS) San Diego was one of more than a dozen centralized naval communications facilities around the globe. Originally called Naval Communications Stations (NCS), as satellite communications became more common in the late 1970s, they officially changed their names to reflect the change in duties. NCTS coordinated radio, satellite, and telephone communications, including the fleet broadcast for its region. The ships of the Pacific Fleet relied upon the stations for access to the officers on shore who directed fleet activities as well as routine logistic information. Although transmitter stations were located separately, the central communications station was located at the Naval Air Station North Island at the north end of the Coronado peninsula on San Diego Bay.

By 1997, the US Navy had merged the official radioman rate with data processing technicians to create a new rating, called Information System Technicians, or ITs, and the radioman became a part of history. The ITs who staffed NCTS worked shifts of eight hours: day watch was 8 am to 4 pm; evening watch was 4 pm to midnight, and mid-watch was midnight to 8 am. NCTS was operational twenty-four hours a day every day of the year. A razor wire fence surrounded the facility, and even though it was in the middle of a secure naval base, it was separately guarded, partly for the critical mission and partly because of the plethora of classified information that passed through its equipment. Sailors greatly desired to be stationed at NCTS. It was a much-coveted shore duty and was often handed out as an incentive for sailors to reenlist.

That Friday morning at 7:00 am, the sun was just rising over the buildings as a gray forklift with three fifty-gallon drums on a pallet pulled up to the marine guard station at NCTS. The driver, an older man with a large gray beard and horn-rimmed glasses, wearing the familiar coveralls of the naval supply depot staff, pulled out an ID and said good morning to the marine.

"Little early for deliveries, isn't it?" the marine inquired.

"Tell me about it," said the man. "Can't imagine why floor cleaner is so crucial at this time of day."

The marine smiled and opened the gate to allow the driver in. The driver pulled through, waving, and drove the forklift down the road next to the main building. The staff entrance to NCTS was around the corner, and the marine watched as the forklift turned and disappeared. In fifteen minutes, the driver was back. The marine opened the gate, and the driver pulled through, once again giving a wave. The marine looked at his watch. 7:30 a.m. The day watch would arrive at any moment, and his shift would soon be over.

At 7:45, the first sailors arrived for their shifts, the guard checking IDs and sending them into the property. The first people in the group walked down the sidewalk next to the facility and turned the corner toward the staff entrance. As they turned the corner, screams and shouts funneled their way back to the marine. Not knowing what was happening and not wishing to leave his duty station, he called for support. Five marines exited the building. Before them was an almost unbelievable sight. An older man, in his underwear, was standing on a 50-gallon drum, screaming and crying. There were two other drums next to the man, and all three were connected by wires.

The marines, with weapons raised, approached the man on the drums.

"No, no, don't come any closer!" the man cried out.

A staff sergeant ran around the corner. He looked at the man on the barrels, looked at the barrels, and finally, looked at the two objects the man was holding.

In his hands were two devices with buttons on them, which the man was tightly gripping with his thumbs. Two objects had wires that went to the barrels. The man was wrapped in square packages, duct-taped around his chest, his belly, and his thighs. The marine turned to the crowd, screaming at the top of his voice, "Run! It's a bomb!"

As panic ensued, the man on the barrel cried to the marine, "I'm Morris Lester. I'm the guy they are looking for from Leavenworth. I'm standing on a bomb. Under my feet is a pressure plate so I can't get down. If I stop pushing these buttons, the bomb will go off! You've got to help! I don't want to die!"

"Just calm down, Mr. Lester," the marine said, attempting to sound calm. "We're going to get you down. Help is on the way. In the meantime, just stay calm, and whatever you do, don't panic. Just keep pressing those buttons and try to keep yourself under control."

"I will," Lester mumbled. "I didn't do this. Really. It's someone else!"

The marine sergeant took a step toward Lester. He had holstered his sidearm and was holding his hands out as a symbol of safety. "While we're waiting for help, sir, please let me know who did this to you?"

Those were the last words the marine would speak. Although Lester had kept the buttons pushed, a man in coveralls with a bushy beard and horn-rimmed glasses had his own detonator. The two in Lester's hands were merely decoys. The man smiled to himself, as he quietly whispered the words, "*tri, dva, odin, poka poka Moe,*"and pressed the detonator.

Two of the barrels exploded simultaneously, sending shrapnel and flames hundreds of feet into the air. The initial blast was so strong that it destroyed the entire main building of NTCS, sending a fireball hundreds of feet into the air, along with debris and building pieces, which became missiles, as some were tossed over a quarter mile away. Cars in the parking lot were scattered and collided with one another as though they were tiny toys. A massive cloud of dust and debris precluded any view of the tumult happening within the area of the communications station. Over the course of the next few minutes, the dust began settling, revealing a horrifying scene. The entire building was a pile of rubble. Those that were far enough away not to be harmed stood, speechless, unable to believe what had just happened before their eyes.

The man with the beard casually walked behind a building, removed his coveralls to expose a US Navy Commander's uniform. He took a thumbtack from his pocket and a piece of paper and pinned the paper to the forehead of the dead man lying next to the forklift. He put on sunglasses and began casually walking toward the exit of the naval base.

Rescue teams arrived on the scene within minutes as firefighters extinguished flames from what was left of the building. A pile of rubble twenty or thirty feet high belied the obvious. It was inevitable that virtually everyone who was in the building was now either dead or buried under the debris. Operational rescue teams were called, and before they could arrive, sailors were grabbing hunks of concrete and twisted metal with their hands in a futile attempt to find anyone who might be alive. Within twenty minutes, FBI and NCIS forensics teams were on site, attempting to sequester and gather any evidence of the source of the explosion. The base was put on lock-down, and equipment was brought in to assist in removing the remains of what was once the NCTS building. For the following three days, teams with dogs would work around the clock searching for survivors.

PULLING OUT ALL THE STOPS

Wednesday, May 24, 2000 (0800 hours, Pacific Time)

Matt, Jake, and the senior staff of the Regional NCIS Office sat in the large conference room of the Commander of the Third Fleet in Point Loma, just a mile or so from the NCIS regional office. In the room's front, a television set was on. No one in the room spoke, and all eyes were locked on the television. Matt sat with his face in his hands, doing his best to wrap his head around what had happened two days before. The television speaker came alive with Peter Jennings's voice saying, "And now the President of the United States is taking the podium."

The President stood behind the podium, momentarily looking down. He took a deep breath, raised his head, and looked into the camera lens. "My fellow Americans," began the President, "As most of you are aware, our US Naval Base in San Diego, California, was brutally attacked by terrorists two days ago, who detonated a bomb that demolished several buildings on the base. Rescue workers have been working night and day to find any survivors of the bombing. The hard work of the rescuers allowed the rescue of fifteen survivors from the rubble, all of whom are in critical condition at Balboa Naval Hospital. It is my sad duty to inform you that the remaining one hundred seventy-three sailors and civilians perished in the bombing. In addition, several hundred people outside of the building were injured. This is the most vicious act of violence on a United States Naval Base since the Japanese attacked Pearl Harbor in 1941, and the deadliest terrorist attack in our country's history. From the moment of the attack, my cabinet and I have treated this brutal assault as an act of war on our country. There is currently no evidence that this was an act of foreign terrorism, and law enforcement is operating on the premise that this was an act of domestic terrorism. I have directed all federal agencies to make the arrest and prosecution of the vile perpetrators of this unforgivable crime their highest priority. I have directed the Department of Defense, specifically the Secretary of the Navy, to spearhead this effort in partnership with the Federal Bureau of Investigation. As your President and the Commander-in-Chief of our armed forces, I make a solemn vow to you, the citizens of our country, that these criminals shall be brought to justice swiftly and without mercy. The Secretary of the Navy, Jefferson Poe, and the Chief of Naval Operations, Admiral Dylan Myricks, will hold a press conference this afternoon at 4 pm Eastern time to bring you up to date on the progress of the investigation. It is my promise to keep you informed to the extent we are able without jeopardizing the process, as we expect that you, our country's citizens, will hold your elected officials accountable for taking appropriate action to facilitate the rapid conclusion of this investigation."

From a chair in the room's front, a stout man in a blue suit stood, approached the television, and turned it off. He motioned to another man wearing a suit that appeared remarkably similar to the first man's. The second man approached the first and stood next to him. "Good morning, ladies and gentlemen. I am NCIS Deputy Assistant Director Gomez, and this is Executive Assistant Director Jordan, who heads the FBI's Criminal, Cyber, Response, and Services Branch. The President and the Secretary of the Navy have appointed the two of us to supervise the investigation. We have reviewed the NCIS investigation up to the point of the bombing two days ago. We have decided to keep Aldrich Sowles, Special Agent in Charge at NCIS San Diego, as our field investigation chief. We have delegated him responsibility for the work you all will be doing. There are one hundred of you in this room, about half FBI and half NCIS, and you will be working together to bring this matter to a successful conclusion."

"I know we are all feeling a great deal of pressure to find these perpetrators and bring them to justice. The President will be anxious to be able to offer positive news to the public as soon as we have any, so I'm not going to waste words blabbing about the importance of our job now. SAC Sowles will be handing out an organizational chart that we have created and a list of each individual assignment. SAC Sowles will be reporting to us each morning on your progress."

"You men and women are all consummate professionals and represent the best in the field. I have no doubt you will quickly find these criminals, and Executive Assistant Director Jordan and I will do our best to stay out of your way. In the meantime, our mission this morning will be for you to meet one another and assemble a status report for SECNAV and the CNO's press conference this afternoon. Now, we've got a plane to catch back to D.C., so I'll turn things over to SAC Sowles."

The two men exited the room while Aldrich passed out the organization charts and assignments. "You'll notice the executive team assignments on the first page. I want to meet with this team in fifteen minutes for a short orientation, so the rest of you grab a cup of coffee, and your team leaders will muster you shortly."

"Well, the Washington bureaucrats have come, papered us with bullshit organizational charts, and are sailing off to make plans for their promotions as soon as we do the actual job," Matt said as Aldrich handed him the pile of paper.

"Matthew, I'm *shocked* that you are so cynical," Aldrich said with a smile. "They'll be tucked safely on a plane in no time so we can do our job." Every agent knew that the bureaucrats with their powerpoint presentations and red tape, only get in the way of getting the job done. They have to do something to make themselves look important in an attempt to justify a future promotion. Matt and Aldrich were both extremely happy to see them leave.

Guessing What's Coming Next

Matt, Jake Packer, and three senior special agents sat in Matt's office assembling the summary of the investigation for the press conference that afternoon. "You realize they aren't going to have a helluva lot to say, right, Matt?" Jake blurted out.

"We've got enough for them to reassure the public that we are making some progress on the case. And we have more physical evidence from the bombing than Wilson's first two appearances. About three hours after the bombing, we found an abandoned forklift. Base police searching the area found the body of a supply worker, and a note was thumbtacked to his forehead. It simply said, *It's now ten billion.*"

"We got the preliminaries from the bombing back from forensics, and I think it gives us at least a little more to go on. It looks like the bomb is almost a duplicate of the Oklahoma City bomb from five years ago, with a couple of exceptions. The bomb Timothy McVeigh used to attack the Alfred P. Murrah Federal Building was much larger than this one, but most of the ingredients were the same. Ammonium nitrate fertilizer, mixed with liquid nitromethane and birthday candles of Tovex sausages. While McVeigh had sixteen 55-gallon drums of explosive, Wilson only had two. One big difference is between Oklahoma City and NCTS is that we know McVeigh intended to use hydrazine rocket fuel to boost the force of the detonation, but he couldn't afford it. Apparently, Wilson didn't have that problem, as each drum also contained the rocket fuel. Otherwise, the ingredients of Wilson's bomb were identical, just on a smaller scale. In addition, Lester had ten packages of C-4 taped to his body, providing additional explosive power. The rocket fuel most assuredly added significant power to this bomb.

"Each of the filled barrels weighed in the neighborhood of 500 pounds. The fuses appear to be more sophisticated. Once again, he demonstrated his skills with remote detonation as they were initiated by a radio remote control switch from a distance. The pressure detonators Lester had in his hands were fake, which means Wilson always planned to detonate the bomb himself. This also means Wilson was within radio control proximity of the bomb during detonation. This increases the odds that someone saw him at some point or during his escape."

"We've got teams canvassing the base in the hope that he was seen that morning, and we also have teams looking for recent thefts of the materials for the bomb. Most of the ingredients could also have been purchased on the open market, but the Tovex had to have been stolen, as it requires a license to possess it. Even though we have the benefit of computers, our law enforcement computers don't play well with one another at this point, so it's going to take time and labor to get the information we want, none of which the politicians are going to like."

"As for the ransom, the position of our government is simply a big 'fuck you.' I think this assures that Wilson will strike again. Quite frankly, I believe that the whole extortion thing is an attempt to mislead us as to his motive. The guy has a plan, and where it stops, nobody knows. Each successive crime has grown, in damage and in casualties. I can't help but think he'll be headed for an even bigger splash if that's possible. We have naturally added multiple layers of security to all the gates of our bases and our facilities. Still, we also know that Wilson has skills that exceed anything we've ever seen before this series of crimes.

"A large ceremony is now scheduled at the site of the bombing in ten days, on Saturday the 27th, and the CNO and SECNAV will both be in attendance. The base CO says it's going to take that long to extract all the bodies and clean up the blood and body parts so that it's presentable on TV. Thankfully, the President will not be there as he will be in Brussels for some bullshit economic summit. I don't have to say this, but I will: it would be a perfect opportunity for Wilson to pull more shenanigans. He's smart enough to know that we will be preparing for it, but he may be tempted by the fact that he will get much more media coverage if he pulls off something while being broadcast live on all the national networks. It could also be an opportunity to distract our attention from something else; something unexpected and far from NAS North Island. So, we have to be on guard for suspicious activity outside and inside the memorial. Now, let's get this into talking points for the press conference so we can get back on the street and nail this lunatic."

An hour later, with the information faxed to D.C., Matt and Jake were poring over details of the bombing. Matt's office door crashed open, and a young special agent rushed in, breathless. Both looked up with questioning looks on their faces. "I'm sorry to barge in, but I think we have something big. There is a quarry that mines aggregate just east of Los Angeles. They were broken into three days before the explosion and lost a case of Tovex."

"Good to know there was a theft, but is there anything that links it to Wilson?" asked Matt.

"Not sure. We've got forensics teams climbing all over the place right now. But here's the clincher: They had surveillance cameras and caught a man on tape stealing the Tovex. The DVR is on its way here right now. In fact, it should be here any minute."

Matt smiled. "Good job, Neely," he said. "Let's hope Wilson screwed this one up." The skeptic in his head said *that'll be the day*.

Within half an hour, the DVR arrived, and Matt and Jake went to the technology office, where a technician was already going through the recording. They looked over the technician's shoulder with anticipation. DVR technology was in its infancy in 2000 but was a huge technological leap for surveillance cameras in that it didn't require VHS cassettes that someone needed to change regularly. Nine times out of ten, someone would forget to change the tape, and the camera would be rendered useless. The DVR could hold more data, and the data quality far exceeded VHS, which meant the recordings were much clearer. It could also be stored more easily than the bulky VHS tapes.

Within a few minutes, the technician had advanced the recording to the break-in time. Matt was astounded at how distinctly they could see the building, the details of the stock on shelves, and a man with a flashlight apparently looking for something in particular. They watched the man, who had his back turned toward the camera. The man took bolt cutters out of his backpack and snapped a chain on a locker. He spent a few minutes rooting around in the vault, finally removing a box of Tovex. He emptied the box into his backpack and put it on his back.

"Come on, come on," Matt said. "Turn around so we can have a look at you." The man was not rushing to exit the storage room for some reason. And then, to Matt's astonishment, the man stood to make his escape, not heading for the door, but turned directly toward the camera. He walked a few steps closer to the camera, and looked directly into the lens, giving them a clear view of the man's face. He then held up his hand and waved at the camera, his lips moving. Matt didn't need a lip reader to see what he was saying. The technician paused the DVR.

"Holy fuck," said Matt.

"You know who it is?" Jake asked anxiously.

"Yeah. It's former Senior Chief Radioman Morris Lester." Matt stared at Jake for a moment with a look of disbelief on his face. "Somebody explain to me how our perpetrator can also be a murder victim, and why was he saying, 'help me'?"

UNCOMMON COMMONALITIES

Wednesday, May 24, 2000 (2100 hours, Pacific Time)

At 9 pm that evening, an exhausted Matt Bertram walked into his small apartment next to the Naval Base. He immediately went to a cabinet and pulled out a bottle of Jack Daniel's Single Barrel Reserve Proof Whiskey. He poured a large glass, perhaps better described as a tumbler, neat, sat down in his easy chair, and sighed an exhausted exhalation. He put the briefcase of homework for the night on his coffee table. Matt loosened his tie, extracted his cell phone from his jacket, and pushed number one on his speed dial. The voice on the other end said, "So, sailor, do anything interesting today?"

"Just the usual saving the world from the evil genius kind of day for me," Matt said with a tired smile. "Why don't we get married and run away to the Jemez, get a couple of horses and spend our days trying to identify the weird birds sitting on the fence?"

Randy laughed and said, "I can't run away with the man who is going to save the US Navy. Besides, Aldrich would hunt you down and kill you with his bare hands!" She quickly changed the subject by asking Matt to bring her up to date on things. Matt updated her on the day and the big news that they had surveillance footage of the break-in at the quarry. "I hope you're sitting down, Randy. You won't believe this one."

"What, the Loch Ness Monster? What?"

"Randy, there on the film, plain as day, stood Morris Lester!" She was stunned when he told her about Lester being the one to steal the Tovex. "We're scratching our heads on that one, Randy. The pieces are just not fitting together. He has an accomplice break him out of Leavenworth, brutally killing six men. A few days later, he willingly steals explosives from a quarry, and it was obvious he wanted us to know it was him. Then three days later, he goes from being a co-conspirator in the building of the bomb to becoming its first victim. Where do you go with that one?"

"That's going to take some analysis, Matt. But it sounds like Lester was a victim, not a perpetrator. You've got a damn good team there, and I know you will crack this. I know it. You can be a very systematic thinker in this kind of situation. You're a brilliant investigator. You've got this. Speaking of which, I'll be coming out on Saturday, a week before the memorial, leading the advance team for the SECNAV and CNO visit. We are all naturally incredibly nervous about it, so I will need the time to do everything I can to keep them from being the next victims, but I was hoping I could crash with you while I'm there."

"I was hoping you'd ask," said Matt. "I not only need your body, but I also need that amazing mind. I'm hoping that your perspective will help to give us some ideas to go on. This puzzle is a tricky one."

"It's a working trip, Matt," Randy interjected.

"Even working people need to eat, sleep, drink, get massages and such."

"I don't want to set you up for too much disappointment, but, yes, I think having a week before the arrival of my protectees will give us at least enough time for a 'massage' or two. Please keep me informed, and I'll let you know the details when I have them."

"You got it. Hey?" Matt said.

"I love you too," said Randy.

Matt took another sip of his Jack Daniels and opened his briefcase and pulled out reports to review. He had barely started on the first report when there was a knock on his door. A quick look out the peephole revealed Jake Packer holding up a six-pack in one hand and a pizza in the other.

Smiling, Matt opened the door to let Jake in. "I hope that's not whiskey in your Big Gulp cup, Bertram," Jake said.

"Guessed right, my friend," Matt replied. "I got another just like it in the cupboard."

"Whoa, I'm a beer guy," said Jake. "The hard stuff turns me into an asshole."

"And how would that be any different from your day-to-day attitude?" Matt retorted. "So, I figured you'd be in your hotel room watching *James Bond* movies."

"I've got all of that dialogue memorized," answered Jake. "All five lines. Besides, I've got some ideas whirling around in my head, and I just couldn't wait until tomorrow to talk to you about them. I figured you probably hadn't eaten anything, so I thought I'd stop and pick up the five food groups for us."

"Five food groups?"

"Yeah. Bread, meat, cheese, fruit, and beer. Pizza is a health food, man!"

Jake dug into the pizza while Matt took a long draw on his whiskey. With his mouth still stuffed with pizza, Jake started talking. "There are so many things happening that I just don't completely understand. Nothing about this makes any sense to me. So, your assignment to me was to think like the bad guy, right? As you requested, I've been spending all my waking hours and half my sleeping hours imagining what's going on in Wilson's head. I'm so far in his head that I can see out of his eyes.

"I'm going to go out on a limb and make some bold statements; but I think I can back them up. First, I agree with the profilers that we are dealing with one person. When I look at all four of his strikes, I see a man that isn't out for extortion. If he's not out for extortion, then what is his goal? It could be the thrill of getting one over on the navy. It could be that he's just a psycho, and the Navy just happened to be an available target. Or, and my favorite is that he is out for revenge. Nobody this smart or with these skills would be stupid enough to think the United States Government would ever possibly pay him."

"I get that, Jake, but what person with these skills could be that pissed at the US Navy that they would willingly murder hundreds of people?" Matt questioned.

"I've thought about that. I think that the answer might be found in the actions he's taken. You know that old saying, 'You reveal yourself not in what you say, but in what you do'."

"OK," said Matt. "What does each of the three crimes tell us about Wilson?"

"Four." Replied Jake. "There were four crimes, if you include Lester's escape from prison and explosive pureeing, which I think you have to at this point. I'm not a betting man, but if I were, I'd say there is a connection between the targets Wilson has chosen. They weren't random. I haven't spent much time on this, but there's a key there someplace."

Matt gave that some thought. "Yes. Definitely four, and I agree, the guy we're dealing with has a distinct purpose. I've never bought into the extortion gambit. But all four crimes aren't necessarily related. He could be simply focusing on navy targets. He could be a disgruntled sailor; maybe a former SEAL; maybe a Department of Defense contractor or somebody who did covert ops for the navy. Hell, maybe the navy screwed his dad or something."

"Well, I think I'm on to something, and I suggest you put your brainiacs on it too. The guy is too methodical for these not to be connected in some manner. Anyway," Jake said, draining his beer and standing up, "I'll leave you with that to ponder. Oh, and I've spent about a hundred hours trying to connect the name Wilson. I think he intentionally gave us a clue there as well. I've looked at cities, counties, a certain sporting goods company, famous sports stars, famous people, fictional characters, and more. There are a lot of Wilsons out there, and I haven't found one that rises to the top, but I'm not quitting."

Matt nodded in agreement. "Let's have our investigators look at actual people named Wilson in the San Diego area. Let's also look at active and former special forces personnel named Wilson. Who knows, maybe the guy's name is actually Wilson. "Oh, and one thing you might know the answer to: Is it possible to get names of CIA operatives?"

"I have a feeling that would be close to impossible. I'll ask just to see. Anyway, I'm going to get out of your hair and get back to my James Bond movies," Jake said with a smile. "You can ponder the big stuff. I'm just Captain America."

Matt shut the door behind Jake and locked the deadbolt. He returned to his chair, took a sip of his whiskey, and re-opened his briefcase.

Matt thought back to the first time he was introduced to Jack Daniels while serving in the navy. The ship he was stationed on at the time, the USS *Robert E. Peckham,* was in Yokosuka, Japan. For some reason, practically every ship homeported there was out to sea, so the crew of their small ship almost had the base to themselves. Matt got a terrible toothache on a Friday, and the base dental office was closed until Monday. Matt's friends got him through the weekend, swishing Jack Daniels in his mouth and, of course, swallowing it. Since then, Matt had been grateful to Jack for getting him through that weekend.

It had only been in the last few years that Matt discovered that the Jack Daniels Distillery made a very high-quality single-barrel reserve whiskey. While much more expensive than his long-time black label, it was a rare luxury that Matt allowed himself these days. He took a sip of the whiskey into his mouth and let it sit on his tongue for a few moments while his taste buds embraced the complex flavors, then swallowed, waiting for the familiar warm "hug" as the whiskey traveled to his stomach. He closed his eyes, trying, for just a few seconds, to exist "in" the moment.

Matt's mind relaxed just enough to give him some time to ponder Jake's suggestion that each of the targets had something in common with the others. He pulled out a pen and pad and started creating a Venn diagram. He drew a circle for the first attack on the USS *Stilton*. *What's unique about the Stilton?* It was a short list. *Stilton* was a navy ship. It was docked at San Diego. Not much more.

Matt went on to create a circle for attack number two: USS *Alamo*. *Alamo* was a navy ship, homeported in San Diego. OK, two for two with the *Stilton*, but there had to be something else. He wrote *attack was on the radio shack*. Information Systems Technicians, or ITs, were attacked. Matt smiled when he wrote that down. He still had trouble with the fact that his old rating, radioman, had disappeared when ITs were created.

Matt moved on to create a circle for the Naval Computer and Telecommunications Station bombing. It wasn't a ship, but he immediately saw a shared trait with the *Alamo*. ITs were the primary victims. Naval telecommunications were a critical function, so it could have been simply an attempt to paralyze the fleet. It was challenging to find another similarity.

Finally, he created a circle and wrote "Morris Lester" on the page. First on the list: Spy. Second on the list: Life without parole in Leavenworth. Third on the list: Former Senior Chief Radioman. Fourth on the list: Victim of the bombing at NCTS San Diego.

With the list on paper, Matt could see that all four attacks had one similarity in that explosives were used. But three of the four attacks had another similarity: Radiomen/ITs. Wilson had targeted radiomen and/or communications in three of the attacks but not the first. He stared at the paper for what seemed like hours, straining to find some similarity. After an hour of intense thought, Matt took a sip of his whiskey. And then it hit him like a rock in the forehead. Alone in his apartment, he said out loud, "I know what all four have in common. *Shit.*"

THE COMMON THREAD

Matt was in the conference room with Jake and his senior special agents. They were waiting for Aldrich to arrive before beginning the meeting; the others were chatting, or rather arguing, about baseball. Jake, seeming to get a bit heated, said, "I don't care who goes to the series this year, as long as it's not the *fucking* Yankees. Actually, I take that back. I hope the Yankees play the Mets in the series, and they get their asses handed to them on a paper plate."

Matt had been a Red Sox fan since he was a kid. A benefit of growing up in New Mexico was that they had no professional teams of any kind, so he had no pressure to be a fan of the local home team. He always liked the Red Sox, and that meant, by nature, he hated the Yankees as much as Jake. Today, he was barely listening to the conversation. He felt he had a break in the case, but his head was throbbing like a heavy metal drummer was playing inside it, making him wish he hadn't drunk quite so much whiskey last night.

Aldrich came into the room and sat down, several file folders in his arms. "Sorry I'm late. How do I say this delicately? Our new bosses were drilling me a new asshole for our lack of progress. They expressed their desire to produce some progress, and they weren't going easy."

Matt, unable to contain himself, blurted out, "Well, here's your progress, Aldrich. It's *me*. I'm what all four of Wilson's crimes have in common."

Jake looked at Matt. "OK, Matt, I think we need a little more detail on that statement."

"Jake stopped by my apartment last night and inspired me to start thinking more deeply about how these crimes could be related." He pulled out his notes with the Venn diagrams and laid them on the table. "Let's start from the latest crime and work our way back. Wilson blew up NCTS San Diego, a communications station, staffed by what used to be called radiomen. *I* was a radioman when I was in the navy. One step back is Morris Lester's escape from prison, or, rather, most probably, an abduction. *I* went undercover in Lester's radio shack for the NIS, and because of my work, he went to prison for life. One step back is the bombing of the USS *Alamo*. It just so happens that the ship's radio shack was targeted, killing over a dozen ITs, or what we used to call radiomen. *I* was a radioman."

Aldrich Sowles chimed in. "Sorry to interrupt, Matt, but the commonality is communications, too."

"I might agree with you were it not for the two clinchers—first, the sabotage of the USS *Stilton*. The ship was named after my former commanding officer's father, a direct connection with me, and only me as far as I can tell. And the Lester abduction seals it in my mind. He and I are directly connected."

"OK, so let's go with that theory for a moment," said Jake, "Who on earth would hate you enough to go to those extremes?"

"Until Lester became a victim, he would have been my most likely suspect," said Matt.

Aldrich spoke up. "Well, at least we have a computer database these days, so we are able to look at all of your cases. Over 24 years as a criminal investigator, there must be a whole lot of people pissed-off at you."

"I agree," Matt admitted, "but we need to find someone who is not only pissed-off beyond measure but also has *skills* beyond measure to pull this off. That's a tall order. We also have to ask ourselves why on earth someone who is this angry with me didn't just kill me."

Thursday, May 18, 2000 (0700 Hours, Pacific Time)

The attendant knocked on the room door with Jack Wilson's nameplate before opening the door to enter, much as she did each morning promptly at 7:00a.m. Her job was to help Wilson move from his bed to the wheelchair, then to the bathroom, where she would help him take care of his morning urination, defecation, and face-washing. She would then wheel him to the dining room for his breakfast.

However, as she entered the room this morning, she found a surprise. Mr. Wilson was nowhere to be found. She called out to him and received no answer. She entered his bedroom to find the bed neatly made and the wheelchair empty, in the corner, with no occupant. Although she knew he could not walk on his own, she called out toward the bathroom and received no response. She opened the bathroom door to find it empty. A sense of panic seized her chest as she hurried out to the front desk to see if, by chance, another attendant had taken him to breakfast. They deployed a scurry of employees around the home to look for Mr. Wilson, and when there was no sign of him, they called the police. The police patrolled the surrounding neighborhood as they occasionally had to do when one of the residents with less than full mental capacity got lost or wandered away. When they failed to find him, a missing persons report was filed.

By Saturday morning, both the police and employees of the home relegated Mr. Wilson's disappearance to an unsolved mystery. He was an older man. He could have had a heart attack and fallen in a ditch somewhere, and he had no family putting pressure on the police to find him. The police had more important things to do than spend their time looking for an elderly and probably senile old man who had somehow wandered off from his nursing home.

FRIENDS AND SUSPECTS

Saturday, May 20, 2000 (0900 Hours, Pacific Time)

"Well, I've got some bad news about looking for people named Wilson," Jake said with a frown. "Wilson is quite a popular name. It is, in fact, the tenth most popular family name in the United States. I used that internet *Google* thing and found some amazing shit. It's pretty crazy, Matt, what you can find on that site. Well, regarding Wilson, there are just about 275 people for every 100,000 in the United States named Wilson, meaning there are at least 10,000 people named Wilson in the San Diego area. In addition to Google, I searched the NCIS Navy and Marine Corps databases, but there were no SEALs or Force Recon named Wilson that have been prosecuted or dishonorably discharged, *ever*. And, by the way, none of your investigations resulted in the prosecution of anyone named Wilson. The bottom line is that Wilson is a very common name, and that they seem to behave themselves."

"I don't know what this Google thing is, but it sounds like that avenue is not going to work," said Matt. "Let's go one more path and just look at police arrests and reports over the last, say, year, just to see if we have any Wilsons on their radar. San Diego County should have computer resources to pull that up."

While Matt was disappointed that another possible source of information was turning out to be a dead-end, he was distracted by the pleasant thought that Randy would be arriving in San Diego that afternoon in preparation for the CNO and SECNAV presence at the memorial ceremony.

Matt spent the morning reviewing the reports on his desk, searching for any evidence that had been overlooked. At 1 pm, Matt looked at his watch and saw he had about 30 minutes to get to North Island Naval Air Station to pick Randy up. He stood to put his unread reports in his briefcase, and just as he was shutting it, Jake walked in. "You know, this computer thing is something I've got to learn more about. I drove down to San Diego County and asked to put in a request for all the Wilsons listed on arrest records, police reports, and such for the last year. I thought they'd tell me to come back in a week, but no, the officer helping me sat down at a computer and had the reports pulled and printed in about ten minutes. Wow, the job would have been easy enough for a five-year-old to do if I'd had that stuff when I worked at the CIA. Anyway, I haven't had a chance to review these yet, but I'll read them and get back to you tomorrow."

"That's OK, Jake, go ahead and give them to me. I've still got plenty of home-work to do, and I'd like to have a look sooner rather than later," said Matt, taking the reports and stuffing them into his already over-filled briefcase. As he grabbed a set of carpool keys, he headed toward the door. He stopped and looked back. "Thanks for the work, Captain America," Matt said with a smile. "I will call you if I need you but enjoy your Sunday. I'll see you Monday."

Jake shouted back to Matt as the door was shutting, "You be safe, Sherlock. That woman can steal your soul!"

"She's already got my heart," Matt shouted back without turning. "She can have my soul too if she wants it!"

Matt was on the runway's tarmac as he watched the Cessna Citation business jet touch down. As he watched the sleek plane stop, he remembered his travels from an economy seat on a commercial airplane, and thought to himself, *I may have chosen to work in the wrong division of NCIS.* When Matt had routine travel, it was always economy class on the cheapest airline available.

He jumped out of the car and met Randy halfway between the jet and his car. He shook her hand in front of the others and walked her back to the car. Matt shut Randy's door, walked to the driver's side, sat on the seat, and wrapped his arms around his lover. She responded in kind, saying, "We've got to stop meeting like this," and giving him a long, tongue-laced, full-passion kiss.

"Here's where I talk about you running away with me," Matt said.

"And here's where I tell you that I'm arriving one day later than I wanted to, and I've got two hours before my first meeting, sailor, so you better drive fast!"

Matt heeded Randy's advice, and they soon were at Matt's apartment, clothing abandoned, catching up on lost time.

"You really have a meeting today?" Matt said, sounding like a disappointed five-year-old.

"A short one. I've got to get with my team to discuss our plans for the week and what preparations need to be made. Remember, Matt, we think your madman Wilson likely has something planned for the memorial, and we want to be ready. It would be the perfect opportunity for him to grab the headlines again and do even more damage. Much as I feel the tragedy of the deaths of the sailors on the *Alamo* and the communications facility, the assassination of SECNAV or the CNO, or even both, would have disastrous consequences.""I understand," said Matt, with a look on his face that indicated he did not. "And I brought work home on the off chance you ditched me for those security types. Anyway, we've been told here at the office that, except for the core Wilson investigation team, you have all of our human resources at your disposal, too."

"That's meeting number two, but that's Monday after we've had a good night's sleep – or at least a good couple of hours of sleep, if you know what I mean. Tomorrow will be filled with meetings of my staff and the base commanders."

Matt fixed them a quick meal of stuffed mushrooms and bruschetta, before Randy rushed out the door with Matt's car keys. Matt shut the door, realizing he hadn't even had a short "massage." He poured himself a glass of Jack Daniels, sat down in his tattered but ever so comfortable easy chair, and opened the overfed briefcase. He began with follow-up reports on bomb supplies; then moved to summaries of interviews with sailors and staff the morning of the bombing. With some curiosity, he pulled out Jake's copies of the police reports that included the name Wilson. Domestic violence arrests, DUIs, and petty larcenies, all involving nobody with the skills to bring the US Navy to its knees. He was about to put it back in the folder when he happened to notice, at the very end of the report there had been a report of a missing person. It had happened on Thursday. According to the officer's notes in the report, a man went missing from an assisted living home whose name was Jack Wilson. It captured Matt's attention for a moment until he saw that it was a geezer in his 80s. *Fat chance an 80-year-old could pull off the crimes of the century*, Matt thought. He began to move on to the rest of the reports when he saw the missing man was confined to a wheelchair, but the idea of an 80-year-old who was unable to walk disappearing from an old folks' home without his wheelchair aroused his investigator senses. *I wonder how often something like that happens*, he thought to himself.

Randy arrived back at Matt's apartment just before midnight. "Short meeting, huh?" Matt said as he handed Randy a Stone Brewing Company Double Bastard Ale.

"You got my favorite," Randy said, flashing a big smile. She took a long slug, wiped her mouth with the back of her hand, and said, "I need to sit down."

As they sat, Randy explained the massive amount of pressure being placed on their team. "Wilson has been silent since the explosion, so we have no hint of whether or not he's going to try something at the memorial. We have decided to go on the assumption that he *will* try to do something, plan accordingly, and hope that we're not surprised. How in the hell do you plan for that? Anyway, needless to say, this will probably be the highest security event of the year, and we are taking no chances. Snipers, bomb shields, you name it, we have to plan for it. And the shitty thing is that we know this asshole's skills, and I'd never admit this to anyone but you, Bertram; it just feels like if he wants to assassinate some bigwigs, there's very little we can do to stop it. Not that we aren't going to try. Anyway, you're going to get an earful at the meeting Monday. I would love it if you would bring me up to date on your investigation."

Matt gave Randy a summary of the investigation, the evidence discovered, and the hard facts of the case. He took a deep breath and said, "There is something you need to know that I haven't told you. I don't know if this is a break or not, but it surely changes things. We have pretty much concluded that this guy is seeking revenge. And don't freak out, but it seems to be focused on revenge against me."

As Randy sat, eyes as wide as saucers, trying to maintain composure, Matt explained the connections between the four crimes. "The truth is, I can't think of a single person who would hate me enough to do these things that also has the skill to achieve them."

Randy sat, staring at Matt. She took another slug of her beer. "Well, I can think of someone who might be that angry, Matt, but I can't imagine he would have the proficiency to accomplish them."

"Who?" Matt said, leaning forward in his chair.

"What about Clay Young? He was Lester's partner in the USS *Oklahoma City* spy ring. You put him in jail. He spent ten years rotting in Leavenworth. I'd say he's got plenty to be pissed about. And he could have been just as pissed at Lester; perhaps enough to blow him up."

Clay had been Matt's best friend for some time after Matt was assigned to the USS *Oklahoma City*. Clay was an endearing human being, a fellow radioman, and, for a time, Matt thought he was a man of principle. Clay was from Texas, and Matt was constantly in stitches at the number and frequency of Texas collo-quialisms Clay could muster up, or, as Clay would say, "More sayings than you could shake a stick at." Instead of saying, "That's acceptable," for instance, Clay would say, "Might as well. Can't dance, never could sing, and it's too wet to plow." Before the navy, Clay had been a highly talented baseball player and even had a contract to play in the big leagues. The fact was, he hated baseball and only played to please his father. When his father became overbearing, Clay walked off the ball field and joined the navy as an enlisted man, even though he possessed a college degree. Matt was heartbroken when he discovered that Clay had been Lester's right-hand man, and a big part of the *Okie* spy ring.

"I just can't imagine it would be Clay," Matt said. "He helped us escape from Makarov at the hotel in Baguio. Hell, he took a bullet for us. I talked to him in the hospital at the time, and he didn't seem the least angry. He spent a good deal of energy expressing remorse for the role he played. I even spoke for him at his sentencing. And besides, Clay did not have the proficiency and skills to shoot a gun, much less blow up a communications station."

Randy simply sat and listened as Matt worked through his analysis of the possibility that Clay Young could be involved. He stopped, took a big breath, and smiled at Randy, the kind of smile someone who truly loves another has for them. "But ... you're right. He might have a motive, and perhaps he signed up for some super-duper Indiana Jones spy class where he acquired extraordinary skills. I'll check it out. Hell, perhaps Makarov opened a spy school when the Soviet Union fell," Matt said, laughing.

"Matt?" Randy said, staring at him. "You just said something. Something that maybe ... may be important. Oh, probably not, but—but Makarov. There's the guy who has the skills to pull something like this off."

"That seems pretty unlikely, Randy. The last time we saw him, he was making a clean get-away in an executive jet, headed back to the good old USSR. Besides that, I can't imagine he's still alive. He'd have to be in his 80's, long-retired, living the good life in a chateau on the Volga River. Besides, spying was his business. It wasn't personal. He's had to have forgotten me long ago."

"I guess you're right," Randy said with a look of frustration. "I'd at least locate Clay to be sure he's not capable of making this happen."

"I will," Matt promised. "Let me get you in bed, and I'll give you one of my famous Bertram back rubs," knowing that the back rub usually led to more fun for all.

"Your back rubs always seem to end up being front rubs, too," Randy said, smiling.

"Full-service. That's my motto."

BUSY AS A ONE-EYED DOG IN A SMOKEHOUSE

Matt had liked Clay Young from the first minute they met. Clay had been a radioman aboard the USS *Oklahoma City*, CG-5. Clay was from East Texas, and Matt loved to listen to Clay spin yarns using his colorful Texas sayings.

Matt had been recruited by what was then the Naval Investigative Service (NIS) to become an undercover operative for them. The NIS suspected that there was a significant leak of Top-Secret intelligence from someone in the radio shack on the ship. Clay and Matt became fast friends, sharing off-duty time in ports in the Pacific. Sadly, Clay had also been part of a conspiracy with two other radiomen aboard the ship who were spying for the KGB. Their ringleader had been Senior Chief Radioman Lester Morris. Randy Glasscock had been Matt's "handler," and the two became partners in helping to expose the spy ring and bring the three to justice.

When Matt and Randy had been discovered by Moe Lester and his KGB contact, Major Pyotr Makarov, they came within a hair's breadth of being executed. At the last moment, Clay had a change of heart and helped save Matt and Randy. Clay was wounded in the escape. Even though he was helpful to the prosecution, he was found guilty of espionage and sentenced to ten years in prison.

Although Matt did not believe Clay could have had anything to do with the current crimes, he did believe in Randy's adept intuition about things and decided he had better check him out.

"In this day and age of computers, I can't believe we are unable to just tap into the Bureau of Prison's database," Matt said to the special agent attempting to help Matt. "So, you're telling me we have to go to the BOP and ask them to run this information?" Matt said, chagrined.

The SA gave Matt a helpless look. "I'll call over right now, sir," the SA said.

Fifteen minutes later, the SA knocked on Matt's office door, poking his head in. "Now a good time, sir?" the SA asked. Matt motioned him into the office. "Clay Young was released from Leavenworth in 1986," said the SA. "He's living in a town in Texas called, well, I'm not sure how it's pronounced, but here's how it's spelled." The SA showed Matt the word spelled *Lampasas.* "He runs a martial arts business and has had a few minor brushes with the law. He's single, has no children, and lives out of town on a small ranch. The BOP still checks up on him regularly, but they don't have anything else that's helpful."

Matt couldn't resist but use a "Clay Youngism" and said in his best Texas drawl, "Sounds to me like he's happy as a boarding house pup." The SA stared at him, wondering if that required a response. Matt smiled, enjoyed watching the look on the SA's face. "You know, he's safer than granny's snuffbox." Not able to go any further, Matt chuckled and simply said, "I can't imagine Clay has anything to do with this, but it's worth a quick trip to Texas for me. I'm pretty sure there's an army base close to, um, whatever that place is called. The Texas senate delegations of the 1960s did a good job of getting lots of military money there."

Unable to resist one more Clay Young-ism, Matt said, "We are probably just hollerin' down a well, but we'll see."

Because of the foremost priority of the mission, Matt had no problem getting a military executive jet booked for that afternoon. Matt wrangled Jake into going with him, called Randy, and told her where they were heading and that they would probably be back by midnight. Their destination was Fort Hood Army Base in Killeen, a thirty-minute drive to Lampasas.

"We scored, my friend," Jake said. "All we need are some cute flight attendants and refreshments, and we'll be cruising."

"We got the jet because everyone from the custodian in my building to the President wants us to stop this guy," Matt said. "But I must admit, this is way better than economy class on any airline, even if we don't have cocktails!"

As they settled into their flight, Matt updated Jake on Clay and his role in the USS *Oklahoma City* spy ring. "The only thing that causes me to want to talk directly to Clay is that he's developed some skills since leaving prison. I just want to ensure that the skills are limited to martial arts. I'm 90 percent certain we won't find anything, but I just can't leave any stone unturned. And even if he's not Wilson, he might know something that can help the case."

"I get that," Jake said. "Taking the day to check it out is worth the effort. By the way, I heard a rumor that you have been offered the SAC position. Congrats, man!"

"Yeah, thanks, Jake. I originally was not going to take it, and I haven't let Sowles know one way or the other."

"I also heard you were thinking of quitting and moving back to New Mexico," Jake said.

"How the hell did you know that?" Matt said with an incredulous look on his face.

"I was a professional spy, Matt. I kinda have some skills in that area."

Matt shook his head. "I was so close to resigning and heading to New Mexico. I know it's weird to say, but I need to be back in my home, guiding my own destiny. There's just something about New Mexico that stays in my soul. It is with me day and night. Maybe it's just peace I seek. I don't know."

"But I've realized that there's no way I can talk Randy into coming with me, and if I went without her, our relationship would be at great risk. She's the most important thing in the world to me, and I'm not willing to put our life together, as peculiar as it is, in jeopardy. I've come to the conclusion that I have to hang on until we both retire, and then maybe, just maybe, I will convince her to marry me and move to the Jemez."

"Well, I've never been very successful at love, so I can't help you there, Mathew, but I'd have to say, just because someone needs to say it, that being Special Agent in Charge of the largest NCIS office in the world is definitely *not* just hanging on."

The jet landed at Fort Hood, Texas, and the two submitted to the excruciating process of securing a motor pool car, which turned out to be a ten-year-old pickup with a standard transmission and a broken rear-view mirror. "The Army have something against the Navy?" Jake said as they cranked the hesitantly starting engine of the truck.

"I'm surprised they let us have anything," Matt said. "Fair warning, Jake, it's been a long time since I've driven a truck with a manual transmission. Hard to believe they issue vehicles in Texas with no air conditioning. Thank God it's only May, or we'd be in deep trouble!"

The two enjoyed the drive to Lampasas. The Hill Country of Texas was far different than either of them had imagined with rolling hills, tall oak trees, streams, and abundant flowers spread throughout the countryside. Along the sides of the roads were Bluebonnets and Indian Paint Brush, Black-Eyed Susans, and more. Matt's only experience of Texas had been in the northwestern part of the state, and this looked nothing like that area. "I read a little about Lampasas before we left. They originally built the town because it had some mineral springs that people thought had healing powers," Jake pronounced.

"I suppose you found that on Ogle, or Bogle, or whatever that computer thing is," Matt said with a look of disgust. "It's Google, and you'll eventually have to use it yourself. The internet is the wave of the future," Jake responded.

"Well, that's a wave I'd be happy to miss. Computers are for geeks and secretaries."

They stopped at the martial arts studio that Clay owned. One of Clay's instructors was in the studio, and he let the two know Clay was at home today. They had his home address and headed out again, looking for Farm to Market Road 580. They turned on the road, headed past a large reservoir, and finally found a dirt driveway with a ranch gate. The gate wasn't locked, but both noted the sign on the gate saying, "No Trespassing: We are getting tired of burying the bodies."

"That's a joke, right?" Jake said.

"I know Texans take their land rights pretty seriously, but they also have a good sense of humor. It sounds so much like Clay." Matt said.

As Matt drove past four or five abandoned cars, rusted farm equipment, and a longhorn cow, they finally pulled up in front of the main house. Predictably, a man came out carrying a lever-action Marlin model 1833. It was somewhat comforting that he wasn't pointing it at them. Matt immediately recognized Clay. Although it had been 24 years, Clay looked much the same, except for the wrinkles and the long, grey hair.

As Matt got out of the truck, Clay shouted from the porch, "Trespassers are as welcome as a skunk at a lawn party."

Matt walked around the truck and said, "I didn't think a friend would treat me like that."

Clay stared, squinted one eye, then both eyes brightened, and a big smile crossed his face. "Well, look what the cat dragged in. If it ain't my old buddy Bert!" Clay put the rifle down, ran down the porch steps, and gave Matt a suffocating hug. "What in the hell are you doing here in God's country, Bert?"

Matt introduced Jake, and Clay invited the two men up on his porch, sat them down in rocking chairs, and went into the house to get drinks. He came back with a big pitcher of sweet tea and three glasses. Matt's first taste caused his eyes to open wide at the sweetness. *Apparently, Texans like a little tea with their sugar* thought Matt. "Much as I like chewin' the fat with y'all, I'm assuming y'all are not here for a social call," Clay said, looking directly at Matt. He poured more tea, and then sat back. Matt explained the purpose of their visit, what had happened to lead them to want to talk with him, and the seriousness of the situation.

"We're here because you're interrelated in this mess, and we are just hoping that you can give us something that can help. Have you talked with anyone or heard anything?"

"Just what I saw on the TV. It sounds like this no-account fellow would steal the flowers off his grandma's grave." Matt noted, once again, that Clay had no shortage of colorful Texas sayings and had perhaps accumulated more over time.

"I'm afraid I just can't help y'all," Clay said, shaking his head. "I've pretty much kept to myself since I got out of prison. They give you a long list of people you aren't allowed to associate with. Shoot, I'm not even legally allowed to own this rifle. I guess I don't, really. It was my daddy's, and I just kept it when he passed on, God rest his snarly old soul. As I ponder your situation, Bert, there is just one thought that comes to mind. Have you given consideration to –"

At that instant, Clay's head snapped backward. As Matt and Jake watched with horror, they saw the back of Clay's head explode. Blood and brains launched into the window behind him, with a small hole in the middle of his forehead. Jake and Matt fell to the ground. Matt crawled over to Clay, grabbed him in his arms, shouting, "No! no, Clay, you hang in there," knowing that Clay was dead before he hit the ground. Jake began surveying the area, looking in the direction where the shot most likely originated. Matt joined him, weapon drawn, crouching behind a half-wall on the front porch.

"Behind the barn, about 1000 yards away," Jake said. "I'm pretty sure it came from that direction." Matt looked at where Jake was describing. Behind the barn was a hill covered with Texas Cedar trees. The hill had steep slopes that would have prevented the two from pursuing.

"Pretty good location for a sniper attack," agreed Matt. At that moment, they heard the sound of a dirt bike starting and moving away from them. Clay was dead. And the timing was mind-boggling.

Matt and Jake sat in the rocking chairs on the front porch as the coroner bagged Clay's body, and law enforcement did its job. The following two hours were taken with county deputy sheriffs questioning the two. They were told they couldn't leave until they were cleared and thoroughly questioned, which could take hours. Matt was quickly on the phone with Aldrich Sowles. "Don't worry. I've got two FBI agents on their way, and they'll extricate you. What the hell happened, Matt?"

"I wish I could say something different, but this can only be the work of Wilson. How in the hell he could know we would be there is beyond me. I'm getting the creeps like I've never had them before. And here is yet *another* crime that is connected directly to me."

"Just get back on that plane and get back. Clay isn't going to be of any help now."

Matt and Jake flew back to San Diego that evening, Clay's death weighing heavily on his soul. Trying to lower the tension, Jake turned to Matt and said, "Damn government flights. No inflight booze service! I could use a beer right now."

Without responding to the comment or looking in Jake's direction, Matt said, "Clay was a good guy who made some bad choices, but more than made up for them. And now he's dead. There's no doubt his murder is Wilson's doing, and if there was any doubt before, there is none now that Wilson is connecting people and places to me. And, with the exception of the USS *Stilton*, they all are connected to the *Okie* spy ring. There's somebody out there with a huge grudge and the fortitude to make us pay. This is going to take some thinking." For the remainder of the flight Matt said little, and Jake gave Matt his space to grieve.

It was late when Matt returned to his apartment. He took out his keys, turned them in the lock, and opened the door, not an ounce of energy left in him. Matt's mood immediately picked up when he walked in his apartment door to a kiss and a glass of Jack Daniels from Randy. *That was a welcome back that I'd love to have much more often.*

"You just take a deep breath, Matt. Have a seat, and when you're ready, tell me about your day." She took off his shoes and socks and grabbed some moisturizer from the bathroom. She rubbed his feet, and he felt the tension subside, if just a bit.

"Clay's dead," he said, almost without emotion. "Somehow, I don't know how, Wilson was there. He killed Clay right after we had our first sip of Texas sweet tea. It was so good seeing him, Randy. And, suddenly, he was gone. Taken. It was like Wilson was just waiting for that moment so that I could witness the horror." He explained what had happened during the day. He and Randy both shed a tear or two for Clay as they reminisced about the folksy Texan. They readied themselves for bed, and as Matt turned off the light, Randy said, "I just can't help but think the answer is staring us in the face. We'll get it, Matt. I know we will."

Just before he went to sleep, he thought of the old man named Jack Wilson, confined to a wheelchair, who disappeared from the assisted living home. Something just wasn't right about that, but he couldn't put his finger on it.

SHADY PALMS

Tuesday, May 23, 2000 (0800 hours, Pacific Time)

Jake walked into the NCIS office carrying two cups of coffee, knocked on Matt's office door, and walked in without being invited. Matt was hunched over a pile of papers.

"I imagine you've been here a couple of hours already, but I thought you might need your tank refilled," Jake said, setting one of the coffees in front of Matt.

"No such thing as too much coffee on a day like today," Matt responded.

Without looking up from his paperwork, Matt asked, "What are you up to, Jake?"

"Other than fetching coffee like a good intern, just going to be analyzing any new information that came in while we were gone yesterday," said Jake.

"Well, I need you to take off your intern hat and put on your Captain America uniform. I have something on my mind. I'm pretty sure it's just because I'm running out of options, but if you're not doing anything, why don't you take a ride with me?"

"Sure," said Jake. "At least I won't be staring at paper all morning."

When they were in the car, Jake asked, "You going to tell me where we're going?"

"Sure," said Matt. "We are going to Shady Palms Assisted Living Center in Chula Vista. It's the most off-the-wall investigative work I've ever done, and I almost feel foolish doing it. It's most likely a completely wild goose chase. But in all that research you did, I came across an odd occurrence that I just can't seem to get out of my mind."

"And there's some kind of lead there?" Jake said with a sideways glance.

"I don't know. I doubt it. It's probably a waste of time, but in one of the reports, you noted a missing person from this assisted living place, and it just sort of stuck in my head. There's been no trace of him, and he's wheelchair bound, yet the report said they found his wheelchair in his room. His name is Jack Wilson. I know, not much of anything that could be used as evidence. I just can't get the odd Wilson disappearance from the assisted living out of my head. The timing of his disappearance just after the last crime that our Wilson committed just seems to be too coincidental. For someone who can't walk, walking away from an old folks' home screams 'tilt.' I think I need to ask some questions to get the thought of an 80 year with the ability to carry out these actions, out of my head."

"I'm not going to argue with you or tell you it's a waste of time, even though it sounds like you are grasping at straws," Jake said with what could have been interpreted as pity.

When they arrived at Shady Palms, they found a lovely building with Tuscan style architecture, tall orange and yellow flowered Pride of Barbados plants in front, and a circular drive around a courtyard lined with Nasturtiums. The place could easily have been mistaken for a hotel. They parked in the guest parking spot and walked in the door. There was a lobby with a high ceiling and a stone fireplace with a gas fire burning on fake logs. They greeted the receptionist, who, said with a smile, "Welcome to Shady Palms Assisted Living, where life is better! I'm Chantrelle, director of guest services. May I help you?"

Matt showed his credentials, and a minute later, a tall attractive woman who appeared to Matt to be in her mid-forties walked up to them. She had black hair, and it was evident she spent a great deal of time exercising, as she was unusually physically fit. "Agent Bertram, I'm Rita Pacheco, the executive director here at Shady Palms. I understand you have questions about our missing resident, Mr. Wilson."

"This is my associate, Mr. Packer, Ms. Pacheco," said Matt. "And yes, we do have a few questions.""Pardon me for asking, but why is NCIS investigating a missing person?"

Jake chimed in eagerly to engage in conversation with a woman that Matt could quickly tell was in Jake's sights. "It's just a little follow-up on another case we're working on, Ms. Pacheco. May I call you Rita?" Jake stuck out his right hand, inviting her to shake hands with him, and perhaps held the handshake a moment longer than normal for business etiquette.

"Please, do call me Rita," the director replied, belying more than a little reciprocal interest. As they walked toward Jack Wilson's room, the two asked Rita to tell them about him.

"There's not a lot to tell," Rita said as they walked along. "We aren't a nursing home, but an assisted living home, so our residents have varying needs. Mr. Wilson has been here almost a year, keeps to himself, and to my knowledge, has never taken part in any of the activities here. He has never had a visitor, and when he arrived, he explained he had no family living in the country. He didn't say where he originally came from, but I detected a slight accent. Mr. Wilson has difficulty walking, so one of our staff pushes him to his meals, although I suspect he could wheel himself."

"Why do you say that, Ms. Pacheco?" Matt inquired.

"He dresses and undresses, can transfer himself to the bath, and can take care of his toilet habits. If he has sufficient upper body strength to do that, I'm guessing he could get around by himself. Nevertheless, he's paying the bill and requested we provide those services.

"Other than getting Mr. Wilson to and from his room, we don't have a whole lot of contact with him. As I said, he keeps to himself, and I've not seen him engage in conversation with any of our other residents. Ah, here we are at Mr. Wilson's room." Rita turned the master key, opened the door, and let the two into the room.

"Would you mind if we just looked around, Rita?" Jake said with what Matt would have characterized as Jake's best attempt at a flirtatious smile, but looked just a bit lecherous to Matt.

"Just let me know when you leave, and I'll be sure the room is locked back up," Rita said. "Let me know if there's anything else we can help with."

The two men, both with extensive investigation and observation skills, methodically combed the room. They noted it was neat and tidy, with nothing in the living room and kitchen trash cans. There was no food in the refrigerator or the pantry. There were no personal mementos on the walls or tables. The room was on the ground level, and there was a large window looking out onto a grassy area, and beyond was a street. The window opened enough for a person to squeeze through, and there was no screen. As Matt searched the living room, Jake moved into the bedroom. From Matt's perspective, the apartment looked almost as though no one lived there. Jack Wilson lived lightly on the planet.

Finding nothing of interest in the living area or kitchen, Matt went into the bedroom to help Jake. "Anything?" Matt asked quietly.

"I haven't been in the bathroom yet, but I found something odd under the bed. Could be just a bed part or something." He pulled out a steel tube that looked to be around three feet long. It was heavy and strong.

"That's interesting," Matt said, standing and looking toward the bedroom door. Finding what he was looking for, he took the bar and placed it in two brackets near the top of the doorway. It fit perfectly. Matt looked at Jake, who stared back with a quizzical look on his face.

"A chin-up bar?"

"Not just a chin-up bar, but one the user would have to stand to use," Matt said.

"OK," Jake replied. "Not the kind of thing you'd expect to find in the apartment of an eighty-something-year-old man who can't walk."

They finished the search by entering Jack Wilson's bathroom. It was devoid of personal items. Both stood and stared at the mirror. On the mirror was a yellow sticky note. In handwriting, it said:

It's a hell of a thing, killing a man. You take away all he's got and all he's ever gonna have.

"What in the hell does that mean?" Jake exclaimed.

"It means this guy just became a suspect," said Matt. "I want this room locked down and forensics to go over it, inch by inch."

CONFIRMATION

Aldrich Sowles stood in front of Matt's desk, trying to create his most consoling look, which, to Matt, looked a bit like he was going to sneeze. "I'm sorry, Matt, but we have two days until the CNO and SECNAV arrive to attend the memorial service, and I absolutely must have all personnel attending to this. There is no evidence to suggest that Wilson is going to pass on this opportunity, and from the President down, I've been given the practically impossible task of maximizing all of NCIS' resources to make sure the memorial goes smoothly and without unpleasantness. You and Jake can spend the next two days working the case, and as soon as the bigwigs are safely tucked on their jet headed back to D.C., your staff can get back on track. But until then, it's just the two of you."

"I understand, Aldrich. I just think that if I had my staff going at full speed, we might catch Wilson before he can do anything further."

Aldrich shook his head. "Despite your optimism, Matt, you've got something much more than a two-day investigation ahead of you. There's quite a lot of groundwork for you to do even to get close to Wilson. I know you'll get there eventually, but that's just the way it must be. The event on Friday must be our complete focus."

As Sowles was leaving, Jake Packer entered. "Well, forensics went through the apartment top to bottom," he said.

"And let me guess. It was wiped clean," Matt interrupted.

"Quite the contrary. There are fingerprints, DNA from hair, and saliva on pillows. A veritable plethora of evidence of Wilson," Jake said. "I took the liberty of asking the FBI forensics team to look at it, and it's already being run through IAFIS." IAFIS, or the Integrated Automated Fingerprint Identification System, managed by the FBI, had been in operation a full year and had been a breakthrough system in computer-based crime-fighting. "We should have results in less than an hour," Jake said smugly.

"Well, Captain America comes through again," Matt said, smiling. "Let's hope that Wilson is in the system."

"I've been thinking about what was on the sticky note, too," Jake said. "It somehow sounds familiar."

"Don't say it; you're going to run it by Boogle, right?" Matt said.

"I'm not even going to bother to correct you, Bertram. You're intentionally fucking up the name just to piss me off!"

"How's it working?" Matt said playfully.

"Pretty damn well, and yes, I am going to Google it," Jake said, storming out of the office.

"Once you're done Moogling it, I want to go by the Shady Palms again and walk the neighborhood. I want to see if we can find anyone who might have seen an old fart going out a window and through the surrounding area."

"Got it," Jake said from the empty room outside.

Ten minutes later, Matt heard a shout from Jake. "I got it!" he bellowed. He came into Matt's office without knocking and said, "I knew I had heard that line before, and I was right! It came out of Clint Eastwood's mouth in a movie I loved called *Unforgiven*!"

"Please don't tell me that's a cowboy movie," Matt said, looking down.

"It's one of the best I've ever seen," Jake said.

After a long pause, Matt dropped his head to his chest. "Shit," said Matt. "Can it possibly be him?"

"Who?"

"Major Pyotr Ivanovich Makarov, of the First Directorate of the KGB; the guy was bonkers for anything regarding cowboys. He was a western movie devotee and even wore Tony Llama cowboy boots. That is one of the oddest things I've ever seen; a KGB agent wearing cowboy boots. You never forget a sight like that. The few times I heard him talk, he used cowboy movie quotes as often as sailors cuss. That's not something you hear from KGB agents, or anyone else, very often, I'm guessing."

Jake's cell phone rang. He answered and listened for several moments. "Not a thing?" Jake inquired. "Got it. Thanks, Ray." He pushed the "end" button on his phone. "They found fingerprints for Shady Palms staff, and one other print in the apartment, but there is no match in IAFIS. IAFIS recently added Interpol's database also. Apparently, Wilson has never been fingerprinted in the United States or Europe. He's entirely off the radar."

Matt sat in stunned silence for a few moments. "Jake, I'm sure this is an impossible request, but you still have connections with the CIA. Is there any way you could use your connections to find out what happened to Makarov following the *Okie* spy episode?"

"I can make some calls. I still have friends there, but you know how spooks are with their information."

"Please give it a try," said Matt. "And while you're at it, would you use your looker-upper thing to see if there are any cowboy movie characters named Jack Wilson?"

Jake was already halfway out of the door and without turning his head back toward Matt, said, "Got it."

"When you're done with that, let's go for that drive," said Matt as Jake sat down at his computer.

Matt grabbed his phone and called Randy's number. When she answered, he brought her up to date on the events of the day and his suspicion that Makarov was his primary suspect. "I know it's pretty unbelievable, Randy, but everything we discover leads us in this direction."

"OK, Matt, I can see how you're being led there. But there is an awful lot of implausible speculation on your part. First, we are talking about a man who is over eighty accomplishing physical feats a twenty-five-year-old SEAL would find problematic. Second, as you said, he got away and flew home to the USSR without being publicly exposed. I think you put it well: it was just business for him. Third, who in the hell exacts revenge from another person by trying to bring down the entire United States Navy, along with all the people he might hold directly responsible for the failure of his spy ring?"

"I agree. I've done some stretching here. But he has brought down all the people responsible for exposing the *Okie* spy ring, and his sights are clearly set on me. I'm hoping to get my hands on more information that will help us either rule him out or corroborate my suspicions."

"Look, Matt, we are pretty much ready for the memorial service. I have a lot of last-minute details, but I'll be free tonight. I'll stop at the store and get fixings for a good homemade meal. How about I prepare your favorite New Mexico dish, stuffed sopapillas?"

"That sounds wonderful. I'll stop at Blockbuster and get a movie. We'll pretend we're an old married couple," Matt said.

"An old married couple still has crazy monkey sex, right?"

"Of course," Matt said, smiling.

Once again, from the outside room, Jake gave a yell. He came rushing into Matt's office practically out of breath. "Jack Wilson. He was the bad guy in the movie *Shane*. Jack Palance played it marvelously. *Jack Wilson*, Matt."

On Wilson's Heels

Wednesday, May 24, 2000 (1400 Hours, Pacific Time)

Jake and Matt spent much of the afternoon walking the neighborhood around Shady Palms Assisted Living Center, asking residents and passersby whether they had seen an older man walking in the area. As both suspected, they had no luck in this task. "Finding the relationship of the name Jack Wilson to a cowboy bad guy completely sews it up for me," Matt said as they were driving. "It also makes sense that there would be no fingerprints on file. He was a KGB spy, and there would have been no opportunity to collect his fingerprints."

"I'm becoming more convinced of your suspicions, Matt," said Jake. "As implausible as it sounds, I've read about men who are surprisingly fit well into their eighties. I just find it hard to understand why he would have such a massive grudge against you for something that happened twenty-four years ago and which he escaped from unscathed."

"That's why I'm hoping that your connections at the CIA might have information on Makarov that would enlighten us. So far, he's gone after everyone directly connected with the *Okie* spy ring, and it's obvious he's planning something big to get me. That something, for some reason, doesn't involve directly executing me *yet*."

"Well, I've got calls into everyone and anyone who could or might help me," Jake said. "I have an old friend who was Chief of Station (COS) in the Moscow

Embassy during the time the Soviet Union fell. I'll try to locate him, and if anyone can help us, he can."

"I don't mean to be pushy," Matt said, "But time is definitely of the essence."

"Got it."

Matt dropped Jake off at his hotel and headed to the Blockbuster Video close to his home. While he knew he would have trouble staying focused during the evening, he saw Randy so seldom these days that he wanted to push Wilson/Makarov out of his head for a while—almost. He had a slightly ulterior motive in suggesting a movie. There was a particular movie he was looking for. He parked in front of the store, marveling that technology had gotten to the point where he could go to a store and rent a movie to play in his home. Given his work, he had little time for such frivolity in his life, often working seventy hours a week.

Matt had finally broken down and bought a VHS player six months ago. The store clerk told him he should buy a DVD player because VHS was on its way out. On its way out? *I haven't even started with this technology, and it's already obsolete,* he thought. He did not take the clerk's advice and bought a VHS machine. Matt had used the machine exactly twice since he bought it, after persuading his neighbor's sixteen-year-old to son set it up for him.

Matt entered the store and went to the check-out stand. "I'm looking for a certain movie in particular," Matt said. The teenager behind the counter asked him what movie he was looking for and directed Matt to the "Westerns" section of the store. *Unforgiven* was available, and after setting up a Blockbuster account and providing more credit card information than he was comfortable giving, Matt left the building with the movie for the night, along with the warning that if it was not returned within two days, there would be an extra charge. Before heading home, he stopped at the Kash n' Karry in his neighborhood and bought a couple of bottles of wine.

When Matt arrived at his apartment, Randy was already busy in the kitchen. She was wearing a very sexy red dress, and it was evident that she had taken some extra time primping and preening for the evening. He had never really thought about it, but he had only seen her in a dress a couple of times during the entire twenty-four years he had known her. To make things even sexier (for Matt), she wore a blue apron over her dress. True to her word, she was making his favorite dish in the whole world, stuffed sopapillas.

The northern New Mexico dish was rarely found outside the region, and Randy had learned how to make it from Matt's mother, who lived in White Rock. The dish was simple enough. New Mexican sopapillas are a little different from those found outside of New Mexico. While in Texas, they are a desert, in New Mexico, they are usually less sweet and are enjoyed alongside the meal.

As Matt entered the door, he took a moment to take in the wonderful smells: fresh handmade sopapillas, ground beef, and especially the green chili sauce, which made the meal. Matt couldn't help but say, "Hi honey, I'm home!" with a husbandly tone.

Randy didn't skip a beat. She walked over to him, kissed him on the forehead, and said, "I hope you got the milk and cereal for the kids tomorrow."

"To hell with the kids," Matt said. "I brought wine. And might I say you look ravishing in your apron."

"Well, for the wine, you get a hell of a better kiss, my man," Randy said, now sounding much sultrier. "And even more later!" Randy wrapped her arms around Matt and, with one hand, pushed the back of his head toward her lips. "There's your official starter kiss," she said, returning to her cooking.

Matt stopped, took her flour-covered hands in his, and looked into her eyes. "That dress looks beautiful on you, Randy. I do love you so."

Always quick to blush, Randy smiled, saying, "Get that wine open, man. I've got food to prepare!"

Matt opened a bottle of wine, poured them each a glass, and then sat at the kitchen bar. "I'm not sure you want to hear this, but we learned something new this afternoon. We discovered where the name Wilson came from, and particularly our nursing home escapee, Jack Wilson."

Randy put down her wine and looked straight into Matt's face. "Tell me."

"Jack Wilson is a character in the western movie *Shane*. He was the bad guy."

"That's tough to ignore," Randy said, shaking her head.

"With all of Makarov's cowboy fetishes, I can't imagine another person in the world with the skills and cowboy boots to pull this off," Matt stated with a frown.

"I don't know why he's so pissed off, but he is. I just can't figure out why he has so much rage that he would devise such a devastating plan for revenge."

The two ate their dinner, doing their very best to have a conversation that excluded the current situation. They talked about trite, unimportant things while they ate. Following dinner, Matt put in the videotape, and they watched the movie from which the quote on the mirror was derived. When the film was finished, they sat for a moment, staring at the screen.

"OK," Randy said with a look of confusion, "but Clint Eastwood is the good guy in this movie," Randy said.

"Yes and no," Matt said. "He's a former gunslinger who decides to put his gun back on to avenge a wrong while at the same time collecting a bounty. He ends up killing all the lawmen at the very end of the movie. Granted, they are rotten horrible, no-good lawmen, unfit to wear a badge. From my perspective, it's pretty easy to see the psychology going through Makarov's brain. He has come out of retirement, put his guns back on, and plans to kill the rotten no-good lawmen, while, at the same time, at least behaving as though he'll collect a bounty," Matt replied.

"That's just sickening."

"And so much more than just sick," Matt added. "It is twisted, sick, and terrifying what he is willing to do for revenge, if revenge is indeed his reason. He has killed so many people so far. I've got to stop this man if it's the last thing I do."

MEANS, MOTIVE AND OPPORTUNITY

Aldrich Sowles' reputation for being methodical and careful to act was not being displayed by the ranting man pacing behind his desk. Matt and Jake were sitting in the leather seats on the other side, watching Sowles flailing his arms, shouting, and hitting his fists on the desk. "When you told me, Matt, that you thought it was Makarov, I was doubtful, to say the least," he said, finally calming down and having a seat. "But this new information puts an entirely different light on him. I think we must go with *that* theory unless and until we find anything that dissuades us. I know you've started without my permission, but where are you at in finding him?"

"Because we have no fingerprint information in IAFIS, and there are no known photographs of him, at least in files we have ready access to, we have no choice but to do this the hard way," Matt said. "I have a sketch artist from the FBI's Investigative and Prosecutive Graphic Unit (IPGU), along with a San Diego Police Department (PD) artist whom they say is very good, at the rest home, interviewing the staff and attempting to put together a rendering of Wilson."

"It occurred to me the CIA might have a file on Makarov and even old photos of him. If we could get our eyes on the file, it might give us at least a few clues as to his motives for all of this. Additionally, if they have old pictures of him, the IPGU can do facial age progression and photo retouching, "aging" them to show what the Makarov might look like today. If we can do that, it will make security at the memorial on Saturday more effective because we'll know whom to look for."

"I'm in touch with some friends at the CIA to see if we can get anything on Makarov," said Jake. "I haven't been successful so far."

"Well, that's about to improve," said Sowles, grabbing the phone. He quickly dialed a number and put it on speaker. "Director Thoms," the voice on the other end said.

"Director Thoms, this is SAC Sowles in San Diego, sir."

"Aldrich, what's up? This must be important to use this number."

"It is, sir," replied Aldrich. "I have a request, and it will be tricky and needs to be fast. We need to have the full cooperation of the CIA in getting whatever information they have on a former KGB agent. He is our primary suspect in the Wilson matter, and they have the best chance of having information that could help us in this investigation."

"Let me make a call, Aldrich. Email his name and anything you know about him, and I'll give you a call back in a few minutes."

Ten long minutes went by, and Sowles' line rang. Sowles put the phone back on the speaker. "Aldrich, you'll be getting a call from the Director of the CIA in five minutes. He will provide anything you request," said Director Thoms.

"Wow, that's amazing, sir. How did you do it?"

"I called the Secretary of the Navy, who called the President, who called the Director of the CIA," said Thoms. "This is important on all levels, Aldrich. Nobody wants this resolved more than the President."

"Thank you, sir. I'll keep that in mind," said Sowles.

"You're doing good work out there. Good luck and let me know if I can help any further."

As Director Thoms promised, the Director of the CIA was on the line within five minutes. Sowles, Matt, and Jake gave him a list of what they needed and reiterated how quickly they needed it. The Director assured the men he would make it his highest priority.

Matt called Agent Ryan, the FBI's IPGU agent at Shady Palms, and was told they would need another couple of hours to get preliminary sketches of Wilson. Matt informed them he might have old photos of their suspect, which encouraged the agent considerably. "We have some pretty observant people here at Shady Palms," the agent said. "It's good that Wilson was here for a year, and medical personnel are trained to look at faces to determine distress or illness. I think we will have some success. We have some rudimentary tools for facial aging, but I'm afraid there aren't any reliable computer programs to use. We have to rely upon the artists themselves. It doesn't sound like we would have enough time to bring our anthropologist out to help."

"I'm not sure what an anthropologist is used for, but we need at least a rough picture by tomorrow morning at the very latest," said Matt.

Hanging up the phone, Matt said to Jake, "Let's head out to the memorial site and see how preparations are going. It sounds like we've got a few hours before we'll have a sketch, and God knows how long it will take the CIA to come up with anything."

The two arrived at the memorial site to a scene of frenetic activity. They arrived simultaneously with three buses. Aboard the first bus was a Navy SEAL team and the other two buses had two Marine Force Recon platoons. Randy, clipboard in hand, was barking orders to a Marine colonel and what Matt assumed were ten or so snipers. She had a large table covered with several maps. "Commander Holliston has already plotted the best locations for snipers. He will give you a tour of the locations and will seek your input. Please do not hesitate to disagree with him and offer suggestions. You are the professionals."

Matt and Jake walked up to Randy as she finished. Matt held up a paper bag and a drink. "I bet you haven't eaten all day," he said.

"Oh god, Matt, you're a lifesaver. I hope there's caffeine in the drink!"

"Of course, it's one of those Starbucks Crappocinos or something." Matt said. "And I've got your favorite sandwich in the bag: chicken salad."

"OK, I'm reconsidering that marriage proposal," Randy said.

"I'm glad to see you haven't lost your sense of humor in this. How are things going?"

Randy sat down on a bench and chugged her cold coffee drink, wiped the foam off her lips on her sleeve. "We have almost 1000 extra personnel here. We have two SEAL detachments, three Marine Force recon detachments, every single one of my protective division staff, all your NCIS folks, eleven snipers, bomb dogs, sonar buoys in the harbor, two detachments of navy divers, and me. There will be five helicopters in the air, and we've mapped every square inch of the base. Nobody will be allowed onto the base without going through a metal detector. We've got underwater observation in the harbor, along with the divers. I think we've done everything we can at this point."

"We are working hard to have the FBI IPGU unit have sketches for you first thing tomorrow, so, hopefully, you'll have a better idea of what Makarov looks like at this age," said Matt.

"That will be helpful, but, truthfully, an eighty-year-old man who walks like he's thirty is going to stand out," Randy said. "Although, as we've seen with everything else he's done, we know he can disguise himself."

Just then, Matt's phone rang. The office told him they had just received an email from the CIA. "Gotta go, Randy. We may have something from the CIA."

Randy gave him an air kiss. "I'm staying on base tonight and tomorrow night. It's looking like around the clock from here on out."

Matt gave Randy a sad look and said, "I understand. I'm hoping you'll stay a few days after?"

"We'll see how Saturday goes, Matt. We'll see how it goes."

ON TRACK TO CATCH A BAD GUY

Thursday, May 25, 2000 (1400 Hours, Pacific Time)

It was 2:00 pm when Matt and Jake arrived back at the NCIS office. They walked into his office to find a folder with the label "Makarov" neatly typed on it, along with "TOP SECRET NATO RESTRICTED" stamped on the front and back of the folder. Matt took a breath and opened the folder. Jake sat in a chair opposite Matt, anxiously watching Matt's eyes and facial gestures. "They have some basic information on Makarov and photos of him at his post in the Tokyo Embassy."

Matt sat for a moment, staring at the pictures, and chills went down his spine. It transported him back to the hotel room in Baguio, Philippines, the night Makarov tried to kill him and Randy. Matt's memories were as vivid as the actual experience twenty-four years ago. He pictured the strong, tall man with the cowboy boots and the dissonant way he spoke cowboy cliches with a Russian accent. He was brought back to the moment when Makarov left the room to determine Matt and Randy's fates and the brave change of heart that Clay Young had, saving both of their lives.

"This is mostly biographical information from CIA intelligence analysts," Matt said. Matt read much of it to Jake. "Makarov was a Major in the Soviet Union's Committee for State Security, better known to most as the KGB. His official title at the Soviet Embassy in Tokyo, Japan, was 'Diplomatic Officer'. It looks like he served in the KGB since its formation just after World War II. He has earned a Master of International Relations degree from the University of Moscow State. He speaks six languages fluently. He was a bigwig in the Soviet Union's First Directorate, a sub-organization in the KGB dedicated to external spying." Matt looked up at Jake. "As we've learned since the *Okie* spy ring, recruiting foreigners to conduct espionage against their own countries was one of the KGB's most successful endeavors. He ran the program that RMCS Lester was involved in. There is not much information here, other than the basics, but the email says that they have more information tracing his return to the Soviet Union after our bust. They are digging that information out of the archives. They will try to get it to us by 5:00 pm today. It's important to me that we have the opportunity to see that information. I'm clueless as to his motivation to commit such heinous acts and the level of hatred he must have had for me, as he did for Lester and Clay."

"So, we've got three hours to wait," said Jake.

"At least we can run these pictures over to the sketch artists at Shady Palms and see how they are doing on the composite sketches," Matt said, grabbing his coat.

When they arrived, FBI Agent Ryan and the San Diego PD artist were just finishing up their sketches. "I have a picture of Makarov from twenty-five or so years ago. Do you think that will help?" Matt inquired.

"I think it will help us put some finishing touches on the sketch and confirm how close we have come to his likeness today," Agent Ryan replied. "In the meantime, we have a sketch, and the staff who helped us concur that it's very close to Wilson." Ryan handed the sketch to Matt and Jake. Matt asked the staff to make some copies of the sketch and gave the original back to Agent Ryan. "I'll work tonight on an aging sketch from the pictures, and we'll see how close it is to this one, but I'm pretty satisfied that we have his likeness nailed," declared Ryan.

Matt thanked Agent Ryan and the San Diego PD artist, and they rushed to Matt's car and drove back to the office to make copies for Randy to distribute. It was 6 pm by the time they returned, and, once again, there was a folder on his desk. This time, the folder was an inch thick.

Matt and Jake left the office for Matt's apartment to review the folder's contents. They stopped at Matt's favorite sushi restaurant for some take-out. "I'm not eating raw fish," Jake said. "If God had wanted us to eat raw fish, he would have made it smell better."

"No worries," Matt said. "They have pansy stuff like teriyaki and tempura, too."

At the apartment, Matt cleared his kitchen table, found a couple of legal pads and pens, and poured Jake a beer and himself a Jack Daniels. With chopsticks in their hands, Matt opened the file. The contents were copies of official-looking documents, all in Russian.

"This is almost unbelievable," Matt said, looking at the CIA's note attached to the file. "When the USSR fell in 1991, the new government purged thousands of records, many of which were confidential, at the very least. The governmental transition was, apparently, chaotic. One of our operatives in Moscow discovered that rather than shredding thousands of documents, somebody very careless simply threw them in dumpsters. The CIA had agents dumpster diving behind several government buildings in Moscow. They found a veritable treasure trove of formerly secret Soviet documents simply by going through their trash. The new Russia, led by Boris Yeltsin, was throwing out documents it considered no longer relevant without caring that it had been sensitive information just a few months before the fall of the USSR. Fortunately for us, Makarov's personnel file was among those documents recovered in the trash bin."

"Boy, am I glad you're here," Matt said to Jake. "I'm not sure where we would find a Russian interpreter tonight." As Jake reviewed the Russian documents, he relayed as much as possible to Matt.

"Wow, Matt," Jake said, taking a swig of beer, "Looks like things didn't go well for Makarov when he returned to the USSR. Blame for the fall of the most successful spy operation for the Soviets was placed squarely on the shoulders of the Major. They considered firing and even imprisoning him, it looks like. However, imprisoning a World War II hero and founding KGB agent, was not going to be good for the morale of the agency, so he was quietly shuttled off to a completely remote place called Dikson Island in the Kara Sea, above the Arctic Circle, and he was essentially abandoned by his employer. In 1991, after the fall of the USSR, the Russian government, with the swipe of a pen, removed him from the rolls of the employed as the KGB was dissolved. He lost his pension, never had a family, and was apparently among the unemployed. He ended up working as a janitor in the shipyard, then working in the machine shop, then running the machine shop. The main successor to the KGB, the *Federal'naya sluzhba bezopasnosti Rossiyskoy Federatsii*, or the FSB RF, purged all the 'dead weight' from the organization, and allowed Makarov to be ghosted, even though they seemed to have kept track of him for a while, judging from the notes on his career in the shipyards and machine shop. He lost everything, Matt."

"Well," Matt said, taking a long pull on his Jack Daniels, "If that doesn't make a guy pissed off, I don't know what will. And now I can see where his additional machining skills come from. At least we have an answer to the one question I couldn't fathom. He blames me and everyone directly involved in the *Okie* spy ring and intends to exact revenge by detonating a nuclear bomb, figuratively speaking. And he has been using each crime to send a message that he is coming for me."

"I'm hoping he doesn't have a nuke because if he did, he would probably use it," Jake said, standing up to leave. "Oh, shit," he said, leafing through the papers, once again. "I'm terrible at this cop stuff. I found a fingerprint card in the file."

Matt looked up, stunned. "Holy shit! Now we can compare it to what we found in the apartment and make a solid match."

"I'll call Aldrich and Randy and let them know what we've found, and I'll make sure that the sketches are copied for Randy and her team to use. We can get the print card to the FBI in the morning and should have a solid match within a few hours."

"I'll see you first thing in the a.m.," Jake said. "I'm guessing we'll have plenty to do tomorrow."

"Yeah, I agree," said Matt.

Jake opened the door and began to walk out. "Hey, Jake," Matt said, "I really appreciate your help. I don't think we'd have gotten this far without you."

"I admit I'm an amateur cop," Jake said. "But it's nice to know that at least some of the skills I picked up along the way have been useful. Get some sleep, Sherlock."

"You too, Captain America," Matt replied.

Matt called Aldrich and updated him. "I want to send some special agents over to your place to keep an eye out," Aldrich said.

"I appreciate the offer, Aldrich, but based upon everything we know about Makarov's abilities, skills and his willingness to employ them; I think putting a couple of agents in harm's way will be as useless as a one-legged man at an ass-kicking contest. I'm pretty confident that I'm not the target quite yet, and I'm also of the mind that I'll know when the time is coming."

Matt hung up and called Randy. He explained the day's happenings and offered to drive copies of the sketches over to her. "It won't make any difference tonight. Just get them to me first thing in the morning, and we'll be fine. You be careful, Matthew Bertram," Randy said. "A genuine Bond movie villain is gunning for you."

"You just keep the bigwigs safe. I can handle myself," he said, trying to sound much more confident than he felt. He heard a click as Randy hung up. "Love you," he said into the phone.

It was after 11 pm, so Matt decided to shower and get some sleep. He set his service weapon on the bedside stand along with three extra magazines, for all the good it would do.

However, settling in and turning off the lights didn't turn Matt's brain off. Something was still bothering him. There was some important detail that he was missing, and he couldn't discern what it was. The thought was just out of his reach. He knew he had missed something, but it was just not surfacing. They had made quite a lot of progress today, and he was sure the fingerprint cards would match the prints in the apartment at Shady Palms. But there was something else just out of the reach of his consciousness, and it would cause him to have a very restless night.

MEMORIAL PREPARATIONS

Friday, May 26th, 2000 (One Day Before the Memorial)

By 9:00 am, FBI Agent Ryan let Matt know that they confirmed the sketches he had provided the day prior to be as accurate as their photo-aging techniques. Matt had already provided copies to Aldrich Sowles, who, in turn, provided them to Randy and her security team. Matt and his team spent the morning distributing the sketches to local law enforcement, the FBI, and all military law enforcement agencies. The San Diego Police Department and the California Highway Patrol had issued all-points bulletins and promised to make it the highest priority in their watch briefings. In addition, Interpol had been informed so they could be ready should Makarov attempt to leave the United States.

Matt drove out to the memorial site around 1 pm to see how Randy was doing. As he pulled up, Randy was in line at the Navy Exchange Mobile Canteen, the original food truck, known more commonly as the "Roach Coach" to most sailors. Randy bought chili dogs with onions and a Coke to have a quick lunch with Matt. "I have exactly four minutes to eat this, then I have to get back to work," warned Randy.

"I get it. I just wanted to see you for a minute, anyway." He had updated Randy on his work for the morning and asked how they were doing on Randy's end.

"I think we've just about got it. We've had five dry runs, our escape route is planned along with alternates, and we have arranged to have one half dozen ambulances present, which will be hidden out of sight, around the corner. All of our snipers and plain clothes agents have their positions, and the base is locked down tighter than a drum. The only ones getting on base in the morning are essential personnel with appropriate ID, the press, local government officials, invited guests, medical staff, the ambulances, and, of course, our dignitaries. Everyone has a copy of the sketch you provided, and, by the way, thank you so very much for that. We've got a top staff meeting in about an hour, and I'll have one more meeting with my team at 0530. If we've missed anything, we'll know soon enough."

"How are you holding up?" Matt asked.

"Matt, this is my job. I do it very well, and I'm in my zone."

"Seriously, how are you doing?" Matt asked one more time, cocking his head to the side like a puppy.

"Matt, I'm scared shitless. And that's top-secret information between you and me, SSA Bertram!" Randy said, smiling.

"You've got this, kiddo," Matt said, smiling back. "There's nobody better in the business. As for me, we have a lot to get to, and Sowles wants me at the office tomorrow, along with enough special agents that we can respond, should the worst happen. I don't like not being here, but I'm no security expert, anyway. My job is to catch the bad guy, so I'll be bad guy catching tomorrow and holding down the fort. I just can't help thinking that I've missed something significant in this case, and I can't put my finger on it. Anyway, I don't suppose I can pry you away for a quick supper?"

"I really wish I could, sweetie, but I'll be going 100 miles an hour until the event is finished."

"I get it," Matt said sadly, "Couldn't help but try."

Matt spent the afternoon taking and making calls to law enforcement agencies, ensuring that Southern California airports, Amtrak, and Bus transports were advised to be on the lookout for Marakov. The remainder of his time he spent building his case file. He started revisiting the chemical plant break-ins and purchases of ingredients, making notes of places to follow up with, and generally trying to keep himself busy.

He was still nagged by the feeling that he was missing something important, but it was just out of reach of his mind. He considered heading to a used bookstore to see if he could locate the book Shane, but he remembered that the bad guy in the novel was named *Stark* Wilson, not Jack Wilson, and, for some unknown reason, when the movie was made, the bad guy was renamed Jack. Because of this, he decided that Makarov had chosen the name from the film, not the book.

On the way home, Matt stopped at Blockbuster Video. He asked the owner if they had a copy of the movie, *Shane.* The store had two copies on its shelves, and Matt was a little surprised since the movie was made in 1953. It starred Alan Ladd and Jean Arthur. The bad guy, Jack Wilson, was played by Jack Palance, who rarely played any character other than a bad guy. Matt remembered the movie from his childhood. The novel by Jack Schaefer, on which the film was based was required reading for a class he took in high school. These days, Matt mostly enjoyed crime novels and a new favorite author, Carl Hiassen, who provided him with some much-needed humor in his life. Matt had, in his younger years, gravitated toward spy novels. After his experience with the USS *Oklahoma City* spy ring, he found his fascination with spy novels had waned dramatically. Hiassen was funny and insightful, and his protagonists were always faulted. In his current life, Matt saw much of himself in Hiassen's faulted characters.

Tonight, however, he hoped that seeing the movie from which Makarov took his pseudonym might provide some insights. He turned on the movie, and as he ate and watched, his memory of the film came back. Wilson wasn't introduced until later in the movie. The character he played was a gunslinger, brought in by the real bad guy, a man named Fletcher, who was trying to intimidate homesteaders into giving up their claims. He reached the part in the movie where Shane confronts Wilson and says to him, "I've heard about you."

Wilson replies, "What have you heard, Shane?"

Shane says, "I've heard that you're a low-down Yankee liar."

Wilson responds, "Prove it," which leads to Shane clearing the bad guys out.

The movie ended with Shane riding off into the sunset. The film left Matt with an eerie sense that he knew his job. One that the United States government probably would not officially sanction: to be Shane and terminate Makarov with *extreme prejudice.*

THE MISSED PIECE

Saturday, May 27, 2000 (0930 Hours, Pacific Time)

Matt had arrived at his office at 8 am, rearranging notes into what, for him, would be a coherent flow chart. He had decided to build a separate folder for each item on the timeline. Jake walked in with a coffee in each hand. "Had a feeling you would already be here," Jake said.

"I might as well have spent the night here for all the sleep I got," Matt replied, taking one of the cups. "I have a strong, nagging sense that I'm missing something big, but I just can't quite get my head there. I thought if I built a coherent flow chart, I might wiggle it loose."

"Well," Jake said, showing surprising sympathy for Matt's dilemma, "Let's walk through it again, this time with the confirmation that Wilson is Makarov." They looked at the timeline and the evidence, methodically taking it step-by-step.

"What gets me," Jake finally said, "Is that Makarov knows he's not going to get any money out of this, and he has killed everyone who was directly involved with screwing up his *Okie* spy ring, except for you. Why doesn't he just kill you and be done with it?"

"You've got a point. He has killed everyone associated with the *Okie* spy ring." Matt suddenly exhaled as he felt his stomach and lungs tighten as though they were going to burst, a look of realization and horror coming over his visage. "Oh my God," Matt said, the blood draining from his face.

"What? What, Matt?" Jake said.

Matt paused, almost afraid to put it into words. "He *hasn't* killed everyone who screwed up his spy ring, Jake.""Who has he missed?" Jake asked.

"Randy. Randy was instrumental in bringing him down. She had more to do with bringing the spy ring down than anyone." Matt shook his head in disbelief of his actions. "How in the hell could I have missed that?" Matt paused, took a deep breath, and lowered his head. "He's going to do something to Randy today, *not* SECNAV and the CNO. Oh, they may be collateral damage, but Randy is going to be the primary target. I'm sure of it. All eyes will be on the others, including Randy's. Her personal guard will be down. She will be laser-focused on the dignitaries, not herself." Matt grabbed his cell phone and, in a panic, dialed Randy's number, which took him three tries to get right. The call went straight to voicemail. "It's 10 am," Matt said frantically. "The memorial has just begun. We have to get over there now and warn Randy!"

Saturday, May 26, 2000 (1000 Hours)

Risers had been set up in front of the rubble of the San Diego Naval Computer and Telecommunications Station. To one side was a model of a sculpture that had been commissioned to be placed at the scene. Sitting on the risers was a plethora of dignitaries, including the commander of the naval base, the commander of the seventh fleet, both California senators, the Secretary of the Navy, and the Chief of Naval Operations. Behind the riser was a curtain hung to provide a backdrop and divert attention from the appalling mass of broken concrete and twisted metal beams. There were steps at the back of the riser for the dignitaries to come and go, and marker cones had been set up so that escape would be more easily facilitated in case of the need for a quick exit. Randy stood on the ground at the rear edge of the riser, earphone in, watching. She was uncomfortable that there were more than 300 people in attendance. She would have much preferred a smaller group. As she scanned the audience, she looked for and found each of her agents, in plain clothes, scattered throughout the crowd.

A color guard of sailors and marines marched slowly down the center, made a left-face, and continued to flag stands at the left side of the stage while the Navy Band played the National Anthem. When the National Anthem was finished, the Navy Band played "Anchors Aweigh," the fight song of the United States Naval Academy and the unofficial march song of the United States Navy. As the color guard marched out, the naval base commander stood, approached the podium, and began making his introductory comments. Randy did not listen to the speakers but constantly scanned the audience, the buildings surrounding the event, and her staff. She regularly checked in with the snipers, each one reporting nothing suspicious. Every person who had come through the entrance to the event that morning had been scanned with a metal detector, and an explosive detection dog had been stationed at the metal detector. Most of the attendees, except for the dignitaries and ambulances, were required to park in a designated location, and a shuttle bus brought them to the memorial site. *So far, so good,* Randy thought.

The Chief of Naval Operations was introduced and began his prepared remarks. When he was a few minutes into his speech, a young sailor tapped Randy on the shoulder. He handed her a folded piece of paper and said a man had given it to him and said it was urgent. She thanked the sailor and opened the note. In handwriting, the note said:

Randy: Just got critical info about the attack. Come over to the ambulances quickly
Matt

Just for a moment, Randy realized that since they had entered the electronic age, she didn't really remember what Matt's handwriting looked like, but it seemed close to what she recalled. Matt was left-handed, and his cursive letters leaned in a strange direction. She also remembered that he always put a little curly-cue design under his name, which was on the note. She called her second in command and let him know over the radio that SSA Bertram needed her by the ambulances and asked the special agent to take her place. He arrived in seconds.

Randy turned and ran back through the cones to where the ambulances were parked, expecting to see Matt standing there but saw no one. She thought perhaps he was behind the ambulances. As she started in that direction, from behind, a powerful arm wrapped around her neck, and a voice with a Russian accent said, "How nice to see you again, Special Agent Glasscock." Realizing in an instant who was attacking her and that she should fear for her life, her training and reactions took over. She kicked the assailant's shin in an effort to get him to loosen his grip, to no avail. She then sent an elbow sailing into his solar plexus, and a scream of pain surged through her elbow as though she had hit a wall. While considering her next option, she felt a prick in her neck, and in an instant, everything went black.

An ambulance slowly approached the front gate of the naval station, and the driver stopped and rolled his window down, showing the ambulance company ID. "One of the guests got the green apple nasties, so we're taking her to Balboa to have a look at her," the driver said with a perfect West Texas accent. The guard waved the ambulance through, and it turned in the direction of Balboa Naval Hospital.

Just as the ambulance left the base, Matt and Jake arrived at the scene of the memorial. Matt approached the riser from the rear, knowing where Randy would be. Another special agent was in her place. "Where's SSA Glasscock?" Matt asked, with more than a bit of panic in his voice.

"She radioed that she had been called back to the ambulance area by, um, well, by you, sir."

Matt's stomach felt like it rose into his throat as a wave of panic hit him like a sledgehammer. "We have a huge situation here," Matt said to the agent. "I think SSA Glasscock is in big trouble. I believe *she* is the target here today."

"Sir, we can't leave our posts while the memorial is going on," the agent said helplessly. "Our job is to protect SECNAV and the CNO. I'll call it over the radio, but I just can't leave."

In frustration, Matt turned to Jake with a helpless look on his face. "Let's get to the ambulances," Jake shouted. Matt and Jake ran for the ambulance area, leaving the special agent behind. Matt drew his weapon, a Sig-Sauer P228. When they reached the ambulance area, no one was to be found. They systematically searched each of the ambulances, opening their rear doors. Jake noted that one ambulance parking space was empty, and on the ground was the note Randy had received. Matt picked up the note, realizing that it was a passable forgery for his handwriting, down to the little scroll that he would put under his name when he wrote cards or notes to Randy. Matt grabbed his cell phone and tried to call Aldrich. When he answered, Matt quickly explained the situation. "I think he may be trying to get away in one of the ambulances," Matt yelled.

"I'll get the gates closed to everyone," replied Aldrich. "I suggest you head for the front gate as quickly as you are able."

The two men ran to their car and raced toward the front gate. Matt called the base police while they were enroute and asked them to meet the two there, explaining the possible abduction. When they reached the gate, it had indeed been shut, and marines, unaware of the details of the situation, had M-16s aimed at the cars. Matt got out, waving his NCIS badge as the base police cars arrived.

"Has anyone left in the last five or ten minutes?" Matt questioned.

"Just an ambulance taking somebody to Balboa who was sick," the marine replied.

"Describe the driver for me."

"Some old hillbilly guy, who said the person had something nasty and green, or something--Oh, yeah, he said she had the 'green apple nasties,' whatever that is."

Only Makarov would say something like that, Matt thought. Matt quickly briefed the base police, who said they would call SDPD and get an APB for the ambulance. With Jake driving, the two left the base, heading toward Balboa Naval Hospital, hoping they could spot the ambulance. In the meantime, he called back to the office. Aldrich had just arrived back. "I've informed the police at Lindbergh Field to be on the lookout, Matt. We've got police helicopters in the air looking for the ambulance. It'll be easy to spot." Aldrich paused, then added, "I'm sorry, Matt. We'll find her and get her back."

"If it's the last thing I do, Aldrich, I'm getting her back alive," Matt replied. "You can take that to the bank."

Matt and Jake drove the neighborhood and side streets searching for the ambulance. With a mélange of grief, anger, and self-contempt, Matt hit his fist on the dashboard. "I should have known, Jake!" Matt cried out. "Why didn't I realize that Randy would be on his hit list?" Matt said, rhetorically. "If something happens to her, I'll never forgive myself. How in the hell did Makarov get my handwriting to make the note?"

"As we just discovered, it's amazing what you can find dumpster diving, Matt. We'll find her, Matt. We'll find her," said Jake, which to Matt at that moment sounded only like resoundingly hollow words.

Five minutes later, Matt received a call that the ambulance had been located. Jake steered toward the address, and they pulled up behind an SDPD cruiser. Matt jumped out of the car with his badge in hand. "There's nobody in it as far as we can tell," the officer said as they approached. Matt held his breath as they opened the back door. An empty stretcher sat in the back of the ambulance. On the stretcher was a note. It read:

I am a man of notorious and intemperate disposition. Let's play a little hide and seek. I want her to die in front of you.

Wilson

DR. NIKITA BARANOV

Sunday, May 27, 2000 (1000 Hours, Pacific Time)

S lowly coming out of unconsciousness, Randy heard a peculiar buzzing in her ears, much like lights in a stadium. The darkness gradually receded, and as Randy awakened, she felt the sensation that someone was wiping her face with a sponge, much like the feeling of applying makeup. As consciousness returned, her eyes focused on a terrifying sight. She was shackled into what looked like an antique wheelchair, both hands and feet. She raised her head and saw the face of Makarov, humming a vaguely familiar western cowboy song.

"Ah, the little filly comes back to life—for the moment," Makarov said.

"Fuck you, Makarov," Randy spat back through slightly slurred speech. "Matt's coming for you, and he's going to find you; when he does, he will take you out."

"Well, aren't you in a horn-tossing mood," Makarov shot back. "You see, I'd like nothing better than for that real revolting son of a bitch to do exactly that. In fact, we're going to let him find us—in good time."

"You're not going to get away with this," Randy said, spitting in his face.

"Now, young lady, you'd make a hornet look cuddly," Makarov said, smiling. "And there's nothing to get away with. I'm simply exacting retribution, the Russian way, which is ugly and painful as all hell. Now, I'm sorry to tell you, but you're going to go back to la-la land in a few minutes."

Randy looked around her. There was another wheelchair, this one a modern chair with a headrest and a hanger for an IV bag. She realized she was no longer wearing her clothes but rather she had been changed into something akin to a hospital gown and slippers. Fright embraced her as she realized that her head had been completely shaved. With visions of electronic leads placed along her shaved skull for tortuous purposes it was almost a relief when Makarov brought out a gray wig and fitted it to her head. The relief faded quickly when he smiled as he raised a hypodermic needle and injected the contents into an intravenous (IV) port in her arm. Randy immediately felt light-headed. She sensed that she was gradually losing control of her muscles because, while still conscious, she was unable to lift her head or arms.

"You're probably wondering what in tarnation is going on," said Makarov. "We are going to take a trip, you and I, and it's a rather long distance. I'm sorry to inform you that you are in need of a medical procedure that can only be performed in a certain country, and you'll demonstrate that by not moving or communicating. I've made you a little cocktail that I call, *she's got too many cobwebs in the attic*. You'll stay pretty well conscious, but you'll be paralyzed with a drip of pancuronium bromide, a dab of lorazepam, and a pinch of suvorexant. The pancuronium is great. It's a lot like the poison curare, only it doesn't stop your breathing—*usually*. So, enjoy the trip!"

Makarov dialed his cell phone, and Randy realized the drugs were taking swift effect since she couldn't focus on anything he was saying as he transferred her to the new wheelchair. He pushed her outside in front of the building and locked the door to his workshop behind him. Within ten minutes, a medical transport van arrived. Makarov reached out his hand and introduced himself. The driver loaded Randy into the back of the van. Makarov got into the passenger seat, and the driver headed northwest. Their destination was Gillespie Field Airport, a small commuter airport near El Cajon. It would be approximately a thirty-minute drive.

Although Randy could not move a single muscle in her body, she was aware she was in a van heading somewhere. Her completely immobile body concealed the fright and panic she felt inside. Even with the sedatives, her mind raced through intermittent periods of fog and near unconsciousness. It was utterly terrifying not to be able to move, talk or scream. She was completely helpless. The only external evidence that she was conscious was the stream of tears rolling down her cheeks.

The van pulled through the airfield gate and drove toward a hangar. Makarov directed the driver to the hangar, but the driver was already familiar with the location from previous visits. They parked in front of an office with a connected hangar. A sign above the office door read, "International Air Transport, Inc." Parked in front of the hangar was a Learjet 45, being fueled and prepared for flight.

Out of the door came a jovial, chubby man with baggy pants and a white short-sleeved shirt. He was wearing a tie that had been tied much too short. He had a paunch, and a bushy mustache almost completely covered his mouth. The man walked up to Makarov, put out his hand, and said, "Dr. Nikita Baranov, I presume?"

"Yes, my friend, are you Mr. Adkins?" Makarov inquired.

"Yes sir. Bob Adkins, Doc. Please call me Bob. I understand this is a crisis situation, and the needed procedure is only available in Moscow. I want you to know that we'll take damn good care of you both. Now, I don't know if you've gone through this process before, Doc, but we've gotten your Ukrainian passport and your patient, Ms. Ruell's US passport, pre-approved for leaving the US and arriving in Moscow. The visas are all arranged, and we used our contacts in Moscow to secure a medical van to take Ms. Ruell to Medsi Hospital. There will be stops to refuel in Hawaii and Japan; weather permitting, you'll be in Moscow in time for Ms. Ruell's operation. Now, we'll need to change her to a specially built gurney for the trip, but there's plenty of room to get the wheelchair and your luggage aboard. There's also plenty of food and hydration, so you'll both be comfortable on the trip. Unfortunately, we don't have flight attendants, so it's self-serve."

Randy was listening intently to the discussion. As she did, she systematically scanned her muscles for the ability to move any of her body parts whatsoever. She discovered that she could slightly move one eyelid and could move her eyes to the left and right. As Bob Adkins and the crew were transferring her to the gurney, she attempted to make eye contact with each of them. She winked and moved her eyes in random directions, which was the most she could muster. Tears continued to roll down her face as she felt the frustration of being unable to communicate.

At one moment, she thought she might have captured the attention of Adkins as he looked into her eyes. All he returned was a very sympathetic look. He patted her hand as he looked at her gray hair and said, "Don't you worry, Ms. Ruell. You're going to be just fine, I'm sure."

They loaded the gurney onto the plane along with the wheelchair and two suitcases. After taxiing away from the transport company, the plane turned onto the runway. The pilots pushed the throttle levers forward, and the jet roared to life. The aircraft was just lifting off as it passed where Bob Adkins was standing. He gave them a wave as the jet became airborne, quickly turned west, headed for Hawaii, then Japan, and finally Russia.

To Russia With Love

Sunday had come and gone, with the entire regional office staff working hard to chase down leads and ensure that airports were under surveillance, as well as the highways, bus terminals, and train stations. Every police department in California had received photographs of Randy and the sketch of Makarov. They discovered the ambulance had been stolen, and the ambulance company had not noticed the theft until Sunday. The company reported the theft within two hours of the discovery. Special agents were knocking on every door in the neighborhood where SDPD found the ambulance. So far, this had yielded no usable information.

Matt and Jake were looking at a map of the city with the location they found the ambulance marked. "You know," said Jake, "The ambulance was abandoned only four or five blocks from Shady Palms. I can't help but think we might want to make another visit to the area around the home. If Makarov were traveling to and from Shady Palms on foot, he probably wouldn't have had his workshop terribly far away."

Feeling relieved that they would be doing something more than reviewing paperwork and staring at maps, Matt grabbed his jacket and car keys, and they drove to Shady Palms. They spent an hour or so knocking on doors, with no one having any helpful information. "Let's do five more homes and call it a day," said Matt. On home four, a man was watering his flowers in front of his house. The two men approached him and Matt showed his credentials. He explained a bit about the situation, asking, yet again, if the man had seen anything suspicious.

"Well, not really suspicious, I'd say," said the man, "But my business is in the industrial park a couple of blocks away on Epsilon Street. I didn't see an ambulance, but I did see one of those vans that transport disabled people go by my place yesterday. I just thought it was a little odd seeing something like that in the complex."

"Do you remember the name of the company?" Matt inquired.

"Can't really say I do, but the van was blue and white if that helps any."

The two thanked the man, asked for his name and whether they could come by again if they had more questions. He said he would be happy to oblige.

"Of course, it would make sense for him to have a space in an industrial park," said Matt. "He had to have kept machinery and such somewhere."

Matt called back to the office and asked the agent who answered to start going through local handi-van companies and see if any paint their vehicles blue and white. "Let's go over to that industrial park and see if we can talk to somebody there. Maybe someone saw something."

They drove to the park and found a leasing office. They entered the office and were greeted by a thin, balding, middle-aged man with a name tag above his shirt pocket that said, "Anderson," and below the name was engraved the title, "Manager." Matt showed the man his badge and gave the man a summary of the reason they were there. He asked the manager if he had seen anything going on yesterday, but since it was a Sunday, he was not at work. He promised to ask the tenants on Tuesday. Suddenly inspired, Matt turned to the leasing agent as they were about to leave. "Just out of curiosity, have you leased any space to an older man? He probably looks like he's in his 70's or 80's."

"Now that you mention it, we do have a tenant that's an older guy. Unlike most of the other companies in the park, I've never seen him come and go. He must keep strange hours," said the leasing agent, "But over the past year, he's brought in a ton of machining and printing equipment and lots of stuff in crates."

"Could you tell us his name?" Jake asked.

"Well, I really shouldn't. I'm supposed to keep that information confidential."

Matt implored, "Mr. Anderson, the life of one of our agents is at stake, right now, and time is of the essence. I'm happy to keep it between you and me if you like," Matt said, lying.

The manager relented, went to a file cabinet, and pulled out a file. "There it is," the agent said, "Let's see here. Um, oh yes. Wilson. Jack Wilson."

Matt looked at Jake, then back at Anderson. "Mr. Anderson, is there a possibility that you could let us into that space?"

"I'm sorry, Special Agent Bertram. I couldn't possibly do that without a warrant."

Within an hour, nine NCIS and FBI cars, a forensics van, and three canines were at Anderson's office. Matt had warrants in hand to search for equipment used in manufacturing: extending robotic arms, C-4, and various remote control devices. Anderson let them know that he did not have a key to the space. "That's no problem, Mr. Anderson. NCIS will get in. We'll pay for any damage to the space."

Six minutes later, an Explosive Ordinance Disposal (EOD) team was on the roof of the building, drilling a hole in the roof. They inserted a fiber optic camera into the hole to determine if the space had been booby-trapped. A cadre of government agents, with weapons drawn and wearing full assault gear, were preparing to enter the space. An FBI bomb expert directed the entry as all realized there was a distinct possibility the space was wired to explode. The locks were broken, and with precision, the bomb expert gave the go-ahead to enter. There were no booby-traps. As Matt, Jake, the EOD team and the others entered the space, they found a frightening scenario. The space contained sophisticated machine tools, printing and laminating equipment, and a kitchen. The entire space was completely sound-proofed, and an antique wheelchair with shackles attached sat in an area of the room under an ample mercury vapor light.

As the EOD team searched the space, their bomb dogs discovered the remains of C-4, Tovex, and multiple other explosives and bomb ingredients. There were two 50 gallon drums of potassium nitrate and a large canister of rocket fuel.

Jake looked in the refrigerator and said to Matt, "You better look at this, Matt." Matt walked over to see vials of drugs. On the counter was equipment to start IVs.

"I'm not sure what all this is, but I have a feeling it's some combination of sedatives," Matt said.

A sticky note was on the table in the kitchen. It was similar to the one they had found at Makarov's apartment. All it said was:

Show down at Kazan Theotokos

Matt stared at the note for a moment in utter disbelief. He felt the air drain out of his lungs, sweat broke out on his face, and his head was spinning. He had to take several breaths to regain sufficient composure to say anything. "I don't know where that place is, but I'm going to find it and blow Makarov's brains out."

A special agent approached and said he had gotten a call from the office. They found the name of the handi-van company, and they told him they had done a pick-up yesterday. The drop-off was at Gillespie field. Two special agents were on their way to the airport.

"Let's go ahead and go out to the airfield, Matt. Forensics will be here for hours, and we need to build a plan," Jake said.

"I plan to find that place, go there and blow Makarov's brains out," Matt reiterated.

"Well, Sherlock," Jake said, trying to lighten the moment, "I would suggest we put a little more meat on that plan."

KAZAN

Monday, May 28, 2000 (1300 Hours, Pacific Time)

Matt and Jake arrived at Gillespie Field just as the other two special agents were getting out of their car in front of the offices of International Air Transport. The four went into the building, showed the receptionist their credentials, and were invited into a conference room. A rotund man entered, stuck out his hand, and said, "Hello, officers. I'm Bob Adkins, the manager of this base." Matt introduced all the agents and explained they were with the Naval Criminal Investigative Service.

"Mr. Adkins–"

"Bob. Please call me Bob," the man said with a smile.

"OK, Bob. I understand that a handi-van arrived here at your base yesterday at some point," Matt said.

"Well, sir, we actually had two handi-vans and two ambulances. We had four flights out yesterday."

"You are quite busy, aren't you, Bob?" Matt replied.

"Indeed we are, Special Agent Bertram," Bob said. "We provide a unique service, here, and we are the only air transport in San Diego County that makes international flights."

"Well, in this case, there was probably an older man with a woman, and the woman may not have been conscious," said Matt.

"Ah, yes, that one *was* special. It was a doctor, Dr. Nikita Baranov. He had a patient, Ms. Ruell. This was special because it was our first international flight to Moscow. We fly all over the country and sometimes to Europe and Asia, but we've never transported a patient to Russia. Boy oh boy, Special Agent Bertram, I had to learn a lot quickly about visas and the required paperwork to accomplish this, and our pilots were pretty damned excited about flying there. I have been working on it for a number of weeks now."

"A number of weeks, huh?" said Matt. "And Moscow, too. Was the woman mid-forties with red hair?"

"No, she looked older than that and had gray hair. She was awake but didn't seem to be able to move. She kept moving her eyes in circles, and there were tears on her face, but she didn't say anything. Dr. Baranov let us know that she was going to have a procedure that only one hospital in the world performs, and that's Medsi Hospital in Moscow."

"Must be expensive to get a patient to Russia," Matt proposed.

"Probably the most expensive flight we've done," Bob replied.

Matt pulled out Makarov's sketch and a photo of Randy. "These look like the folks?" Matt inquired.

"Definitely the Doc," Bob replied. "And now that I'm looking at the woman, there's a strong resemblance to the woman. Only the picture makes her look much younger."

"So when does the flight get there?" asked Matt.

"Oh, it's already there. I arranged for an ambulance to take her and the Doc to Medsi hospital from the airport as soon as they cleared customs and immigration in Moscow. I'm expecting a call from the pilots letting me know they are on their way back any minute now."

"Is there a chance we could see your paperwork on this flight?" Matt inquired.

"I'm afraid I'd have to have a warrant for that, Special Agent Bertram," Bob replied.

"It will be on its way as quickly as we can get one signed," Matt said.

"We're keeping the judge pretty busy today," Jake said to Matt with a smile. Matt was in no mood for humor.

Matt thanked Bob for his time. Matt asked Jake to drive back to the office. As soon as the car was in drive, Matt was on the phone with Aldrich. Matt explained the situation. "Let me make some calls and see what's doable, Matt," said Sowles. "We'll put together a plan when you get here."

"I hope you understand how important this is, Aldrich," Matt said, his voice cracking.

"I do, Matt. And we'll do everything we can to get her back."

Monday, May 28, 2000 (0800 Hours Moscow Time)

Vladimir Putin assumed the Presidency of Russia in May of 2000, which was not much of a change as he had been Prime Minister before taking the presidency. The Russian government, seeing an opportunity to draw cash into the country, was actively promoting tourism. After the fall of the Soviet Union, Russia became one of the top ten countries in the world for tourists to visit. Consequently, acquiring visas to enter the country had become a relatively simple matter, and immigration and customs officials had relaxed their standard fine-tooth inspections of those visiting. It was even easier for Makarov to get Randy into the country for medical purposes.

The Learjet touched down and was instructed to park at a specific building off the tarmac after taxiing off the runway. Waiting for the jet was one customs officer and an ambulance and driver. Makarov and the official had a conversation in Russian. Makarov handed the official several hundred US dollars. The official smiled at Makarov, and they placed Randy in the ambulance.

The ambulance driver had been instructed to proceed to Medsi Hospital and began his drive. Makarov engaged the driver in casual conversation on the way. About ten minutes into the trip, Makarov told the driver there was a change in his patient's status and asked him to pull over to the side of the road for a moment to check on her, which he did. Once the van was placed in park, Makarov moved forward behind the driver, bringing a nylon line about two feet long out of his pocket. In one smooth motion, he placed the garrote around the neck of the driver and pulled tight. The line cut into the neck of the driver, and severed both carotid arteries in his neck, which immediately stopped the blood flow to the driver's brain. The driver was dead in seconds. Makarov pulled the driver out of the front seat and laid him next to a terrified Randy, who was awake and aware of the entire scenario, yet still unable to move. Within thirty seconds, the ambulance was back on the road, not to Medsi Hospital, but north and west, leaving downtown Moscow, headed for the village of Yaropolets.

Just A Couple of Tourists

Monday, May 28, 2000 (1500 Hours, Pacific Time)

Matt and Jake arrived back at the NCIS Regional Office and were met by a special agent, who handed them an envelope. Inside the envelope was the paperwork for the air ambulance flight, including copies of both passports and the entry visas into Russia. The picture of Randy was a shock. "Old Bob was right," Jake said, looking at Randy's picture. "She's an old lady."

The two walked to Sowles' office, knocked, and Aldrich shouted to come in. As the men sat down, Sowles appeared very frustrated. "We've spoken with the CIA and the State Department. It's a true political quagmire. Everyone is concerned about the ramifications of helping to rescue Randy. There's only so much they can do to help. They are determined to stay in the background, mostly just observing and listening to police channels in the area and providing any logistic guidance we might need. They aren't willing to take an active role in intercepting Makarov and Randy, as the operatives they have in the embassy are spying undercover as attachés and such in ostensibly diplomatic roles." Sowles sneered, saying, "Like the Russians don't know who they *really* are. In addition, our suspect is a Russian citizen. They recommend involving the Moscow police."

Matt held his breath for a moment before responding to Sowles. He took a deep breath, letting the air out slowly, wanting to sound more measured and sane than he was feeling. "You know, Aldrich, as well as I, the local police will do squat with this one. It will get buried, and we will lose our opportunity to save Randy. I'm not going to let that happen. If we can't get any help from our people in Russia, there's only one choice left. We'll just have to go ourselves—correction, *I'll* have to go myself."

"I'm afraid I can't let you go, Matt. This is an international issue now, and protocol requires us to report it to the local police in Moscow and ask them to handle it. We have pretty good relations with Russia these days," Sowles responded.

"You and I both know, Aldrich, that Makarov wants *me* and that he's got the ability to evade the Russian police if they get involved. If that happens, he'll just kill Randy and modify his plans to come back, find me and kill me. He'll get his way. The only way we have any chance of saving Randy and getting Makarov, is if I do it. Plain and simple."

Sowles stared back at Matt. "I had a feeling you would say that, but I had to hear it from your mouth. This case is of utmost importance at the highest levels, at least behind closed doors, but you know as plain as the nose on your face that Makarov has a trap set for you. You also know that he is aware that he's holding the only bait he knows you'll grab without giving it a moment's thought. So, he will be expecting you and he wants you to pursue him. That was the point of the show down note. He'll have already made plans for you, and he won't be stupid. Look at how he has brought the US Navy to its knees. You have very little chance of success—actually, less than that."

Jake cleared his throat and waved at Sowles like a third grader who knew the answer to a question that was asked. "I don't want to speak out of turn here, Aldrich, but I think that if I go along with Matt, it will even up the odds just a bit. I have a feeling that Makarov is figuring that Matt will go alone. I've spent a whole lot of time inside that asshole's brain, and I think I have a handle on how he thinks. He's a friggin' idiot when it comes to the whole cowboy thing, and if you look at practically every cowboy movie and book, the hero and the bad guy face off alone. I'm sure the *pig fucker* wants a 'High Noon' showdown, just like the movies.

"I can go along. I have some skills of my own, including the ability to speak Russian. I know we can't send in the posse, but we can quietly get to Russia as tourists. With the embassy and the CIA's 'logistical support,' we can find him, get Randy, and get the hell out of there."

"So, Aldrich," Matt said, "Did the note give us a clue as to where we can locate them?"

Sowles said, "We're pretty sure we know. He gave us the location in his note: Kazan Theotokos. We did some research and found that it is actually a place. More accurately, it's known as Kazanskaya Tserkov, or 'The Church of Our Lady of Kazan.' It's an abandoned Russian Orthodox Church just at the edge of a village named Yaropolets. The church is about 80 miles from Moscow. The building was damaged in World War II and never rebuilt, thanks to the anti-religion Soviets, and it's now in such disrepair that it is beyond restoration. There's a razor wire and corrugated steel fence around the church, but few people know about it, so there is no security other than the fence. Occasionally some overly adventurous tourist sneaks in, but, frankly, the Russians couldn't care less about it. It would be the perfect place to set a trap for you."

"Now here's the thing," Sowles said with the most severe expression Matt had ever seen from his friend and boss, "If you are going to do this, and I am strongly advising you *not* to, you have to go as private citizens. This *cannot* be an officially sanctioned NCIS mission. You'll have to pay for your own plane tickets, and you'll have to go without official credentials. You would officially be on vacation. You would be vigilantes on foreign soil. If—no, *when* you return, there's no assurance your expenses will be reimbursed. If you decide to go, you are just two tourists on vacation."

Sowles paused, and then continued, shaking he head. "In anticipation that this was the direction you would be heading, I have managed to persuade the State Department to give you some support. The embassy will covertly provide you with some of the tools you'll need to get the job done. Understand?"

"We're wasting time talking. The decision is already made," said Matt. "I'd like to put in for a couple of weeks of vacation, sir."

"Done. Myers is putting together a research portfolio for you on the town and the church. I have to say, Matt, this is *beyond* dangerous. You'll be flying solo. Some strings have been pulled, and there are, coincidentally, two seats free on Air China nonstop to Moscow, leaving San Francisco at 8 pm tonight." Sowles handed Matt a piece of paper with a number on it. "When you get to Moscow, call this number and ask for Paul. You'll get some help to get you going. I know you are compelled by your relationship with Randy to do this, Matt, but you are most definitely walking into an obvious and perilous trap."

"There is nothing I wouldn't do, nowhere I wouldn't go, and nobody I wouldn't fight to have Randy back," Matt responded.

"I know and I understand, Matt. We'll give you a three-day head start, and then we will contact Russian law enforcement to report this. I wish you success, my friend."

Jake and Matt were packed and at San Diego's Lindbergh Field within the hour. Even though there were no metal detectors at the airport, they knew they would be searched in Moscow, so they travelled with no weapons. They caught a commuter flight from Lindbergh Field to San Francisco International to await their flight to Moscow. It would be about a thirteen-hour flight, and with ten hours of time zone changes, they would arrive at approximately seven pm the following day, which meant they would lose an entire day. They would get a hotel and set out to find Randy the next morning.

The two men arrived at San Francisco International with twenty minutes to spare, ran for the gate, and were seated moments before the door of the Boeing 747 shut. Economy class for a 6-foot-five-inch man was less than comfortable, but Matt gave it no thought. He would have rowed a boat to Russia had it been necessary.

Once the jet was in flight, the flight attendants passed with a drink cart. "Would you like something to drink, sir?" the flight attendant asked.

"I don't suppose you have Jack Daniels," Matt inquired.

"No, sir, but we do have some good whiskey." She brought out two tiny bottles of a generic whiskey, which Matt gratefully took from her, accompanied by a plastic cup. He took a swig and made a face.

"Not up to your Tennessee Whiskey standards?" Jake said.

"Not even close, but it'll slow my brain down for a bit," Matt replied.

During the trip, Matt and Jake read the background information the office had provided. "This church is amazing," said Jake. "They built it in the late 1700s on an estate called The Chernyshev Estate.

"In 1717, a Russian Imperial nobleman by the name of Grigori Chernyshev bought the estate land and developed it. By 1770 the estate had a beautiful stately home and some pretty impressive gardens. Some people called it the 'Russian Versailles.' Apparently, it was a regular stop for Catherine the Great. The whole thing was confiscated by the 'People,' meaning Stalin and his buddies, after the revolution, and they used the home as a sanatorium. I think that's a euphemism for a prison for the enemies of the state. The church's architecture is unusual in that it's composed of two symmetric sections: apses on both ends connected by a broad vestibule. Most churches just have one apse. It was a beautiful freaking church. Nazi bombing and ground fighting heavily damaged the entire estate during the Second World War, and the Soviets never restored it. The house is in ruins, with the gardens overgrown and a crumbling obelisk to Catherine the Great. The church is in awful shape, too. Columns have fallen, paint has peeled off the walls, and there's a lot of damage. The local authorities put a razor wire fence around it a few years ago to keep people out. They think the whole thing could cave in at any moment."

"Not exactly Main Street Deadwood," said Matt, "but creepy enough for Makarov to have his showdown, I guess."

Matt tried, without success, to sleep on the flight, his mind wound up tighter than a noose around a hung man's neck. After many grueling hours in the uncomfortable seat, Matt relaxed a bit as the airliner landed at Sheremetyevo Alexander S. Pushkin International Airport. The former military airfield had recently been renamed from Sheremetyevsky, which was a small village in Russia. The Russians held a contest for a new name, and the Russian poet Alexander Pushkin won the honors.

The two men's passports were scrutinized closely, and their bags were scoured before being released from customs. They rented the only car available, a bright yellow Lada Riva. Jake took the driver's seat and drove a few blocks to find a pay phone. Matt put a ten-ruble coin into the phone and dialed the number Sowles had given him and asked for Paul. "Paul, this is Matt Bertram," Matt said, unsure whether it was wise to have given his name.

"We've been waiting for you to call, Matt. I understand that you will be spending the night in Moscow. Tomorrow morning, we will have your lunch packed and ready for you to pick up. Come to the Russian Sky Hotel, Khimki, International Highway, possession 1, at eight a.m., and your lunch will be ready for you," said Paul. "We'll bring it to you, so you don't have to get out of your car." Immediately, the man hung up.

The two men had a quick supper in their hotel dining room of Ukha and cabbage pie, then fell into bed. Matt was exhausted and knew that he would not be his best the next day without sleep. The twenty-four hours since his last sleep assisted him in falling asleep, but he tossed and turned in a fitful and restless manner; his mind was unable to relax enough for decent sleep.

The following morning, the two grabbed coffees and blini, delicious pastries similar to blintzes. They jumped in the car and headed for the Russian Sky Hotel, just a few minutes from the airport and the hotel in which they had spent the night. When they pulled up in front, a man approached their car, opened the rear door, and put a large box on the back seat. "Enjoy your lunch," the man said, shutting the door and walking away.

The package of information Sowles provided included street maps for Moscow and maps that would help them navigate to Yaropolets and the Chernyshev Estate. As soon as they were safely on the highway, Matt reached into the back seat and retrieved the box. He carefully opened the top. To Matt's surprise, the box contained lunch. "I don't know what these are, but they look good," Matt said.

Jake looked over at the contents. "Ah, there are some golubtsy which are stuffed cabbage leaves, kotlety, which are meatballs, and it looks like kompot, which is a delicious drink they usually make from whatever berries are in season. I'm hoping there's something else underneath them, though."

Matt was already digging through the food to see what was underneath. "I don't know how they taste, but how about two Colt 2000's and ten magazines, and what looks like a couple of Spyderco Civilian fighting knives, two garotes, and two M67 fragmentation grenades?"

"Colts? Colts?" Jake said with some incredulity. "Friggin' CIA is certainly consistent, I'll say."

"What's wrong with Colt 2000s?" Matt questioned Jake. "Seems like fifteen round high-capacity mags, compact design, and a gun built by the company that invented the revolver and changed the course of history isn't bad."

"They just have no imagination," Jake said. "Sig is a much more reliable weapon."

"I'm pretty sure they had to give us what they had on hand," said Matt. "Besides, we're lucky to have anything. I do not know what we would ever do with the frag grenades, but we may think of something. Besides, we will be going against someone who successfully breached secure navy bases three times and killed more people than the Oklahoma City bomber. I'm not sure we could carry enough weapons to feel protected against him."

The two men headed out of Moscow, found the M9 highway, and headed northeast toward the village of Yaroplets. Matt was amazed at how quickly they were out of the city and was surprised at the beauty of the more rural scenery. "I don't know, Jake. Russia was a place I thought was cold and ugly. I sort of imagined the entire country in black and white."

"Much of Russia is a little on the bleak side, but I agree, this is beautiful scenery," Jake responded.

The bright yellow car would provide anything but camouflage as they approached the estate. Matt imagined it looked like a parrot in a park filled with pigeons. "I'm open to any suggestions," Matt said to Jake, "but it seems to me that we would work best if we parked the car and walked the rest of the way just before we got to the estate. I also think it might be the best strategy if we split up, so when Makarov spots us, he only sees me. I can confront him alone, without him knowing that you're with me. You can be hidden away as a backup. That might give us the advantage of surprise since he doesn't expect anyone but me."

"I can't think of a better way to do it," Jake acknowledged. "I'll be as close as I'm able without being spotted."

The journey to Yaroplets was quite breathtaking. The busyness of Moscow quickly gave way to a typically rural scene, with well-kept small farms, grazing cattle, and a fresh breeze. Here, the farmers looked like they had stepped out of time, with ancient tractors tilling the soil, babushkas talking with their neighbors, trading eggs for cabbage pies, and catching up on the local gossip. The country road wound around small properties, many covered with apple trees in full bloom. The land appeared lush and green. Matt could palpably feel time slow here and imagined it to be much as it was a hundred years ago. It occurred to him that perhaps the US had used some serious propaganda to convince its citizens that Russia was a desolate place. *Probably not as lovely in the winter*, Matt thought.

As they followed the road, there were few cars, and those cars they did pass were antiques. Were it not for the business at hand, Matt could have felt himself relax and enjoy the trip through an enchanting countryside. Even so, Matt could feel the world around him settling into the routine of rural life. They passed through the city of Volokolamsk, the last town before Yaroplets, and turned toward their final destination. With the maps provided, they decided that Pushkinskaya Ulitsa street would be the best approach. He gained an appreciation for how much the Russian people must have loved Pushkin, the Russian novelist, poet, and playwright, as his name appeared on many streets and government buildings. The Church of Our Lady of Kazan was on the eastern side of the estate, and from the aerial photographs, it appeared as though there were large trees behind the structure. They hoped the trees would provide the cover they needed to approach the church without being seen – or worse, sniped. Makarov had proved his superior sniper skills when he kidnapped Lester Morris from the prison transport.

It was shortly after 3 p.m. when they arrived at the location they had chosen. Sure enough, their bright yellow Lada stood out like a clown at a funeral. If they approached from this location, Makarov could easily see them. Jake took a left turn on Sadovaya Ulitsa, which brought them around south of their location, well hidden by trees at the rear of the church.

They parked the car a quarter mile away under cover. They took their time reviewing the maps and the floor plan of the church and talking through their plan, step-by-step. "I know you know, Jake, that we have one chance, and it has to go perfectly. If we screw up just a bit, Makarov will successfully complete the execution of his plan. Randy and I, and probably you, too, will be toast."

"You don't have to tell me that, Sherlock," Jake said. "And we will make our one chance count; bet on it."

Matt took one of the Colts and five magazines, and Jake took the others. Each took a grenade and a knife. Matt felt more comfortable with the blade than the gun. While training for his black belt in Hapkido, he was also required to learn how to handle two weapons. Matt had chosen the bo, a long fighting stick, and the knife. Over the years, his Hapkido training had led him to believe that in close quarters, a knife was more often superior to a handgun. Unfortunately, law enforcement didn't agree, so the pistol was the primary weapon of choice in his day-to-day investigative activities even for close quarters.

Once each of them was properly armed, Matt put his hand on Jake's shoulder. "Jake, I need to ask you for a favor."

"Anything, Matt," replied Jake.

"If there is ever any question about whom to protect, it *has* to be Randy. If you need to sacrifice someone, please ensure that it's me and not Randy."

"Do you forget who you're talking to?" Jake said with a grin. "I'm Captain America. The only one who's likely to be sacrificed will be that ass-wipe Makarov."

"Don't forget." Matt repeated.

"I won't, Matt."

The two awkwardly slapped one another on the shoulder and set out to rescue Randy and end Makarov's life.

A Church?

Wednesday, May 30, 2000 (1600 Hours, Moscow Standard Time)

For the past hour, Randy had gradually felt some ability to move her muscles, as the sedative drugs were slowly leaving her system. As she gradually became more coherent, she began to grasp how horrifying her situation actually was. She saw she was inside a dilapidated building. There were several columns, which at one time must have been majestic, but had now toppled to their sides. The ceilings were domed and arched. Randy guessed they were perhaps thirty feet high. There were tall, arched windows in the walls, most of which were broken. She could tell the walls had once been painted a brilliant color of blue, with ceiling molding painted white, most of which was now faded or fallen down. There was graffiti carved into several of the walls, and the floor was littered with rubble. The building resembled a church, and she could see that she was restrained in a room that could have once been an apse. Yet there was no altar present. The building looked to her as though it could collapse at any moment, and her fear was punctuated by intermittent creaking and random pieces of plaster falling.

With each passing moment, Randy's head cleared a bit more. She turned her attention to herself as she felt intense pain in her shoulders. She had straps, or perhaps ropes, looped underneath her armpits, which were connected to a rope above her that was somehow attached to the ceiling. Her hands were tied behind her back, and she was suspended about fifteen feet in the air. Directly below her, the floor had a large hole, approximately three feet in diameter. It was too dark to see what lay inside the hole. As the sedatives wore off, her level of panic intensified. She had no idea where she was. All she knew was that Makarov was her captor, although she could not see him at the moment.

Randy gasped as she heard echoing footsteps in the building, quickly coming nearer. An older man turned the corner and walked toward her. He was wearing cowboy boots. She remembered Makarov liked to wear boots, but what was astounding was that he was also wearing a cowboy hat, a *black* cowboy hat. The man walked toward Randy and stopped about ten feet from where she was hanging. "Well, hello there, little lady," he said, "You look about as nervous as a long-tailed cat in a room full of rocking chairs."

"Listen, sicko," Randy said with as much bravado as she could muster. "Let me down, and I'll show you who should be nervous."

"You're a spirited little filly. I'll grant you that," Makarov replied. "But I've got a much higher calling for you. You're my bait. And I'm about to catch me a big ol' mattfish."

Randy looked at Makarov with a mix of shock and fear. *That's what this is about? He's going to lure Matt here to kill him and probably me. How can anyone possibly be that angry?* As the stupor from the drugs gradually lifted, she began to look for a means—any means—of escape, to avoid what appeared to be an inevitable execution.

Makarov went to the end of the room and brought back a chair and sat in it. "I just checked outside, and my prey has not arrived yet. But I still have a few friends left in this country, and they let me know he's on the way. So, it won't be but just a few minutes, and the two of you will be together again. It'll be a warm reunion, if a bit short."

Randy struggled to find a way to loosen her hands. "You must be pretty pissed off to have gone to all this trouble," Randy said.

"What do you think of your prison?" Makarov said, ignoring Randy's statement, to which Randy made no reply. "It's called The Church of Our Lady of Kazan, and you, my dear, are in Mother Russia. Granted, this poor edifice has seen better days, but it's got a damn dramatic ambiance. I used to play *Cossacks and Bandits* here when I was a child, before the war, when it was still beautiful. There were glorious gardens with beautiful flowers in the summertime. I would picnic with my parents, and they would tell stories of the people who had lived here before the revolution. The Soviet Leadership thought that this building was a Russian Orthodox Church, and, yes, it was used for that purpose, but there are *two* apses unlike any other church in Russia. One was for the Christians, and I happen to know that the other apse, when Catherine the Great was not visiting, was used as a Masonic temple. That hole in the floor is the vault of the admiral himself. More honestly, it used to be a vault many years ago. Nothing has been there for a long time except the remnants of the former bas-reliefs and modern garbage left behind by trespassers. What you see here, little girl, results from the Russian Revolution. Our revolution took the delusion of God away and taught us that religion is only for weak people. The only actual strength is in the power of the People. The State acquired the property during the revolution, and, unfortunately for the admiral, his wealth was redistributed to the People. Under different circumstances, I would show you around. This space feels like a time machine."

"Now, in a few minutes, your friend, whose brain cavity wouldn't make a drinking cup for a canary, will come through that door, and I'll have the joy of making him pay dearly for fucking up my life. That *mudak's* knife is so dull it wouldn't cut hot butter, so even though he knows I'm waiting for him, he will come anyway. I will teach him what pain is because I'm ornery enough that I'd fight a rattler and give him the first bite. That piece of shit caused me to lose my life's work, impoverished me, and made me sweep floors to survive. I was a loyal major in the KGB. He'll pay. Oh, he'll pay, just like your navy paid."

"Please," implored Randy. "It doesn't have to end this way. Maybe there's a way that we can help you. Maybe there's something we can do. I'm certain we can help to right those wrongs."

Ignoring Randy's pleas, Makarov simply said, "I have a few duties to attend to in the next few minutes to get ready for the deputy to arrive, so why don't you just relax. You are in for a helluva show. I've got a few aces in the hole for your friend."

With that, Makarov got out of the chair, and left it in place. He went through a doorway in the side of the building, leaving Randy alone. Immediately, Randy resumed her attempts to loosen the knots of the rope around her hands. After several minutes she realized that the cord was knotted so that each time she struggled, the knots became tighter. Her body was now screaming at her. She felt as though her shoulders were going to be ripped from her body at any moment. Still groggy from the sedatives, the pain caused her to reluctantly slip back into unconsciousness, grateful for the relief from her pain.

THE SHOWDOWN

As planned, the two men split up when they left the car. Matt walked due north, straight toward the church. The research they had been provided described a hole in the fence by the church, just large enough for a person to enter if they squeezed hard enough. The plan was for Jake to enter through that hole five minutes after Matt, then to enter through the back of the church. Matt had to walk through a quarter mile of the old grounds. Although it was in complete disrepair, he could see the remnants of once beautiful gardens, homes, and outbuildings. He walked through a virtual wilderness that had once been the immaculate gardens of the estate. Matt wondered what it would have been like to have one's entire life turned upside down by the followers of an errant philosophy of government that executed the czarist imperial Russian aristocracy. As he approached the church, Matt found, as he had been told, a corrugated sheet metal fence surrounding the building, topped by razor wire. Behind the fence was a breathtaking building. He had read that the church had been Catherine the Great's favorite church in all of Russia.

The intelligence provided by Matt's office had indicated that the hole in the fence in the building's rear had been cut open by adventurous tourists and local teens who used it to enter the immediate grounds of the church. He slipped through the hole in the fence, walked from the back of the building, around the side to what had been the main entrance. Although there were four entrances, he realized that Makarov would have spotted him as soon as he came through the hole in the fence, so there was no purpose in taking cover at this point. As he entered the church, he drew his Colt, racked the slide, and chambered a round in his pistol.

Matt entered the church and saw that the room he was in appeared to be a gathering place, or narthex. To the right and left were long hallways leading to huge separate rooms, each with a dome. Looking to the right, he saw nothing. As he looked to the left, his heart jumped into his throat. There was a chair in the middle of the domed room, and he could see the bottom half of someone's legs hanging from the top of the dome. He hurried in that direction until he came close to the entrance, which, from its appearance, was where church services may have once been held. Randy was hanging from a rope in the middle of the room. It took every bit of restraint Matt could muster to stay calm and aware. Saying nothing, he scanned the room for Makarov. Not seeing him, he entered the room. Randy immediately saw him. Matt held his finger to his mouth, indicating she should not say anything, which she did not. Matt searched once again for Makarov, looking behind him, around corners, and behind collapsed columns, but he could not see him.

From around a corner came a voice. "Well, look what the cat dragged in. You were quick out of the chute, weren't you, deputy?" came Makarov's voice from a place Matt couldn't identify. "Before you start firing rounds off in every direction, let me educate you on the situation. It's imperative that you think through your next move because I've seen your work, and it seems to me you are one bubble off plumb. I want you to look up at the top of the rope your sweet little love is tied to. You see that black box?"

"Makarov, I'm going to kill you," Matt said, immediately regretting that this was perhaps not the most diplomatic introduction.

"Now hold your mustangs, deputy," Makarov responded. "I'm trying to show you the lay of the land. In that box above her head are some explosives. They have a wireless connection to a dead man's switch I am holding in my left hand." He held his hand up to show Matt he was telling the truth. "You shoot me, the box goes boom, little lady comes down, and so does about sixty thousand pounds of ceiling. Not even Rooster Cogburn could survive that. You might get me, but you'll also kill that cute little ol' ginger-haired lady of the line. I don't think you would want that now, would you?"

"OK, Makarov, so you're running the show," Matt said with a sneer. "Where do we go from here?"

"Well, now, I'm glad you asked that question 'cause I've got a damn good answer for you. I'm going to come out, and we'll have a little chat. Now, we both know you have got more guts than you could hang on a fence, but bravery comes in different colors. Today, bravery is doing what I say." A man in his eighties appeared from around the corner, wearing a black beaver Resistol cowboy hat, cowboy boots, and a bandana around his neck. He was wearing a leather vest, trying to look as much like Western villain as he could muster. It would have been funny if the situation had not been so desperate. Strapped around Makarov's waist was a hand-tooled black leather gun belt with a tether strapped to his right leg. In the holster on his right hip was what appeared to be a Colt Single Action Army revolver—The Peacemaker.

This guy is absolute crackers! Were it not for the gravity of the situation, Matt would have laughed outright, witnessing this comical parody. *How can someone so evil be so ridiculous?* However, in twenty-four years as a special agent with the NCIS, he had learned that the crazy ones were the most dangerous. Makarov had orchestrated the deaths of hundreds of people and the loss of billions of dollars of property, all for this moment. It was indeed a dangerous moment, a very crazy dangerous moment.

"Before we start, I got about a hundred bones to pick with you, deputy," Makarov began. He drew his gun and slowly pulled back on the hammer. "Oh, don't worry. There won't be any shooting just quite yet. First, I'd like you to, very carefully, set that shooting iron in your hand on the ground and kick it over here in my direction. Just so we don't have anything go boom too soon."

Matt slowly did as Makarov requested, laying his weapon on the ground. "Now, if you look over to your left, you'll see a bag. Slowly walk over to that bag and get what is inside it." Matt did so. As he opened the bag, he saw that it contained a blond leather western gun belt, and in the holster was a single action revolver—another Peacemaker, and a white Stetson cowboy hat. "You go on and strap that shooting iron to your waist, and feel free to open it up. You'll see you got real live .45 caliber bullets." Matt opened the cylinder, pulled one of the bullets out to be certain it was a real load, then holstered the pistol and strapped the gun belt to his waist.

"I suppose you want me to put the hat on, too," Matt said with no shortage of agitation.

"I think that would be fine as frog fur. It really ain't a shoot-out without the right hat."

"Shoot out?" questioned Matt. *And where in the hell is Jake?*

"Deputy, I've been waiting for this moment for an awfully long time. I've been angry as a rabid hornet for twenty-four years at a stupid sailor who didn't even know the shooting side of a gun, besting me, in front of my men. I was one of the most intelligent and skilled KGB agents in the history of my country, and some stupid country bumpkin brought me to my knees. You don't do that to a man like me. A man like me will unleash the hounds of hell to get his revenge. I sent the navy you protect into a tailspin. I killed hundreds of people who did your job, and I hope some of them were your friends. I took the love of your life away from you, and now I will, most likely, take both of your lives.

"I thought about just shooting you, but then I thought it might be more fun to have a good old-fashioned shoot-out. I'm 84 years old. I'm not going to live forever. I decided that rather than just taking your life, I would make you suffer, just a little bit of what I suffered during the last two decades. I'm going to take your life, but before that, I will make you watch your girlfriend die in front of you. Now that sounds like fun. But just killing her wouldn't be that much fun. I decided that maybe we should make this a little bit more real. Perhaps you'd put up a real fight if you thought you had a chance of beating me to the punch. So, I thought to myself that we should do this cowboy style. You're from cowboy country, and I know more about western movies than anyone. So, I'm going to make this fun by introducing a chance. A chance for you to stop me, here and now, save your girlfriend and yourself, and kill me. All you have to do is outdraw me and shoot me. Then you go home. I've got to say that I don't think there's a snowball's chance in Texas of that happening. As it happens, I've been practicing quite a lot for some time now. But at least it's a little chance. I'm getting old, slowing down a bit, and that might just give you the edge you need to outdraw me. And that's better than nothing, even though I speculate you've got no more chance than a June bug in a chicken coop."

"Why in the hell are you going to all this trouble, Makarov?" Matt inquired. *Jake, where the hell are you?*

"Because you made my life hell, and I'm going to give it all back to you today. And because I'm in control, we get to do it my way. And you are witnessing my way!"

"Now, here's how it goes down, just in case you haven't seen a good old-fashioned western shoot-out. You and I stand in the middle of the hall. We face each other. I'll even let you make the first move and start to draw your gun first. When you do, well, you know the rest. If I get you first, I'll release the deadman's switch, and you can watch the ceiling come down on your lady friend. That'll be the last thing you see."

Matt looked at Randy, then looked at Makarov. "If I shoot you first, she's dead anyway because you have the deadman's trigger." *Come on, Jake, where the hell are you?*

"Well, aren't you smart as a hooty owl," Makarov sneered. "You got me there. OK, I'll make the pot a little richer for you. Before we start, I'll turn off the trigger. Of course, you're not going to get your gun out of the holster before I draw and fire, so I'm not really risking anything. Fair enough?"

Matt looked at Randy, tears streaming down her face. "I love you, Randy," Matt said, tearing up. "I'm going to get us through this."

Randy looked back. "Damn, I wish I'd have married you, Matthew Bertram. I love you too, and no matter what happens, I always will."

"Enough of this, pardners. It's time for High Noon," said Makarov.

"Let's do this," said Matt. He felt every muscle in his body trembling. His knees were weak, and he felt like he just might throw up at any moment. He had a passing vision of being on the beach on Squid Island off the coast of Cambodia twenty-five years earlier, as his team was trying to support a group of stranded marines under attack from the Khmer Rouge. This fear was no different. He could hear the beat of his heart thundering in his ears. He knew the odds, but he hoped he could overcome them. He thought his chances would be much better if Jake made an appearance. *Where the hell are you, Jake?*

The two squared off in the center of the hall, no more than twenty-five feet from one another. "OK, don't do anything stupid, Bertram," Makarov said. He raised his left hand with the switch, raising his thumb to turn it off using a switch on the side.

Before Makarov could slide the switch, from a side entrance, Jake appeared. *Finally, Jake, where the hell have you been?*

"Freeze, Makarov!" Jake screamed.

Makarov looked past Matt to Jake, surprisingly stunned to see that Matt had brought help. Makarov reached for his revolver, and as he did, Jake fired two rounds from his pistol. "No Jake!" Matt screamed. "Makarov has a dead man's switch!"

Jake's first round missed completely, but the other hit Makarov in the left shoulder. The force of the bullet snapped his shoulder back. Matt watched with horror as Makarov raised his arm in the air and opened his hand. The switch left his hand, flying in the air above Makarov's head. Time, for Matt, slowed to a tenth of normal. Matt looked up at the switch, then his eyes focused on Randy, a terrified expression on her face. In an instant, the bomb above her head exploded, severing the rope holding Randy in the air. As she fell from her position more than a dozen feet above the hole in the floor, her eyes never left Matt's eyes until her body disappeared into the hole. Matt stood, helpless to do anything but watch the disaster unfold.

"What's happening?" Jake was screaming as Matt looked up to see the entire room ceiling in which Randy was restrained, crumble. Vast blocks of brick and concrete began falling directly on top of where Randy had fallen. The roof split into hundreds of pieces, raining down upon the floor. Makarov watched for a moment, smiled, and then disappeared out the door of the apse. For the next several minutes, the ceiling continued to descend onto the floor where Randy had fallen until, at last, it stopped and left a cloud of dust that filled the church.

Matt ran to the rubble, which appeared to be at least ten feet high. He began screaming at the top of his lungs, "Randy! Randy! Talk to me!" all the while knowing the odds that she could hear him now were virtually nonexistent. Matt began throwing rocks off the pile in a rabid and rapid attempt to retrieve his love from the brick and concrete avalanche that had just swallowed her. Jake grabbed Matt. "It's no use, Matt; she couldn't have survived that."

Matt turned and swung at Jake, who deflected the punch. "Why did you shoot when he had a dead man's switch? Where were you? What the fuck, Jake?" Matt screamed, crying.

"I … I didn't know he had a switch, Matt. Some cops stopped me as I tried to get through the fence, and I had to talk my way out of it. I ran as quickly as possible to the church. As I arrived, I saw the two of you squaring off. I didn't know he had a switch. Honest. I'm so sorry, Matt," Jake said, crying.

"There's a chance she's in there alive, Jake. Call the police. I have to go get that asshole and end his pathetic life."

"You go, Matt. I'll get the authorities here to help. I'm so sorry. I'm so sorry."

Matt grabbed his Colt SAA from the floor, dropped the western gunbelt and wiped away his tears. "I'm going to kill that son of a bitch, Jake. No matter what! Please find Randy. *Please*."

"I will, my friend. I'll do my best. Now go!"

Matt stood tall and ran to the door in the apse that Makarov had used to exit the church. He stopped at the doorway, turning back and looking at the rubble and dust. Looking at the massive amounts of brick and masonry, he knew in his heart that it was doubtful Randy had survived. Matt was not a praying man, but there are no atheists in desperate moments. He looked to the sky and with tears obscuring his vision, said, "Please, God. Save her." He wiped the tears and ran outside the church, looking for the man he intended to kill.

A Desperate Pursuit

Wednesday, May 30, 2000 (1800 Hours, Moscow Standard Time)

It was getting late in the day, and Matt could see the sun quickly approaching the skyline. He needed to find Makarov before he lost the light. He ran around the side of the church, hoping to spot his enemy. There was a road close to the fence around the church. Beyond the road was an open field, and beyond the field was the road, Pushkinskaya Ulitsa, where they had initially intended to park. He looked across the field and beyond the road. The area past the road quickly became heavily forested. As he was about to give up, he spotted Makarov disappearing into the forested area. Without hesitation, Matt took out on a dead sprint, hoping that Makarov's gunshot wound would slow him down and he could catch up quickly.

The evening was quickly approaching; what little activity there was in that portion of the village had ceased. The local residents were tucked inside their homes, beginning to cook their dinners of borscht or stroganoff or solyanka soup. The temperature this time of year was usually comfortable with highs in the 70s and lows in the 50s, unlike winter temperatures, which were perpetually well below freezing. Matt appreciated the lack of witnesses, as he had no intention of allowing Makarov to survive and was pursuing him with a blind rage.

Matt reached the beginning of the forest. Although far from being a tracker, Matt was able to follow the trail of Makarov's blood on trees and the ground. It appeared to Matt as though Makarov had taken a path, leading him southwest.

He wished he had looked at the aerial photos of the entire estate more thoroughly instead of focusing only on the church. He did recall seeing forests, a small lake and a river, somewhere in the direction he was traveling.

Although they had crossed two roads, Matt remembered that the Chernyshev Estate extended well into the area they were traveling. To his right, he could catch glimpses of the Usad'ba Chernyshevfkh, the manor where the Russian admiral had lived. Like the church, it, too, was in ruins, but it was even more decayed. There were no roofs on any of the buildings, and many of the walls had crumbled into ruins. Unlike the church, there were no fences, and it appeared from the trash on the ground that people visited this area frequently. Even with the significant deterioration, it was an impressive set of buildings.

Matt saw that Makarov had skirted around the buildings, apparently not wanting to be cornered there. Instead, Makarov's path was taking him southeast. Matt could see in the distance that the forest diminished a bit, replaced by what appeared to be an old park, now overgrown. He continued traveling in that direction, hoping Makarov had not switched back or changed direction. Just as he thought he had lost Makarov, Matt caught a quick glimpse of him. Makarov was reaching the end of the more open area of the park, and was running into another stand of trees, much denser than the first stand. Matt had decreased the distance between them by about half, but still had a significant gap before he could get close enough for an accurate shot.

Following as quickly as he was able, Matt gave no thought of keeping himself covered. He was a man on a mission, and at that point, could not have cared less about his own safety. The love of his life was gone. Life would never be the same for him, and at this moment, he would happily give up his life, as he had Randy, he realized, was his reason for living.

For Makarov, Matt's unguarded boldness was an opportunity. Winded, wounded, and eighty-four years old, Makarov realized he could not outrun his pursuer, nor did he intend to. He simply needed the right opportunity to end the mudak's life. This stand of dense forest afforded him the chance to ambush Matt. At the end of this portion of the forest was a small clearing he remembered well from his childhood. It was the spot where the obelisk was located.

Makarov approached the obelisk, recalling from his childhood that his father had told him it had been a tribute by Chernyshev to Catherine the Great. As he approached it he could see it was large enough at the base to provide him the cover he needed for his ambush. He saw that the bleeding from the gunshot was soaking his shirt, so he tore the bottom of the sleeve off and wrapped his wound, hoping it would slow the flow of blood. Once that was accomplished, he crouched behind the obelisk. From here, he could see Matt leave the cover of the trees. He was trying hard to catch his breath and push the searing pain from his shoulder into the recesses of his mind, as he had learned to do in his career. A survival tactic he had learned so long ago; first as an officer in the Russian Army during World War II, and later as a KGB agent. Putting this skill to use, he gradually calmed his breathing and his heart rate. He was grateful he had been hit in his left shoulder rather than his right shoulder. That meant he still had full use of his right arm, which now held his Colt Single Action Army revolver. He pulled the hammer of the gun back to cock it and listened, waiting to hear Matt leaving cover.

As Makarov anticipated, a few moments later, like a grizzly bear crashing through the forest, Matt reached the end of the trees. When he did, he stopped, oriented himself to his surroundings, and especially noted the obelisk twenty feet ahead. Without hesitation, Makarov spun around the corner of the obelisk, and fired at Matt. As he did, Matt turned his body to the side and threw himself to the ground. The barrel of Makarov's Peacemaker exploded with smoke and fury as a .45 caliber bullet hurtled in Matt's direction. Had Matt not dived to the ground, the bullet would have hit him in the center of his chest. Instead, the bullet made contact with Makarov's enemy in his calf. Matt screamed in pain. He pointed his own Colt 2000 in Makarov's direction without taking time to aim, and from the ground, he fired. The bullet missed its mark by an inch or two and hit the obelisk just beyond Makarov's head, scattering sharp bits of brick and mortar. One piece grazed Makarov in the forehead. Makarov saw that he had not dealt a mortal wound to his enemy and fully understood that while Makarov had a fine weapon in his hand, it only held six rounds, one of which he had expended. It was no match for the semiautomatic weapon with a high-capacity magazine pointed in his direction. Prudently, Makarov decided to take advantage of the moment.

He turned and ran into the forest, leaving what he hoped was a greatly disabled adversary on the ground.

Matt quickly assessed his injury and was relieved when he saw the bullet had only grazed his calf. The muscles seemed intact, and the quantity of blood leaving his body was negligible. He stood to test his abilities and found he could walk. Painfully, but he could still walk. *OK, Matt, you need to be more careful.* He resumed his pursuit, this time using his police and military training to decrease the chances Makarov would surprise him again. *Being reckless won't help you, Bertram. Be smart.*

The hunter and prey had gone a little more than half a mile from the church. The density of the forest had slowed them both down, and because of that, Makarov decided to follow a path heading southeast, as he needed to keep his lead. It was evident that this part of the park was visited frequently by people seeking local recreation. The trail they were following had been compacted by many feet over the years. Matt and Makarov both hoped people had left the park for the night, as it would make their mutual intentions for murder much easier.

In the distance, Matt heard police sirens, and they seemed to be heading toward the church. *Good, Jake's getting help.* Matt could only hope that Jake would have the authority's help, as he was a trespasser in a government-owned monument. *Jake can handle himself,* Matt thought, as he turned his attention back to Makarov. He had to find and kill him as quickly as possible so he could get back to the church to help dig out and hopefully save Randy.

The forest gradually became thick again, forcing Makarov to stay on a well-worn path that the feet of thousands of tourists had carved into the forest floor over the years. The route took Makarov around a very large pond. While he was running, Makarov had hatched another plan to ambush Matt. Even though he had not been to this spot since he was a child, Makarov remembered a place where he ultimately wanted to lead Matt. It was a good place for an ultimate showdown. He had been this way hundreds of times as a child and knew where he would have the advantage against this *mudak.*

Forced to slow his run to a walk because the leg wound was extremely painful, Matt was now struggling to walk. He realized that his wound was more severe than he originally thought. He stopped for a moment to look at the damage. His original observation that he had been grazed was errant. The bullet had traveled through his shin. It crossed his mind that perhaps the adrenaline had given him the energy to stand up and keep walking earlier. There was noticeably more blood on his pants and his shoe. Yet he was now single-minded in his pursuit. He knew that if it were the last thing he did in his life, he would end the life of Makarov. After that, if Randy were indeed gone, nothing else would ever matter. Matt looked at the sky and could see that the sun had moved below the tree line. He had perhaps thirty minutes more of sufficient light to take care of Makarov. If it became dark it would be difficult, if not impossible to find him, and Makarov would slip through his fingers. The thought of missing his opportunity bolstered Matt. He realized that he would not be able to live with himself if he allowed Makarov to escape. Yet he was limited by the gunshot wound and his newfound caution. He knew that Makarov was armed and could ambush him at any time. He slowed his pace in order to take in more of his surroundings as he carefully looked for places that Makarov could use to ambush him.

Behind Makarov, Matt followed the path the tourists carved around the large pond. They were following a trail moving clockwise around the pond, and as long as it continued to go in this direction, Matt would not be able to get a clear shot. Matt turned a sharper corner, and the crack from the branch of a tree by his side, followed immediately by the sound of the gunshot, once again caused him to dive to the ground. *That's four more bullets left*, Matt thought, keeping close count.

The trail ended at the far side of the pond, across from the area where they originally started. They had made a large semi-circle to this point. At the trail's end was a concrete sidewalk, skirting a riverbank. There were short concrete fences in strategic places, which were about four feet high. Matt assumed the reason for the fences was to keep visitors on the far side of the wall away from the river. Every fifteen feet or so was a concrete pillar, which Matt used as cover to move closer to where Makarov should be. Another gunshot came from one of the other pillars, missing its target, but allowing Matt to locate Makarov. *Three more bullets*, thought Matt. As Makarov ran toward the next pillar, Matt aimed and fired, his bullet also missing its target. At the next post, Makarov jumped behind it and aimed. Matt quickly looked for a pillar, but finding none, he fired two or three successive shots to provide his own cover. Makarov, unscathed by the move, returned fire. The shot missed, but Makarov, undaunted, fired again. This time he found his target. The bullet hit Matt's upper right arm, his hand reflexively releasing its grip on his pistol, which was now soaring in the air. He watched as it fell into the river. Pain stabbed Matt's arm as the force of the impact twisted his body.

Rage overcame Matt as he charged toward Makarov, knowing Makarov still had one bullet remaining in the pistol's cylinder. Matt did not stop to care. Uncontrolled rage was now making decisions for Matt. Matt charged at Makarov like an NFL fullback. Makarov stopped, stood tall, and took aim. Rather than firing, however, he smiled. Makarov pointed the pistol at Matt's head and shouted, "Stop!"

In a split second, Matt realized that if he did not stop, it was all over. Makarov would have won the entire war. Lester was dead, Clay was dead, Randy was, most likely dead, nearly 200 sailors were dead, and he would also be dead. He had only one chance, and that would be to buy a few seconds in which, perhaps, karma would give him the opportunity to find the high ground. And so Matt stopped, and raised his hands.

"Sage move, sidewinder," said Makarov.

"Enough of the cowboy shit," Matt replied.

"I think at this point, you have no power in this conversation," Makarov said with a smile. "The game is over, and I will have my revenge. Do you like the scenery?" Makarov said.

"Yeah, sure, real nice," Matt said sarcastically.

"This is a rather famous place in Russia," said Makarov. "It's the first hydroelectric power plant ever built in Russia. The river that flows into it is the Lama, which runs about 139 kilometers through the town here and a much nicer town upriver called Volokolamsk. It's a lovely city. You should go there sometime—oh, I forgot, you'll never see it as I am about to kill you. If you look behind you, the river has a small circular shaped dam with water cascading over it about twenty feet to the bottom. It doesn't provide that much power, but when it was built, it was enough to power both Yarpolets and Volokolamsk. Now, mostly people come to swim in the summer, and, unfortunately, the turbines that run the power are very old, very sharp, and very dangerous, so the police must keep people out of the turbine area. Every year, a few brave people on dares, go through the fence and face the consequences of the turbines, which is not pretty. Of course, the river is frozen over in the winter, so, no power. People here are very proud of this place, and it is where your body will be ground into what we Russians call *gamburger*. I probably don't have to translate for you. But now, deputy, it's time for your boots to be pushing up sod."

Makarov, knowing he had the upper hand and knowing that Matt had wounds in two places and was just barely able to stand, let his guard down, believing Matt was too weak to fight.

And then a flash of thought crossed Matt's mind. *Thank you, karma*, he reflected. With every bit of effort he could summon, in one swift action, Matt jammed his fingers into Makarov's eyes in a clawing posture. Immediately, he punched Makarov's throat with his other hand. This was his wounded arm, and the movement sent waves of searing pain throughout Matt's body. Makarov involuntarily stepped back, dropped his gun, and grabbed his throat. Almost simultaneously with the prior two moves, Matt gave a swift knee to Makarov's groin, sending Makarov to the ground. Matt grabbed Makarov, lifted him up to his eyes, and spat the words in Makarov's face, "And that, pardner, is called the Trinity!"

Matt, holding Makarov's shirt, turned him around. Makarov, helpless, fighting for air, a look of terror on his face, knew what was coming next. Matt leaned him against the rail of the dam and said, "This is for Randy," and without hesitation pushed Makarov over the edge of the wall. Makarov's body fell thirty feet to the dam, the water carrying him over the edge. The dam's turbines put a finishing touch on the move, grinding Makarov's body into Russian gamburger. Matt ran to the other side of the bridge and peered over. Red colored water and a few small body parts flowed out the other side. Makarov and his evil behavior were both gone.

Matt leaned against the wall; his leg had difficulty supporting him as he slid to the ground. He gave himself a few moments, took off his shoe and sock, and tied the sock around his calf as a bandage. With a most extraordinary effort, Matt stood and leaned against the rail, watching the red water change back into its original light brown.

Matt's head was spinning. As the adrenaline began leaving his system, it was replaced by agonizing pain in his shoulder and calf. With all his strength, he started limping back to the church. Because his chase had been in a circle, he could walk on a road back to the church. Within minutes he could see the church in the distance. He followed the road that crossed the bridge over the power plant, relieved that he did not have to retrace his steps through the woods. It was slow going, and with each step, he could feel the energy draining from his body. When he was within a few hundred feet of the church, he could clearly see several police cars and a fire truck. Matt's head was now spinning, and he was sweating, unsure he could maintain consciousness for long as he felt the symptoms of shock beginning to take hold. As he approached the police cars, he could see Jake, handcuffed and in the back seat of one of the cars. A police officer approached Matt, and as he did, shock took over, and the world went black.

A Change of Plans

Friday, June 1, 2000 (0900 Hours, Moscow Standard Time)

Consciousness gradually returned. Matt opened his eyes to see a hospital room. He was in bed, dressed in a typical hospital gown, an IV in one arm, a catheter in his urethra, and his other arm handcuffed to the bedrail. A nurse was standing over him, taking his blood pressure. "Amerikanets prosypayet·sya," she said over her shoulder.

A man in a dark gray wool suit stood and walked over to the bed. He smiled at Matt and with a heavy Russian accent, said, "Good morning, Mr. Bertram. I am Sergeant Vitaliy Sergeev. Like Ricky Ricardo say, "You got some 'splainin' to do."

What's with these Russians and their wacko American fetishes? Matt thought to himself. "I'm not sure what you mean, Sergeant." Matt thought feigning ignorance might be the best tactic at this point.

"You and your friend, Jake, *tourists* in Russia, go to Kazanskaya Tserkov' and blow-up roof of a Russian national treasure, and someone shoots you twice. We find an American Colt revolver at the power plant, and Mr. Packer claims there is person under the rubble. Seems to me like explanation might be in order," the Sergeant said.

Just at that moment, another man and a woman entered the room. The Sergeant stood at attention and saluted the man. "V pokoye serzhant," the man said. The woman walked to Matt's bedside. "Good morning, Mr. Bertram," said the woman. "I am Deputy Chief of Mission of the Russian Embassy, Angela

Redmond. With me is Mikhail Popo, the Assistant Chief of the Moscow Police. They are considering charging you with criminal trespass and destruction of property. We at the embassy are chatting with them and various government officials about overlooking these charges and sending you and Mr. Packer back to the US as soon as you can move. I have a feeling Jake will be happy about that, as he is currently spending his days in jail. Russian jails aren't that nice."

"We have spoken with your employer about your situation. They are willing to write a check for reparations to the Russian government, which the Russians will accept, provided you give a written confession and leave the country permanently. They also know that you believe you have a friend buried under the rubble, and they are in the process of clearing the rubble to bring her out alive, hopefully, or to find the body. They will require that you agree not to return to the church and immediately leave the country. We've pulled some strings, and if you agree to this, you'll be on a plane back to the US this evening."

Matt sat for a moment in stunned silence. Leave Russia without Randy? He would be willing to confess and didn't care that he could never visit Russia again. Knowing that they had not yet found Randy, he wanted to be at the church, helping.

"Mr. Bertram, I'm afraid we need an answer right now," the Assistant Chief said, "Or no deal."

Matt took a long, deep breath. "As long as I have your assurance that you will find Randy and inform me of the situation," he reluctantly said.

"We will inform the US Embassy as soon as we know," said the Assistant Chief.

"Then fine. We'll go."

"Thank you, Mr. Bertram," said Deputy Redmond. "I know this is very hard, but it's the right thing. We will stay on top of it and keep you informed."

The sergeant took the handcuffs off Matt, and the two officers left the room. Deputy Redmond remained for a moment. "Matt, I know this is tough. They are flying you back to D.C. to meet with the Director and debrief. I hope you were successful in your quest."

"Makarov's dead, but I failed in my quest," said Matt, tears streaming down his face.

By late evening, Matt and Jake were shuttled to a China Airways 747 and on their way to Washington D.C., by way of Tokyo, Honolulu, and Los Angeles. The plane had been in the air for an hour, and neither had spoken a word to one another.

"Matt," Jake finally said, unable to cope with the uncomfortable silence.

"Look, Jake," Matt replied. "I do *not* hold you responsible for Randy. You couldn't have known about the dead man's switch, and had I been in your situation, I would have done the same thing. I'm not angry with you. I'm angry with myself. I should have realized that Randy would be a target much sooner than I did. If I had, this could have been prevented. It was my fault."

"It was Makarov's fault, Matt," Jake responded. "Makarov decided to unleash his evil on us. It was him. And he's dead, the son of a bitch. He's the one who killed Randy, and I hope he's rotting in hell."

Matt turned to Jake and stared him in the eyes. "Randy's not dead. Not until I see her body. She's still alive, at least in my mind, until then."

"I get it, Matt," Jake said. His friend was so broken. His grief oozed from his head to his feet. Jake had never seen this confident man so dispirited.

Matt sat quietly, staring out of the window of the plane for the remainder of the trip. Jake chose to assuage his grief by pouring down Bloody Marys in as great a quantity as he was capable.

When they were in the air on the last leg of their trip from Los Angeles to Washington D.C., Matt turned to Jake and smiled at him. "You know, Captain America, you've become a great friend. I'm so very appreciative that you went to Russia with me. I can't imagine how things would have turned out had you not been there. Thank you. And I hate to admit this, but your stupid Trinity move saved my life."

"What? How?"

"When we were on the bridge over the power plant; Makarov had shot me twice, and he still had one bullet in his gun. He had me dead to rights. I thought I was sunk. And then I remembered you teaching that stupid move at our conference, and even more so, you said it was a move that even your granny could do. I had about as much power and energy as a granny, and I was fresh out of juice, so I did it, and it worked. It's the only reason I'm still alive."

Jake laughed and clapped his hands together. "I can't believe it! I'm so going to revise my book to tell everyone the story! Um ... with your permission, of course."

"You know, Jake, I've been thinking a lot during this flight home. The only reason I stayed at NCIS for as long as I did was because of Randy. I knew that if I went anywhere else, we would lose our connection. Jake, I must have asked her a hundred times to marry me, but she was married to the job. She thought I was also, but if I was, it was for different reasons. I've never made my own decision regarding my future because it was what I wanted to do. The stakes were too high. I couldn't lose her. If she doesn't come home, I'm not staying."

"What, Matt? You've got to be kidding. What in the hell will you do?"

"I'll go back home to New Mexico. I'll buy some acreage in the Jemez, a couple of horses, some chickens, and spend my life trying to forget any of this happened. The only time I'll pick up a gun is to scare the black bears away."

"I can understand that you might feel that way now, but you've got a pretty full and exciting life. I just can't see you sitting on the front porch of a cabin whittling, Matt. Not you. You'd be bored shitless."

"I think a little boring is exactly what I need," said Matt, turning back to look out the window.

After an excruciating sojourn from Moscow, the final leg of their trip ended as their plane touched down at Washington Dulles Airport. A driver and a car were waiting for them outside of baggage collection, and they made their way to NCIS Headquarters in the Russell-Knox Building aboard the Marine Corps Base in Quantico, Virginia. They were ushered into a conference room and told the Director would be in momentarily. There was a knock on the door, and Aldrich Sowles, along with the NCIS Deputy Director of Operations, the Deputy Director of Operational Support, and NCIS Director Guthrie Chambers entered the room. Both Jake and Matt stood as they entered the conference room. Director Chambers walked to Matt, grabbed his hand, and clasped both hands together. "It's good to see you again, SSA Bertram," said the Director.

"I hate to be impertinent, Director Chambers, but do you have word on Randy?" Matt inquired immediately.

"I'm afraid the news isn't hopeful, Matt," said the Director. "They were attempting to clear the rubble above where SSA Glasscock would have fallen, and the remainder of the ceiling and one of the walls fell in, injuring several workers. The Russians immediately called off the work and have told us in no uncertain terms that they won't be going back inside the church. I'm sorry, Matt."

Matt did his best to keep control of his emotions. "I understand, sir," Matt said, a single tear dropping from his eye and down his cheek.

"We want you to know that we are very proud of your work to stop that madman. There was no way he would have been captured alive, and you provided the justice that hundreds of navy families need. Your country is greatly in your debt. I'd like you to take a month off, Matt. Go home and do your grieving. I have approved your promotion to Special Agent in Charge of the San Diego Field Office. You and SAC Sowles will transition as he retires when you get back. We are very excited to have you in that position."

"I appreciate your confidence, Director," Matt replied. "But I need to inform you that I won't be taking that job. In fact, I'm tendering my resignation right now. I'm going to head back home to New Mexico."

After a moment of stunned silence, Aldrich said, "Matt. You've been through a lot. Don't be hasty. Take the thirty days and give it some consideration. Please. I'm asking you."

"I'm sorry, Aldrich. I've realized that Randy was the only reason I have been at NCIS as long as I have. If she's not here, then I can't be here either. I'm afraid my decision is absolutely final."

AFTERWARD

April 1, 2001 (Early morning)

As Matt rode his palomino, Zany, down the last mile of the trail from Peralta Ridge and back onto his ranch property after an early morning ride, he couldn't help but notice that the snow was quickly receding. While he had been high on the mountain he had looked toward Los Alamos and the devastation that the Cerro Grande fire had caused just less than a year before, destroying most of the town he grew up in and charring the surrounding mountains. He felt fortunate that it had not come any further east, or it would have devastated the property he now owned.

The winter had been colder than he expected, and since it was his first snow in his new home, he had been learning important lessons to help him thrive and stay warmer the following winter. He was glad to see bits of green grass poking up and the first of the blue iris and rocky mountain penstemon, which would soon paint his field in hues of blue. Summer was on its way, and he had to admit he was looking forward to warmer temperatures.

He rode past his first outbuilding and down to the corral, dismounted, tied the horse to the rail by his barn, and reached in his pocket for an apple biscuit that Zany was already sniffing for. It was a traditional end-of-the-ride treat.

As Matt took Zany's saddle off, he looked back up the hill. "Where is that dang dog?" Matt said, giving a whistle. A flash of gray, white and wagging tale came out of a stand of aspen trees a couple of hundred yards away as Matt's cattle dog, Jake, raced toward Matt. "You go on up to the porch," Matt said to the dog, almost matter-of-factly. The dog responded immediately, ran to the steps, bounded up two at a time, slid into his water bowl, and slurped a well-deserved drink. He then curled up on an old blanket on the porch, eyes closed; job done.

Matt took the saddle blanket off Zany and was about to grab Zany's brush when Jake began growling. Matt looked down to the bottom of his property and saw that a Sandoval County Sheriff's truck had turned off State Road Four and onto his dirt road. Jake intensified his growl, and Matt said, once again in a calm, quiet tone, "Friend." With that, Jake closed his eyes and resumed his nap.

The car pulled up in front of Matt's barn, and out stepped a man of medium height and build, wearing a khaki shirt and pants and a traditional police officer's hat with gold oak leaf clusters on the brim. "Hey cowboy!" the officer said.

"What are you doing so far from home, Hector?" Matt replied, walking toward him.

"Haven't had a chance to get out of Bernalillo in months, my friend," said Hector. "Thought I'd come have a cup of coffee with an old shipmate and shoot the shit for a bit."

"Well, you've come to the right place. I just got back from a beautiful ride up to Peralta Ridge. There's still two feet of snow up there. I couldn't make it all the way. Come on in, and I'll get some coffee on."

They walked up the porch of Matt's cabin. Matt had grown up driving past this ranch as a kid and always wanted to know what kind of wealthy people lived there. The property had belonged to some good friends of Pat Dunigan. Pat had owned the entire Valle Grande ranch, a sprawling 100,000 acre ranch that included the caldera of the world's largest extinct volcano. The locals referred to the ranch as the Baca location. Dunigan sold off fifty acres in the 1960s as he was trying to raise money to purchase the timber rights to the land. He was upset that the beautiful Jemez forests were being decimated by logging. As Matt started looking for a small piece of land in the Jemez, he met the owners, who were putting the fifty acres up for sale.

The $2 million price tag was far out of Matt's reach until an unexpected check arrived in the mail one day. Randy had made him the beneficiary of a $3 million life insurance policy. In shock, Matt bought the ranch and renamed it the Circle R, after Randy.

The federal government purchased the entire Valle Grande Ranch in the 1990s and turned it into a National Preserve. In the past year, President Clinton signed the Valles Caldera Preservation Act of 2000. With that law, Matt now lived across the highway from a 100,000-acre wildlife and nature preserve, and the east fork of the Jemez River flowed through his ranch.

Matt had used much of the remaining insurance money to update the cabin. He completely remodeled the cabin into a 3,000 square foot lodge, with a two-story river rock fireplace in the great room and four bedrooms, each with an on-suite bath. He wasn't sure why he had gone to such extremes, except that he wanted to be confident that when friends visited, they would be comfortable.

Hector sat in an oversized and overstuffed brown leather chair next to the fireplace, which was now crackling with the sweet-smelling piñon wood for which New Mexico was famous. Matt brought Hector a large mug of coffee and sat beside him. Matt warmed his hands with his warm mug of coffee as they were still a bit stiff from the cold morning ride.

Hector Vigil was sheriff of Sandoval County, New Mexico. It spanned from just west of Los Alamos, Matt's hometown, on the east, to Rio Rancho, just north of Albuquerque, to North of Cuba, New Mexico, in the North. It was a huge county that was growing in population every day. The county included the pueblos of Jemez, Zia, Santa Ana, Sandia, Cochiti, Santo Domingo, and San Felipe, portions of the Navajo Nation, and the Jicarilla Apache Reservation. The town of Rio Rancho, a golfing community, was growing by leaps and bounds. In the next year Intel would complete its new plant which would bring over a thousand employees to the small city. The Sheriff's office also worked closely with all the pueblos doing direct law enforcement. There were several pueblos that did not have their own police forces, including the Jemez Pueblo, closest to Matt's ranch.

Matt had met Hector years before when they served together in the Navy. They had stayed in touch over the succeeding 25 years, each watching the other's career in law enforcement closely. Hector had done well for himself and now managed a staff that covered a large land mass containing diverse cultures. It was not a simple job.

"Ok, Hector, now that you have coffee in your hands, you can tell me why you came all this way to see me. Bernalillo is an hour and a half from here," Matt said.

"All right, Matt, no bullshit," said Hector. "I'm here to offer you a job."

"I've got a job, Hector? Have you seen this place?" Matt said with a smile.

"Well, this one is right up your alley," Hector said. "We need to put a full-time deputy in this area, and one with the credentials of a detective would be *un regalo de Dios*. There are so damn many folks who work in Los Alamos, or want to retire in the Jemez, that the population and the crime increase merits having a detective in the office. I can't think of anyone better to serve as a deputy here. It's close to home, the hours are OK, the pay is incredible ... not ... but it's independent, and I really need someone who knows the area and who is an experienced detective. The fact is, I probably couldn't find anyone more qualified, and certainly nobody who would do the job for the shit we pay."

"So, I thought I'd give you the winter to play cowboy, and maybe, just maybe, you'd be inclined to dust the cobwebs out of your head and put all that experience to use helping the people of Sandoval County."

"Let me give it some thought," said Matt. "I'm just not sure I can find that guy again."

"The offer is open, my friend. You would pretty much be on your own up here, and I know how you like your independence."

Matt saw Hector off, put up Zany's tack, fed the chickens, and brushed both Zany and Adobe, his mare. He walked back to the cabin, took a framed picture of Randy off the hearth, and sat in front of the fireplace. He alternately stared at the fire and the image. "Randy," he said, "I'm 45 years old. I'm not sure I can be successfully retired for thirty or forty years. Maybe I've got a little more gas in the tank."

He touched two fingers to his lips and pressed them against Randy's lips in the picture. In his mind, he heard Randy say, "Matt, this time, you're the one who gets to decide."

Glossary of Acronyms and Jargon

When I arrived at my first duty station from service school in the Navy, I had a chief petty officer who gave me some advice. "The military is an FLA. Learn them quickly, and you'll understand what you're doing more quickly." An "FLA" I learned, is an acronym for "Four Letter Acronym," a bit of irony. As I have written this book and the previous two, I have been conscious that many of my readers will not have a fluency with FLA's, which I've come to know can have many more than four letters. With the help and at the suggestion of my editor Ray Tuttle, who contributed substantially to this list, I am providing a resource just in case you are confused by some of the massive numbers of FLA's.

APB – All Points Bulletin

ASAC - Assistant Special Agent in Charge

ASAP – As soon as possible

BOP - Bureau of Prisons

CAC - US Army Combined Arms Center

CIA - Central Intelligence Agency

CIC - Combat Information Center

CITP - Criminal Investigator Training Program

CNO -- Chief of Naval Operations

CO – Commanding Officer

CPO – Chief Petty Officer

DPV – Diver Propulsion Vehicle

EOD - Explosive Ordinance Disposal

FBI - Federal Bureau of Investigation

FLETC - Federal Law Enforcement Training Center

IAFIS - Integrated Automated Fingerprint Identification System

Intel – Intelligence data

IPGU - Investigative and Prosecutive Graphic Unit

IRS – Internal Revenue Service

IV - intravenous

KGB - Komitet Gosudarstvennoy Bezopasnost which translates to Committee for State Security in English

LAMPS - Light Airborne Multi-Purpose System

MBA – Masters of Business Administration

MCID - Marine Corps Criminal Investigation Division

NAS – Naval Air Station

NCS – Naval Communication Station

NIS – Naval Investigative Service

NCIS - Naval Criminal Investigative Service

NCTS - Naval Computer and Telecommunications Station

NWS - Naval Weapons Station

OFS - Office of Forensic Support

ONI - Office of Naval Intelligence

OOD – Officer Of The Deck

PAO – Public Affairs Officer

PD - Police Department

Perp – slang for perpetrator

Prepper – slang term for one who prepares for the fall of civilization through natural disasters or civil disorder

SA - Special Agent

SAC - Special Agent in Charge

SCUBA - Self-Contained Underwater Breathing Apparatus

SDPD - San Diego Police Department

SEAL - Sea Air and Land Teams

SECNAV - Secretary of the Navy

SSA - Supervisory Special Agent

SSES - Ship's Signal Exploitation Space

SVR - Sluzhba vneshney razvedki Rossiyskoy Federatsii whose mission is to conduct intelligence and espionage outside the Russian Federation.

TRADOC - US Army Training and Doctrine Command

USDB - United States Disciplinary Barracks

USSR - Union of Soviet Socialist Republics

USSS - United States Secret Service

WP – White Phosphorous aka Willie Pete

WTF – Well, you know

XO - Executive Officer is the second in command of a Naval Ship or Naval Base

ABOUT MARK DAVID ALBERTSON

Mark David Albertson jokingly likes to tell people that he was born and raised in Texas, which is true if you look at an 1845 map of the Republic of Texas, which at that time incorporated what was to become his hometown of Los Alamos, New Mexico. Los Alamos, known as "The Atomic City," was the birthplace of the atomic bomb. Tucked in the mountains of northern New Mexico, Mark grew up in a secured city with gates, armed guards, and mountain patrols in the surrounding mountains.

Although Los Alamos was a wonderful place to grow up, Mark longed for adventure. He joined the Navy after graduating from high school and set off for the adventure only a sailor could have. In his time in the navy, he became a radioman and visited 19 countries. Mark left the navy with an idea for a novel, based in part upon his experiences and those of his shipmates. Little did he know that it would take forty-two years to accomplish this goal.

Following his discharge from the navy, Mark moved to San Antonio, Texas, where he went to college and served in the Texas Air National Guard as a police staff sergeant. Upon graduating from college, Mark attended law school at St. Mary's University. Following his law school graduation, he moved to Washington State, where he lived and practiced law for the next thirty-four years.

Mark's career and the raising of three children took precedent over novels but not his writing. During his law career, Mark wrote dozens of articles, two law books, and collaborated on several more over his career. On the side he built a successful private investigation practice and a speaking practice. Mark spoke to dozens of organizations and gave over a thousand seminars and speeches.

When the 2000s came Mark suffered a series of painful events. His 24-year marriage ended in 2005, he was diagnosed with a rare cancer with little hope of surviving and became involved in a twelve-year relationship that was far from functional. In 2017 he decided to leave his career and extract himself from the dysfunctional relationship and learn to live a life he had chosen, which he did. It turned out to be the best choice of his life as he met a wonderful, kind, and loving life partner and wife, who encouraged him to finish the book that had been in his head for all those years. They moved from Washington, bought a small ranch (Mark says "It's 90 acres shy of 100") in the Hill Country of Texas, and both Mark and his beloved Astóre both began writing professionally.

Mark's first book, *Steaming*, was the completion of a 42-year goal, followed closely by his second book, *Spying* in 2021. His third book, *Stalking*, is the final book in what he calls his "Sea Story" series. He is already hard at work on his next novel, *Jemez*, with a goal of publication in November of 2023. The book will take his protagonist, Matt Bertram to the Jemez Mountains of Northern New Mexico.

To learn more and keep up to date on Mark's writing, you can find his website at www.mdalbertson.com